"Why me?" I asked.

"Why him?" Smith as

each other for a second. S

headbutt me. Which would not have been a good plan on his part because, hello, duckbill? I can drive this thing through a wooden door if I have to. They should never have told me I was too late for the breakfast special.

I had to agree with him here, though. "Yeah, why me? Why can't somebody else do it? Somebody more qualified? Somebody with some training in realigning and all that?" Somebody willing to die for their country. Because, honestly? I was willing to get bruised a bit but that was about it. That's what happens when you get taxed too much and told you can't cross state lines without notifying the Wildlife and Gaming Commission first, just to be safe. They'd ticked me off, so I saw no reason to help them out now.

No Small Bills

Bills

Aaron Rosenberg

CRAZY 8 PRESS

For Jenifer, Adara, and Arthur, who fill my life with love and laughter

With thanks to Alex, Eugene, Gareth, Laura, Dave G., and Bob
for their many helpful suggestions.

And to Nova—really, this is all your fault.

Chapter One
DuckBob, meet the Universe.
Universe, meet DuckBob.

Ever have one of those days where nothing ever seems to go quite right? Where you miss the train by seconds each time, fumble your change at the snack machine, click away from the porn site too slow to fool your supervisor, kick yourself in the head when you're trying to tie your shoe, take a swig of your beer only to realize it's a canister of baking soda instead?

That's pretty much every day for me.

The name's DuckBob. DuckBob Spinowitz. No, that's not a nickname or a pet name or any of that other funny stuff. It's my name. I had it legally changed. Figured it was easier to join 'em than try to stop 'em, and when you beat 'em to the punch, it stops being funny. A little. Sometimes. Why "DuckBob"? Well, okay, here's the thing—

—I've got the head of a duck.

I know, right now you're thinking, "oh, he's got a flat nose" or "he's got a weak chin and a high forehead" or "he must have feathery blond hair." No. That's not it at all.

I.

Have.

The head of.

A duck.

Really. My head? It's that of a mallard—a Wood Duck, to be precise. Complete with black-tipped red-and-white bill, white below the bill and down the front of the neck, a touch of yellow rising up from the bill and leading to a white streaks above red eyes, and emerald green feathers covering the rest, with a few white streaks mixed in.

A duck.

Only, y'know, man-sized.

I've also got webbed feet. And feathers instead of hair. All over. Soft downy feathers, looks just like fine hair until you feel it. Speckled brown down the chest and on the feet, tan across the arms and hands, emerald green on the back (yes, all the way down!), and white on the belly, groin, and legs.

It's pretty slick-looking, actually. If I were a crazed xenobiologist with leanings toward ornithology, I'd say I was an impressive specimen. I even won a few awards at bird shows, before I was disqualified—seems the entry and the owner can't be the same person. Purists.

Plus there was that whole "disrobing in public" thing. But hey, is it my fault they wouldn't take my word for it about the feathers, y'know, Down Below?

On the plus side, I can walk in the rain and not get wet. And swimming? Fuggedaboutit.

No, I wasn't born this way. And no, I don't want to talk about it. Just another example of the colossal bad luck that routinely plagues my life. Because that's what it was—bad luck. I mean, was it my fault I was hiking through a restricted area in the

Catskills in the dead of night, waving a lighter in one hand and a neon-orange fishing pole in the other? While naked?

Long story. There was a girl involved. At least I certainly hope so, because otherwise I've got no excuse.

Beyond that—let's just say that, all those stories about alien abductions and crazy experiments? They don't know the half of it. Those little gray buggers are downright cruel.

So you're probably thinking, "Okay, this guy's half man, half duck. That's weird. I'll bet he's a superhero, with a face like that—DuckBob the Aquatic Avenger. Or a mad scientist. Or a professional deep-sea diver. Or at least a sunglasses model."

Nope. Sorry. I'm just your ordinary average guy, and when I'm dressed I look completely normal, 'cept for the whole duck-head thing. I'm no superhero. I work at—aw hell, does it even matter what the name is, really? It's an office job, okay? I'm a pencil pusher, and not even a glorified one. I shuffle papers and push buttons in a little cubicle all day. Then I leave.

Whee.

Some life, huh? Well, it beats the alternatives. At least that's what I like to tell myself. Hey, whatever it takes to get through the day. For me that usually includes watching a few minutes from old Donald Duck cartoons at some point. It's about the only way I can convince myself things could be worse. Look like this, not be able to talk straight, and be forced to walk around with my butt and my business hanging out all the time? Yeah, that would pretty much be the last straw.

Anyway, I'm used to being the butt of some cosmic joke. That being said, I was still surprised when I walked into work one Tuesday and two guys suddenly showed up alongside me and grabbed me by the arms. Big guys, too—they lifted me right off my feet, and I'm not small myself. Plus the bill weighs a lot—I've got amazing neck muscles.

"Hey, what's the big idea?" I demanded as they turned and carried me back out the door. "I've gotta punch in!"

"Mr. Spinowitz?" One of them asked. He had a face like a microwaved potato—squishy and overflowing—and a voice like a hoarse bulldog. He was wearing a suit, a dark one, and I was pretty sure I heard fabric tear each time he shifted.

"Yeah. Who the hell are you guys?"

"We need to speak with you about an urgent matter of national security," the other guy said. He was taller than his buddy, athletic where Mr. Potato Head was just squat. (I'm big-boned and slightly rotund, by the way. It's the slacker lifestyle that does it.) Matching suit, though. I thought that was sweet. Like jewelry but washable.

"National security? I was just curious what sort of brownie recipes it had," I said quickly. "I didn't try any of the other stuff, and even if I did Missus Gries down the hall had it coming! I'm sure the twitching will stop soon!"

The shorter guy raised an eyebrow but shook his head. "That's not why we're here."

"What, then?" I thought for a second, then gasped. "Oh, come on! I know the porn was from Yugoslavia but I only traded an old Steve McQueen movie for it! It's not like I was selling state secrets! It's not even a clean copy!"

By this time we'd reached the curb, and a big black sedan

idling there. Mr. Potato Head opened the passenger door and slid in, then Mr. Tall shoved me in after him. I've never understood the whole "dark sedan with government plates" thing, actually. Why that kind of car? Why not those crazy monster SUVs, so the agents can drive over anyone who gets in their way? And nobody'd escape custody—it's not like you can get out of one of those without a ladder and some pitons. Or go for sports cars, classy and great in a car chase. Or the old kidnapper classic, the white Econoline van—cheap, ubiquitous, and now with faster sliding doors! Or maybe something to counteract their whole "we're not really on your side after all" image. I bet government agencies wouldn't seem half as scary if they all drove brightly colored compact cars or minivans with "My Kid's an Honors Student" bumper stickers.

Instead, there I was in the back of a dark sedan. The windows were tinted—I could have made faces at my co-workers and they'd never have known. Not that I can do many faces anymore—duckbills are not very versatile. I'm great at Charades, though. As long as it involves water fowl.

"Where're we going?" I asked as the car pulled away—there must have been a third guy driving but I couldn't see him. "Who are you? What do you want from me? Say, what's that?" That last one I asked while pointing at the Empire State Building, just to get a reaction. I did. They looked at me like I was a moron. I know that look all too well.

With a head like mine, it's hard getting people to take you seriously.

"Our superiors want to speak with you," the taller guy answered.

"They never heard of the phone?"

He glared at me. "It's a matter of national security."

"Yeah, you said that already. Couldn't they have used a nationally secure phone?"

That got snorts from both of them, and I think from the driver as well. "No such thing," Mr. Potato Head said. "You have any idea how easy it is to tap into a cell phone conversation?"

"No. Could you show me? I'd love to know what my boss says about me." Though actually I think I have a pretty good idea. "Quack, quack" is surprisingly easy to lip read.

They didn't answer, and we spent the rest of the ride in silence. I hate silence. It gives me time to think.

Finally we pulled into a building down near the south piers. A warehouse, it looked like, on a narrow street full of warehouses. I didn't see a sign or a street number or anything. Which I guess was the point.

"Out," Mr. Tall demanded once we'd stopped and the garage door clanked shut again. He got out first and Mr. Potato Head shoved me from behind to make me move, then clambered out after me. Maybe his door was broken. I looked around as I got out but it just looked like a warehouse. There was a guy standing there watching us, though. Average height, skinny as a razor blade, with features to match and glossy black hair that looked painted on. Same suit as my escorts but his looked better on him.

"Mr. Spinowitz? I'm Mr. Smith," he said, offering his hand. "Thank you for joining us."

"I didn't really have a choice," I pointed out, but I shook

hands with him anyway. Hell, I was in a nondescript warehouse somewhere in Manhattan with at least four guys, all of them probably armed. Being rude didn't sound like a good idea.

"I apologize for our insistence," Smith explained. "But this is an urgent matter and we couldn't risk you refusing our invitation."

"Okay, so I'm here." I glanced around again. Nothing to see but rusty walls and stairs and railings, concrete floor, the car we'd pulled up in, and us. "What's this all about?"

Smith started to say something, stopped, and started again. "We have a situation, and we think you may be uniquely qualified to handle it for us," he said finally.

"Qualified? Me? You haven't read my performance reviews. What makes me so qualified?"

Smith pointed at my head. "That."

"Oh."

"Yes. You see, we've been approached by extraterrestrials. We have no idea what they want, and none of our attempts to communicate have worked. But you've encountered them before—we hoped that might have granted you some rapport with them."

I stared at him, at the guys behind me, and then back at him again. "Let me get this straight—you've got some aliens you want to talk to, and you want me to do the talking because I got abducted and given a duck head so you figure I can relate to them better? Are you mental?" Okay, I might have forgot about the whole not-pissing-off-the-men-with-guns thing.

"You may be correct," Smith admitted. He actually didn't

look pissed-off at all, which was unusual for anyone I talk to. "But we have little to lose at this point, and it seemed an avenue worth exploring. Would you be willing to make the attempt? For the good of your country?" Man, this guy was good! Those callers from the Fraternal Order of Police had nothing on him!

I took time to think about it, though. I didn't want to just jump into anything. "Yeah, okay, sure."

"Excellent!" He actually rubbed his hands together. I thought they only did that in cheesy movies. "Come along, it's right this way." I followed him to the back of the warehouse, which had several doors. The floor above continued back past this point so I was looking at the doors to several rooms rather than a whole set of back doors. Which makes sense because why would anyone need more than one back door, especially all in a row? Why not just have one great big giant door? Smith gestured toward the door to the left. "After you."

"Oh, the alien's in there?" He nodded. "And you want me to talk to it?" Another nod. "Alone?" Nod number three—one more and I walked. "But you just said 'after you'—doesn't that mean you're going in with me?"

Smith smiled then, which looked like something you'd see on a buzzard that suddenly found itself at a breakfast buffet. "I lied." He indicated the door again, and rested one hand on his side. Right below the bulge I suspected was his gun—either that or he had a hideous growth under his left arm. Either way I figured I'd better do what he wanted.

"Okay, okay, I'm going." I turned the knob and pulled the door halfway open. At least it looked dark on the other side, no blinding lights and sets of examining tables and rows of glistening tools. Not that I think about such things. Much. Ever.

"Right." I took a deep breath. "Here goes." And I stepped inside.

And promptly screamed as the door slammed shut behind me. Then the lights came on, showing me four plain metal chairs and a small folding table—and the little figure sitting in one of the chairs facing the table.

Short, skinny, gray skin, huge head, huge eyes, no hair. An alien. Just like the ones who . . . anyway, an alien.

Though I wondered where he'd gotten the Halloween-themed footy pajamas. Those didn't seem like standard issue. At least the black-bat pattern went with his skin tone and his eyes.

I was trying hard not to panic. I figured I could always do that later, in a pinch. I'm good at spontaneous panic. Also, shooting spitballs. I've got wicked velocity.

Right now, though, I figured the best thing was just to get this over with. Face my fear. All that.

"Uh, hi." I like to think my voice didn't shake much at all. I walked over to the table and leaned over it so we were roughly face-to-face. "I'm Bob. DuckBob. Um, have we met?"

Chapter Two
We do not all look alike!

It stared at me. Okay, strike one. I took one of the remaining chairs, swung it around to the far side of the table, and sat down. Up close these guys didn't look all that scary. Kind of cute, actually, like a kid with a really horrible skin disease and a seriously malformed head. Okay, cuter than that sounds. But not dangerous or threatening. Of course, the fact that there was only one of them, he didn't have any of his Mad Scientist equipment, and he was wearing footies probably helped.

"So," I said, "what can we do for you?" It just stared at me with those enormous eyes. Strike two. One more and I was out—and where had all the baseball metaphors come from all of a sudden? It seemed an odd choice for me. I'd never been particularly good at baseball. I was even worse at it now. Crappy depth perception, and the bill kept obscuring the ball. Though at least I could get beaned in the head and it didn't hurt as much.

"Look," I said, leaning forward, "you came to us, right?" Actually I had no idea if that was true or not—for all I know the Suits out in the main room had nabbed this little guy on his way to some intergalactic slumber party. It would explain the PJs. "So you must want something. And I'm willing to listen. What's

going on? What do you want? Why are you here?" I pointed off
to the side. "And what the hell is that?"

There wasn't anything there, of course. But it got the alien
to look, which was more reaction than I'd gotten so far, so I
considered it one for the Win column. And when it turned back
to me it was doing something seriously creepy.

It was smiling.

Ever seen one of those circular pencil cases with the top that
zips all the way around so you can slide your pencils in and
out more easily? Yeah, its mouth was like that. It had a little
tiny chin anyway—seriously, its whole head was shaped like a
triangle or one of those giant cartoon teeth, enormous at the top
and tiny at the bottom—and its mouth seemed to go all the way
around. And it had little tiny teeth—little tiny sharp teeth, like
a row of needles. Two rows. Maybe three. It was not a pleasant
sight.

And then it spoke.

"Ah, nonlinear thought," it said. "You are clearly a more
advanced member of your species, most likely due to your increased
cranial capacity. And you have already been appropriately
modified. Yes, you will be an acceptable intermediary."

Huh?

I guess the Suits were listening at the door—rude, much?—
and understood it, though, because they came bustling in.
Smith took a seat next to me, while Potato Head and Tall stood
behind us, arms crossed. The alien didn't even glance at them,
though. It was staring at me the whole time. I'd probably have
run if I didn't know the Suits would just grab me and shove

me back in my chair again.

"Ask it what it wants," Smith whispered to me.

"Duh!" I whispered back. "I tried that!" But I asked again. "So what can we do for you?"

This time it replied! "The quantum singularities are converging," it said. "Vector forces are multiplying. The onslaught is imminent, and we are unable to withstand it unaided. Thus we have come here to obtain sufficient assistance to bulwark ourselves and stabilize the region."

Again—huh?

"Something is coming?" Smith asked. "What? How do we stop it?" When it continued to ignore him—which clearly pissed him off and which I found pretty darn funny—he elbowed me. Ouch!

"What is coming, exactly?" I asked. "And how do we stop it?"

The alien nodded as if it thought these were good questions. I was pretty pleased with them myself. Then it reached into its footies—footy PJs with pockets? Cool!—and pulled out something that looked like a cross between a TV remote, a fancy pen, and a baby octopus. And it clicked or pressed or stroked something to make the end light up. It glowed for a second, bright blue then bright pink then bright red then blue again, and then stopped.

"Be on alert!" Smith shouted, and behind me Tall and Potato Head both dropped into these really efficient-looking combat stances, pulling massive handguns from inside their jackets and holding them out with both hands while scanning the area. Me, I put my hands over my head, or tried to. Have I mentioned I have a huge noggin now? It probably looked like I was trying to cover a basketball with a pair of Q-tips.

"What'd you do?" I asked the alien.

"Summoned one who has been equipped to aid you in your endeavors," it replied.

Okay, that one I understood. It had called for help. Good. Maybe whoever it called spoke more clearly, and in smaller words. But I wasn't willing to bet on it.

Behind the alien, the back of the room started to glow like there was a light over there, even though there wasn't. It was a faint blue at first, but getting brighter and brighter. Then it shifted to pink, red, and back to blue before flaring up so brightly I had to look away.

When I looked back there was someone there.

And what a someone! Tall, leggy, busty—all kinds of "y"! She looked liked a supermodel, if a supermodel actually, y'know, ate properly and had muscle and real curves instead of resembling a wire hanger with hair. Her face was gorgeous but stern, her eyes like sapphires, and she had black hair pulled back in a thick braid that hung over her shoulder and down across her really impressive chest. She was wearing a lab coat, though I was pretty sure no one had ever tailored a lab coat to fit like that before. It was like every fantasy about a hot substitute science teacher come to life. (Oh, come on, don't even pretend you didn't have those!)

"Hello," she said, and I shivered. She had one of those deep sexy voices, the kind that rumbles right through you. What, just because I've got a duck head doesn't mean I'm not interested any more, okay? It just means my dating options are usually limited to fanatic animal lovers and horny swans. Don't go there.

"Hi," I replied. "I'm Bob. DuckBob."

"Yes, I can see that." She studied me for a second, and I'd have broken into a sweat if I still sweated. "Partial body modification, full head reconstruction. Impressive."

"Thanks." I didn't get called "impressive" much, except at costume contests. "Who're you? And how'd you do that little lightshow?"

"I am MR3971XJKA. The 'lightshow' you refer to was a translocation effect. The Grays use it for short-range travel but it requires precise coordinates and typically a signal emitter on both ends."

That sounded kinky but I was too busy trying to remember her digits to pay too much attention. "MR39 what? How about Mary? Does that work?"

She studied me again, then nodded. "Mary will suffice." There was one chair left at the table and she slid into it, which made me shiver. Damn! She could make a video of that, just sliding into the chair, and sell it online. There'd be men all over the world suddenly wishing they were cheap furniture.

Even the Suits were affected. It was the first hint I'd had that they were human after all. "I'm Mr. Smith," Smith said, offering his hand. He was trying to look all commanding but his voice cracked like a nervous teenager. "I'm in charge here."

Mary nodded at him but didn't take the hand. "We know who you are."

"We?" I leaned forward, both to hear her better and to get

another gander at her chest. Hey, I'm not proud. "You're not one of them, are you?" I guess I've seen that before, really—gorgeous women with hideous little men. But this was an extreme example.

"I am not a Gray, no," she acknowledged. "I am human, but I have been extensively modified to serve as an intermediary. I can communicate with the Grays and utilize much of their technology, and I have been fully versed on the problem at hand."

"What exactly is the problem?" Smith demanded. "All it told us was something about singularities and vectors and an onslaught. Are you under attack?"

"We all are," Mary answered. "This entire region of space is about to be invaded. And if we cannot withstand the assault, everything here will be obliterated."

"So what can we do?" Smith asked. "How can we help to stop it?"

"You cannot," Mary told him. "Only he can." And she turned those amazing blue eyes on me.

"Me?" I sat back and gulped air. Damn, no pressure!

"Yes, you," I was totally lost in those eyes. "You, DuckBob, are the only hope for the universe."

I've had fantasies like this—what self-respecting geek hasn't? Amazingly hot chick shows up and tells you you're the only one who can save the universe. Of course, then it turns out that you can help by getting with the amazingly hot chick and everything veers into Skinemax territory. I had a bad feeling that wasn't going to be the case this time.

"So what, exactly, do you need me to do?"

She smiled at me. So did the alien next to her. And both of them had the exact same smile—the kind you give a nice juicy steak, just before you take that first bite. And trust me, I'm sensitive to that kind of look. You'd be surprised how many people see me as a month's worth of Duck L'Orange. I've taken to wearing orange all the time, just as a precaution.

Chapter Three
You want me to do what now?

"**You will** need to realign the quantum fluctuation matrix," Mary announced. She gave me a little nod then, like "okay, go to it."

"Realign the what now?" I shook my head—damn, I missed having external ears! "The quantum fluctuation matrix? Is that like the math-geek version of a jigsaw puzzle?"

Mary frowned. It didn't make her any less hot, and that's a feat—most people, no matter how attractive, look butt-ugly when they frown. I think that's the real reason people try to make their loved ones happy all the time, not because their happiness matters but because they don't want to look at that frown all the time. Not her, though. I could have watched her frown all day.

Man, I was desperate.

But she was speaking again. "The quantum fluctuation matrix. You must realign it. That will prevent the invasion and protect this quadrant from any subsequent incursion."

I glanced at Smith, but for once he looked just as lost as I felt. Ha, served him right! "I don't know anything about a universal whatsits," I admitted. "Or how to realign it. Hell, I can't even realign my spine properly—every time I go to a chiropractor he bursts into giggles and can't come near me. And then there're those other ones, the ones with the down allergy. That ain't pretty." I shook my head, trying to dislodge that memory—not many people could singlehandedly shut down an entire chiropractic clinic, and I wasn't proud about it. "So explain, please."

Mary's frown had deepened, and she glanced at the little alien—the Gray, she'd called it—beside her. Its eyes narrowed and its little mouth turned down as well. It was like watching a claymation version of a baby trying to mimic human expressions, incredibly cute and extremely creepy at the same time.

"You are not familiar with the quantum fluctuation matrix?" she asked. She was obviously translating for the Gray, though I hadn't seen them exchange anything beyond that glance. Still, looks were worth a thousand words or something like that, so she still had several hundred to spare. "How is that possible?"

"I was probably absent that day," I told her. "It happens a lot. When I was a kid I was never in a single yearbook—my name was a permanent fixture in the 'Not Pictured' section at the bottom. The one time I was there for the pictures, nobody believed I was me—Robby Pierson got stuck with my picture instead, which confused the hell out of his parents and started a whole weird custody-battle thing with some lady from Guatemala. Not that that's important. Just tell me how to find this matrix thingy and what I need to do to realign it and I'll get right on it."

But Mary shook her head. "No, you must be attuned to the matrix in order to realign it. If you are not, you will be unable to approach it, much less affect it. And if you do not already sense the matrix and its current inoperable state, you must not be attuned." The frown deepened—she had the sexiest worry lines I've ever seen. "This bodes ill for our quadrant."

"We have many agents," Smith offered, "all well-trained and ready to lay down their lives to protect our country—our world. Our quadrant." He was tripping all over himself to try to win her approval. It was like watching an eager little puppy with a disapproving owner. You couldn't help but feel for the guy.

Especially when she shot him down with barely a glance. "No. It must be DuckBob. He is the only one with any chance of success." Ouch! No love for you, Mr. Smith!

"Why me?" I asked.

"Why him?" Smith asked at the same time. We glared at each other for a second. Seriously, I thought he was about to headbutt me. Which would not have been a good plan on his part because, hello, duckbill? I can drive this thing through a wooden door if I have to. They should never have told me I was too late for the breakfast special.

I had to agree with him here, though. "Yeah, why me? Why can't somebody else do it? Somebody more qualified? Somebody with some training in realigning and all that?" Somebody willing to die for their country. Because, honestly? I was willing to get bruised a bit but that was about it. That's what happens when you get taxed too much and told you can't cross state lines without notifying the Wildlife and Gaming Commission first, just to be safe. They'd ticked me off, so I saw no reason to help them out now.

"He has already been altered," Mary explained, "and by

that modification his body has been brought more in sequence with the quantum fluctuation matrix. But he should have been exposed to it fully during the modification process, and thus already attuned." She stared at me again. Hey, stare at me all you want, baby, I don't mind. "We must consider this matter," she announced finally. The Gray pulled out that weird little octopus-pen thingy again, there was a brief lightshow—and both of them vanished.

Smith and I sat there in complete silence for a minute. Potato Head and Tall stood behind us, equally silent. It was like one of those "Who can stay quiet the longest?" games you played back in kindergarten.

Yeah, I always lost those things.

"Well, that went well, huh?" I drummed my fingers on the table. "So, can I get a ride back to work now? And will someone explain this to my supervisor?"

"You idiot!" Smith turned on me like a rabid dog—in his case one of those greyhounds that've never had a proper meal in their life, so who can blame him for tearing into me like a Thanksgiving turkey? Or in my case probably a Christmas goose? "Do you realize what you've done? They came to us for help, for aid, the first step in open communication and collaboration—and you sent them away!"

"What? Hey, hold on now, Charlie," I objected, pushing back from the table and conveniently getting clear of his jabbing index finger at the same time. "I didn't do anything! They said I wasn't aligned to this thingamawhosis so they couldn't use me to realign it! That's not my fault! If anything, it's their fault—

they did this to me in the first place! Figures they couldn't even finish the job right!"

Smith stood too, and looked like he was going to take another lunge at me—then stopped. "You're right," he admitted after a second, smoothing his tie and straightening his suit jacket. "This isn't your fault." He shook his head. "And you did attempt to communicate with them. I apologize." He sighed. "I lost my temper. It was unfair."

"Oh. Well, no problem. Sorry I couldn't help more." Smith being apologetic was a lot weirder than Smith being angry, and it scared me more. I had no idea what he was going to do next. I was afraid he might break out in song. Then Potato Head and Tall would start singing chorus and I'd be stuck with the girl's part. There's a reason I'm never going back to junior high theater. Ever.

"What now, boss?" Tall asked Smith. He and Potato Head hadn't moved a muscle the whole time Mary had been here, as far as I could tell. Well, okay, Tall kept flexing his biceps and I think I caught Potato Head shifting his feet once, but that was it. Otherwise they were like statues. Ugly, suit-wearing statues. With guns.

"Now? Now we wait." Smith shook his head again. "There is little else we can do. We must hope they will contact us again once they have devised some other solution to the problem. In the meantime—" He turned to talk to the knuckleheads more directly, which is why he didn't see the lightshow reappear. But I did, and so did Tall and Potato Head—they both stiffened, which made Smith whirl back around. All four of us were staring across the table when Mary and the Gray reappeared. This time they had company.

It wasn't a Gray. It also wasn't a crazy-hot X-Files chick like Mary. It was—a plumber.

Okay, that was my first impression. But that felt right. He was short and a bit round, with stubby arms and legs though they looked like they could extend somehow. He had a flat face—I mean actually flat, perfectly flat, like a cartoon character that's just run into a wall—but his features were broad and doughy. He could have been Potato Head's cousin, if his cousin was an unhealthy shade of green and had tufts of hair like broccoli just above batlike ears. And maybe his cousin is. I'm the last person who should be making fun of how other people look. Which doesn't mean I don't, it just means I have that little twinge of guilt every time I do. Not with this guy, though. I'd have felt guilty not making fun of him, like the one person who refuses to join in the game. And he looked like a plumber. A weird alien plumber.

The fact that he was wearing overalls and a T-shirt and a New York Mets baseball cap probably didn't help.

"How you doing?" he said as soon as the lights faded. He focused on me. "Oh, yeah, I see what you mean. Yep. I can fix it, no problem." He had a tool belt slung around his waist—or roughly where his waist would be, if there was any change in width across the middle—and started rummaging through the pouches there.

"We have devised a solution," Mary informed us. Her voice made me shiver all over again. "We have brought a technician to complete DuckBob's modification and attune him to the quantum fluctuation matrix."

"Excellent!" Smith said. He smiled, which was just as unpleasant as it had been the first time, and clapped me on the back. "Go right ahead!"

"What? Hey, hold on a second," I argued. "What do you mean, 'complete my modification'? I've already been modified plenty, thanks! I don't need any more! Actually, a little less would be nice—like having a real face again!"

"Now, don't be difficult, Mr. Spinowitz," Smith muttered. "You said you wished you could have done more to help, remember? Now you can. I assume," he said, raising his voice and turning back toward Mary, "that once he has been attuned he will be able to align the quantum fluctuation matrix and prevent the invasion?"

"That is our hope," Mary agreed.

"Well, there you go, Mr. Spinowitz," Smith exclaimed, slapping my back again. I wish he'd quit that. Did he think pain and discomfort would make me more pliable? Maybe he did, at that—he was part of the government, after all. "You will be able to save the universe after all!"

Oh, joy.

Chapter Four
Well, isn't that just ducky?

The alien plumber—okay, I guess alien techie-guy would be more accurate—came around the table at me, still fiddling with his tool belt. "Hold still," he said. "This shouldn't hurt too much."

"Too much? Define 'too much.'" I put the table between us again, which coincidentally put me on the same side as Mary. Win-win. "'Too much' being 'a routine tooth extraction' or 'having your spine torn out by a pair of rabid gerbils'?"

"Somewhere in between," he admitted. "Aha!" That last was because he stopped fiddling and pulled out—okay, I have no idea what it was. It looked like—well, at first glance I thought he was holding a dead rat. Then I thought he had an ice cream scoop, the kind with the little sweeper arm that drops the ice cream into your bowl (or, if you were in a frat like I was, directly into your open mouth) with one little click of the button. Then I thought he was holding a pen, one of those with all the colors on it that always get stuck and always on orange. But it wasn't really any of those. "I knew it was in here somewhere! Okay, just give me a second and I'll have this all taken care of."

"Now look here," I said, maneuvering behind Mary for protection—and yes, I admit it, for a better view of her keister. I don't think I've ever believed in a higher power before, but I sure did after that. "Can we just— I don't even know your name!"

"Ned."

That made me stop ducking, and even made me forget about Mary's astounding rear end. For a second, anyway. "Ned? What is that, short for NE3QR7and so on?"

Ned scratched his head. "No, it's my name. Ned. Pleased ta meetcha." And he held out his hand, the one that didn't have the thingiewhatsit in it.

"Your name is Ned? Not something unpronounceable that starts with a sound most closely approximated by the human sounds 'ne' and 'deh'?"

"Nope."

I stared at him. "Oh, okay, I get it. You're from here, right? They did experiments on you, too. And here I thought I had it bad!"

"No, I'm from round about Betelgeuse, originally," Ned corrected cheerfully. "Decided I wanted to travel a bit, see the cosmos and all that. Hooked up with the Grays and here I am." He advanced again.

"You're from Betelgeuse?"

"A small planetoid in the region, but nobody's ever heard of it so I just tell them Betelgeuse to make it easier."

"But—but you've got a Brooklyn accent?"

"I do?" He thought about it for a second, then shrugged.

"Wacky coincidence, I guess. So, you ready?"

I tried to dodge out of the way as he moved around Mary—he barely even spared her a glance, which proved he really was an alien—but Smith and Tall were suddenly there boxing me in. I had nowhere to go!

"He's ready," Smith replied. "Go ahead."

"Gotcha." Ned raised his doohickey and started, well, caressing it here and there. I felt like I should look away, give him some alone time—what a man does with his rat-scoop-pen-thing should be private, after all. But I couldn't help staring. It was quivering and vibrating in places, and glowing through the fur and metal here and there. After a minute of that Ned grunted and waved the thing over me like an airport security wand. Wherever it approached got all tingly. It was kinda nice, actually.

"All set," Ned said finally, and stroked the thing until it was quiet again, then returned it to his tool belt.

"That's it?" I didn't feel any different, and as far as I could tell I looked the same too, though that wasn't necessarily a selling point. "I thought you had to finish the modification process or something?"

"Yep. Did that. You're good to go." He gave Mary and the Gray a thumbs-up.

"I thought you were gonna turn me into a full-on duck," I muttered, examining my hands. I still had fingers, which was a relief. I'd half-expected to have wings and feathers and nothing else, which would have been great for going on vacation but hell for actually doing anything once I got there.

Thank God for bendy straws, anyway.

"Not my job," Ned explained. "I just needed to finish your attunement to the quantum fluctuation matrix. So I did." Figures—leave it to a techie to do exactly what he was told and not an inch more. He was probably union, too.

"Okay, so now what?" I glanced at Mary. "I'm all attuned? I can reset this thing and that's that, no more invasion, no more threat, the universe all safe and sound?"

Mary nodded. "Precisely."

"Great!" I rubbed my hands—my still very human hands, thank you very much—together. "Point me to it and let's get this over with. Though I'm not going back to work today, no matter what. I've earned a sick day, for real this time—not like when I said I had the avian flu. For three weeks."

Mary turned to the Gray and they conversed—at least I think that's what they were doing. It was just a lot of high-pitched squeaking and head-tilting from where I stood. But damn she did a great head-tilt!

After a minute she shifted her gaze back to me. "Very well. We are prepared to convey you to the matrix."

"Right." I took that as an excuse to step closer to her. She smelled like an old lizard I'd had when I was a kid, probably from all her time with the Grays, but I figured I could work past that. Would she be offended if I bought her perfume? Or room sanitizer? "Are you the one taking me? Let's go!"

She shook her head and actually smiled a little. "We will send you by translocation," she explained. "No accompaniment is required. Stand still." She stepped back and I resisted the urge to follow her. Down, boy. Then there was a shimmer of lights around me and I felt a little tingle again, like one of those Magic Fingers hotel beds without the noise or the constant demand for quarters. Ah, sweet memories of summer vacations with my Aunt Lee and Uncle Tom and cousins Bill and Moe at their home—or Room 314, as we used to call it. The tingle got stronger, spreading all over my body, and the rest of the room seemed to fade a bit, like the image on an old picture-tube TV when you shut it off.

Then the tingle stopped. And the room got clearer again.

"Was that it? Are we done? That was easy—I didn't even have to do anything. Was it just me being near the matrix that reset it, like a proximity sensor? Cool!" But Mary was shaking her head, and the Gray was frowning.

"The translocation failed," Mary informed us. "Something has blocked the transmission." She communed with the Gray again for a second. "This can only mean one thing," she concluded after they'd finished beeping at each other. "The incursion has already begun. The quantum frequencies have shifted slightly as a result of the impending convergence, and as a result our translocation devices can no longer function."

"So that's it?" I asked. "We were too late? We failed?"

"Not necessarily," Mary replied. "The convergence has not fully occurred, and until it does we can still realign the matrix. Doing so will seal the barriers again—any invaders that have already seeped through will be trapped within and must be dealt with, but no more can follow and the frequencies will return to their normal wavelengths."

"Okay, so we've still got a shot." I thought about what she'd said. "But you can't send me there. Right?" She and the Gray both nodded—so did Smith, though he sneered like he was annoyed it had taken me that long to catch on. So I had thought Mensa was a candy with obnoxious ads. Sue me. "So how do I get there?"

"Translocation was merely the quickest method," Mary answered. "There are other paths. We will simply travel the long way around."

"The long way. Right." I reached into my front pocket. MetroCard, check. "So where is this matrix thingy, anyway?"

"Galactic coordinates X3597.124 by Y7794.390 by Z0189.242."

I scratched my head. "And where's that, then? It sounds pretty far. Staten Island? Delaware?"

"Try the galactic core," Ned told me. "That's about forty-three million light years away. Give or take a few."

I stared at him. "Forty-three million light years away? How the hell are we gonna get there, then? Unless you've got a spaceship ready and waiting." That might be kind of cool, actually. I'd always wanted to see the inside of a spaceship. Of course, the last time I had I'd been—no, no, not going there, nope. I quickly walled off that memory, spackled and painted for good measure, hung a little "Don't Touch While Wet" sign, and turned back to the business at hand.

"Our ships would not be fast enough," Mary was admitting, and I breathed a little sigh of relief. I'd lost my enthusiasm for spaceships all of a sudden. "We cannot afford to lose that much time. We must take the bus instead."

Bus? I guess it was a good thing I'd checked for my MetroCard, after all.

Chapter Five
Excuse me, do you stop there?

"Right, where's the bus stop? I don't suppose you've got a map?"
I held out my hand.

"You will not find the bus without me," Mary said, and
maybe it was just my imagination but she looked quietly happy
about that. "I must accompany you."

Well, hot damn! This whole saving-the-universe thing had
just gotten better, and suddenly my old geek fantasies were
back on track! "Works for me," I told her, trying to be cool.
"Shall we?"

"I'd better come along," Ned announced, hitching up his
tool belt—you'd think guys like him would wear a harness
rig instead, distribute the weight across the shoulders so it
didn't keep sliding now, but I guess that wasn't macho enough.
And it didn't create the infamous "plumber butt," which was
apparently universal. "You'll probably need me to get you in
there."

Mary nodded, and now we had a chaperone. Swell.

"Agent Thomas will join you," Smith informed us, and
until he nodded at Tall I had no idea who he meant. So that was
the guy's name! I still preferred Tall, though Tall Thomas also

worked. "That way you have a direct link to our agency if you need us." More like "that way we can spy on you the whole time and steal any new technology we see!"

But Mary was in charge of our little expedition and she nodded, so now we were four. A merry little band we were, too—a hot half-alien chick, a weird little all-alien techie, a stone-faced government suit, and me, the guy with the duck head. I'm sure wherever we were going we'd blend right in.

"First we must equip you both," Mary told Tall and me. Cool, I thought. Alien death-rays, jetpacks, rocket boots—I'm ready! But instead we got—a shot.

"Ow! Hey, what the hell?" I asked, rubbing the back of my neck where she'd stuck me. I wasn't even sure where the needle had come from, and shuddered a little at the idea that she might have more of them hidden about her person. That could make late-night groping awkward: "Oh, sorry I nicked a vein, but you should have kept your hands to yourself!"

"Nanites," she explained, stabbing Tall as well. He barely moved. If not for the way his tie shifted slightly with each breath, I would have sworn he was already dead.

"Nanites? Like little tiny machines that build stuff?" Hey, I read comic books! I know lots of useful stuff. Especially if you need help with your cape.

"Exactly," she said. "These particular nanites are currently rebuilding your lungs and your skin." That didn't sound good! I hoped they were setting up some kind of backup system while they worked, because if they were anything like most IT guys, I could be stuck suffocating while my lungs had a little "we're sorry for the inconvenience—please check back later" sign around them. "When they have finished, your body will be capable of absorbing elemental particles and converting them to oxygen."

Oh. That sounded—promising. "So I can breathe in space?"

"You can breathe in space," she agreed. "Not a complete vacuum, but those are incredibly rare. Most of space is in fact filled with tiny particles, and thus your body will be able to sustain itself under all normal conditions." I didn't exactly consider "wandering through outer space without a spacesuit" to be a normal condition, but whatever.

"Okay, so how do we get there?" I asked Mary as she led the way out of the warehouse. "And what kind of bus is it, anyway? I'm pretty sure Greyhound doesn't extend beyond the moon, or Mars at the utmost."

"'Bus' is not strictly accurate," Mary replied. She'd stopped just beyond the warehouse door and I actually ran into her a little. Okay, sort of on purpose. What, a guy's supposed to save the whole friggin' universe and can't cop a little feel? She didn't even seem to notice, anyway. Probably I wasn't alien enough for her. Hell, I'd met furries—even went out with a few (there's a subset that's into . . . never mind)—so why not alien-lovers or Gray-ladies or something? "It is merely the closest analogy to this transportation model," she continued.

"Okay, when is a bus not a bus? Got it." I backed up to give her a little space. "So what is it, then?"

"It is a regularized mass transit system created by an alien race that allows other spacefaring peoples to travel to various points through the universe without a contrivance of their own."

"It's also dirty, smelly, unreliable, misses stops half the time, and breaks down a lot," Ned added.

Yep, that's a bus, all right.

"So it has a stop here on Earth?" I asked. I was picturing a little addition to Penn Station, with signs indicating "Interstellar Mass Transport—Track 59."

"No, but its route passes between Earth and the Moon," Mary answered. "We will be able to latch onto the bus and pull ourselves on board."

Oh great, now we even had to run for the bus! This was just like my morning commute. I wondered if there would be the alien equivalent of the jerk who stands in the door and refuses to let people in or out, or the punk who sprawls across three seats and pretends to be asleep whenever anyone approaches.

"I can get us into low orbit," Tall offered. "Though I need a few hours to arrange the details." He already had a cell phone out.

"Unnecessary," Mary told him. "I can reach the bus from here. Nor do we have hours to spare—the next bus will pass this way in approximately twenty-one minutes." Yikes! I had a feeling they didn't come through often, either. "We will need a conveyance of some sort, however—it is best not to attempt the transition without proper shielding."

"You mean like an escape pod?" I asked.

"A pod, yes," Mary agreed. "Anything within which we can encapsulate ourselves. Ned can enhance it to provide adequate protection."

I turned to Tall. "Hey, what about your car? It's still here, right?"

He scowled at me but nodded. "It's in the warehouse. Late-model Ford sedan, four-door, tinted windows, bulletproof glass. Will that do?"

Mary glanced at Ned, who nodded. "Yeah, I can work with that, no problem." So Tall turned and headed back into the warehouse. I had a sudden urge to run—with or without my two new alien buddies—but a few seconds later we heard the rumble of a car engine, followed by the clank and whir of a garage door, and then he was pulling the sedan up in front of us.

"Get in," Mary told me, pointing to the front passenger seat. "I will maneuver the vehicle," she instructed Tall, who glowered again but surrendered the driver's seat and moved behind it instead. Ned pulled out a few more weird-looking tools and got to work modifying the car.

I was curious what this little green guy was doing to the thing. Maybe it would wind up with a duckbill of its own. If so, I could claim it as my official vehicle. The Duckmobile! I wondered if the license plate was taken yet.

"All set," Ned announced after a few minutes, climbing into the rear passenger seat and slamming the door shut behind him. I actually heard Tall wince. "Start her up while I seal things from in here." He had another device out and I thought I heard a funny little whine as he used it somehow. The car itself didn't look any different but I noticed our surroundings seemed hazy, like there was fog everywhere but us. Or wrapping around us and nowhere else.

"Contact with the bus is imminent," Mary warned, turning the car on and revving the engine. I noticed she'd pulled a strange little metal-and-glass doohickey from somewhere—I didn't want to think too hard about where, not if I wanted to be able to see straight—and had somehow attached it to the dash just above the speedometer and odometer and other gauges. "Everyone please fasten safety restraints." I hastily buckled my seatbelt and hoped that, if we wound up needing them, the airbags went all the way up.

"Shields in place," Ned assured her. "Inertial dampeners active. Gravitational modulators online."

Mary nodded. "Very well." She glanced at her doohickey. "Bus arrival in one minute and counting."

We waited.

And waited.

And waited some more.

"Typical bus," I muttered after at least three minutes had passed. "Either early when you're running late or late when you're on time."

"Its schedule is typically measured in weeks and months," Ned told me from behind. "Not minutes."

"Even so."

Then the doohickey began to blink. "Bus approaching intersection point," Mary called out. "Activating synchronous motion accelerator in three, two, one—now!" She hit the gas and the car peeled out from the curb—

—and lifted off!

"Holy crap, we're in a flying car!" I looked out the window, watching the ground fall away with alarming speed and the buildings rocket past as we shot up into the sky. "That is so cool! When we get back can I keep it? This is a lot better than getting stuck with wings for arms!" I'm pretty sure Tall was glaring at me but I didn't care—if I was going to save the universe I should get something for my troubles, right?

"The car itself is not capable of flight," Mary explained, never taking her eyes off her gadget. "It is merely locked into the bus's travel path and being carried along in an intersecting flight vector. We are being pulled closer and closer and will soon reach the bus itself, at which point we can exit this vehicle altogether."

"Oh. It's not a flying car, just a shuttle to the bus. Got it." That was too bad—I'd really liked the idea of tooling around in a flying car. "So how soon do we reach the bus?"

"A matter of minutes."

"And what, we glide up alongside it, pop a connecting tube, and sidle across?" I caught her quick frown. "No? So it has a docking bay and we slide into that?" The frown deepened. "Okay, how do we get on board?"

"Our paths intersect. Once that occurs we will terminate this vehicle's separate vector and continue along the bus's original course with it."

"Okay, right. But what does that actually mean?"

"It means we ram the damn bus," Ned informed me quietly. "Hard and fast. And hope we can breach its shields before our own collapse."

Oh. Great. Somehow I'd wound up in the Great Train

Robbery. Only it was in outer space. And if we made it, we didn't even get any loot.

Still, we were going to ram a bus. That might be worth it, all by itself.

Chapter Six
Do you have a ticket?

"Are you crazy?" I demanded. "You want to ram a bus—an intergalactic bus, no less—with a car? With a late-model Ford?"

"With bulletproof glass," Tall pointed out. "That may help."

I glared at him. "We're not dealing with bullets, you moron! It's us against a spaceship! That's like sending a fly against a Sherman tank! We're talking escape-velocity spatter—and we're the spatter! There won't be anything left of us but smears on the metaphorical windshield!"

Tall looked to Mary for a denial of that last statement, and gulped audibly when she shrugged. "There is no way to be certain we will survive the collision," she admitted. "The likelihood is very high, however."

"We should be fine," Ned assured all of us. "I know the bus's schematics, and I've calibrated this car's shields to take full advantage of the vulnerabilities in their emitters. Our shields should hold for a tenth of a nanosecond longer than theirs." He actually had the nerve to look pleased with himself about that, while Mary stared straight ahead and Tall and I both visibly contemplated strangling him with his own tool belt. A tenth of a nanosecond? Was that even enough time for the whole "life flashing before your eyes" thing? Or would I get stuck seeing only up to second grade? Because Mrs. Herkel's class hadn't exactly been my finest hour.

"What can we do to help?" Tall asked, and I rolled my eyes. Yes, ducks can roll their eyes—you don't believe me? Try offering one of them anything less than seven-grain bread. Snotty little mothers.

"There is nothing you can do," Mary replied. Duh! Unless he was offering to play human shield—which didn't exactly work right now, given the whole "zooming through space" thing—I wasn't sure what he'd expected. Did he have some kind of forcefield projector tucked away in his suit, right next to the pocketknife and the cell phone and the miniature blowtorch? Maybe he figured he could ward off danger by looking stalwart, or something. I had no idea.

Me, I was under no illusions. I was useless, and likely to remain that way. I just concentrated on making sure my seatbelt was properly fastened, and wondering how much velocity those airbags could take.

We exited the Earth's atmosphere, which should have left me giddy with delight and all-consuming fear. But I was too busy worrying about the whole "smack into a bus" thing to really notice either. I did admire the view—man, the stars are really bright once you get past all that air, and there are a ton of them! It's a wonder aliens can sleep at all, given all those little twinkling lights everywhere! But after a second I was distracted by a comet blazing toward us.

"Is that—?"

Mary nodded. "That is the bus, yes."

Great. I looked at it again. It looked just like you always see in those cartoon depictions of comets—a blazing trail of sparks and fire and dust shooting across the sky. And we were going to crash into and try hitching a ride on that?

"Intersection in five seconds," Mary warned.

"Five seconds?" I gripped the door handle. I dunno, maybe I thought I could bail out if things went wrong—not that it would help any, since that would leave me floating in outer space without a suit. I'd seen enough movies and TV shows and even PBS documentaries to know that would be bad. I could hold my breath underwater for a ridiculously long time—I know because I'd done it a few times, both to impress ladies and to freak out lifeguards. But outer space? Not so much.

The comet was freaking huge now, and right in front of us. It was a mass of swirling colors, and I thought I could just make out shapes within it—and faces pressed up against the glass, staring at us and shouting in horror. But maybe I was imagining that last part.

Tall was muttering something that sounded suspiciously like a prayer. Amazing. Ned was calmly fingering one of his weird little tools. At least I hoped it was a tool—it was the same color he was, and, well, if you were about to die why wouldn't you, really? Mary had one hand on the steering wheel and the other tapping buttons on the doohickey.

"Three," she called out, "two, one—impact!"

The car shuddered and squealed and all of us were thrown against our seatbelts, back against our seats, and from side to side. It was like one of those horrible "let's simulate an earthquake" amusement park rides. Light and sound were everywhere, suffocating me, and I was sure we were toast. Flattened intergalactic toast. Then the squealing softened, and the lights dimmed a bit so I could see the spots behind my eyes, and the air backed off enough that I could breathe again.

"Successful entry," Mary announced happily—I couldn't help noticing, and noticing again, and staring, that she also took a deep breath and let it out. Slowly. Man, I could almost enjoy a near-death experience for that.

"We must exit the vehicle and blend in with the other passengers," she informed us, undoing her seatbelt and shoving the driver's side door open. It was dented inward a bit, and the roof was crumpled toward us as well—I guess one-tenth of a nanosecond doesn't buy you a lot of leeway. So much for the Flying Fed Car. Once Tall got over sobbing in relief he'd probably be pissed.

"Right, out of the car. Going." I clicked free of my belt, kicked the door open, and hopped out. Who knew what'd happen to the car next? They might have some sort of alarm system on board that would detect it, realize it didn't belong, and flush it like a used tissue in one of those airplane toilets, and if that happened I definitely didn't want to still be inside it. Ned and Tall were emerging as well, and I glanced around to see where we were.

The walls were swirling. At first I thought that was just the concussion talking, but when I turned to Mary she was still in focus. So no, the walls were swirling—there was color and light moving through them, shifting and dancing just enough that you were never quite sure what you were seeing. It was disorienting, to say the least, but not completely unpleasant.

There wasn't any furniture, or any passengers. Just those swirls, us, the car—and a bunch of shapes, like odd packages, most of them gift-wrapped in glittery metallic paper. Some were stacked here and there, others were webbed to the walls or suspended from the ceiling. If you crossed a magpie, a spider, and a crazed holiday shopper, we were probably in her lair.

"Baggage car," Ned told us, looking around. "Nice shot, Mary!"

"Thank you." She brushed herself off—I almost offered to help—and gestured toward a wall, which I noticed had a circular window set at head-level, and another one below that at waist level. Either the creatures here came in all heights and sizes or they just really liked crotch-gazing. It could have gone either way. "The passenger compartment is that way. Shall we?"

I was quick to scoot up behind her, and Ned and Tall were stuck following me. Hah, sorry, guys—victory goes to the swift! She waved a hand before those windows and the wall slid aside, allowing us access.

It's a good thing Ned was right behind me and could shove me forward, or I'd have just stood there, frozen despite the increasing distance between myself and Mary's inspiring backside.

Chaos. Complete chaos. That's the only way to describe it. I know I was staring at a long, wide, tall room, but beyond that my brain was having trouble processing anything.

"Go on in," Ned hissed behind me. "Hurry up! We don't want anyone to notice we came from the baggage car!"

Notice? Who was going to notice? I doubted they'd notice if we suddenly whipped out instruments and began performing "Ragtime." While breathing fire. And riding unicycles. Shaped like elephant tusks.

There were aliens everywhere. I know they were aliens because they were moving and talking—I think it was talking—and eating—I hope it was eating—and drinking and doing everything else you see people on busses doing that they're told not to do. Yes, everything. I'm scarred for life. But I couldn't really tell you anything about them except they were alien. Oh, I spotted one or two like Ned—mostly human-looking, with maybe some weird color and a few odd limbs thrown in. But others! I swear I saw a pair of coral with long wispy beards and waving snail-stalk eyes and hands like Mickey Mouse, playing cards off in a corner. There was something kind of like the Yeti, if he suddenly became a rock star and wore enough bling to bankrupt the EU. I thought someone had left their drink sitting out until it blinked and extended a stream to turn the pages of its newspaper. It was insane. I don't think I'll ever be able to look at anything the same way again—I'll always worry that the crumpled candy wrapper on the floor or the coffee stain on the desk is another alien, and I'll spend the rest of my life saying "excuse me" and "have you got the time?" and "got change for a dollar?" to inanimate objects and dirt.

"This way." Mary was beckoning, and the sight of her in all this mess helped snap me back. Hey, it's amazing what good a gorgeous woman can do your sanity. At least until she starts laughing at you. Anyway she led us through the crowd and to what looked almost like a park bench made of cut and folded paper. It was empty and she sat down, which reassured me that it wasn't going to get up and storm off in a huff, then gestured for the rest of us to join her. I did. I was only too happy to squeeze in close so Ned and Tall could fit beside me.

"We made it onto the bus!" I was thrilled. "That's awesome! What now?"

"Now," Mary replied, leaning back slightly, "we stay on this bus until it nears the matrix location. It will not take us directly there, but within enough proximity that we can then use more localized transportation to cover the remaining distance."

Right. Stay on the bus. Cool. I could handle that.

"Do we need a ticket?" I asked after a second. I did mention that I'd always sucked at those quiet games, right? "I mean, are they gonna come around asking for tickets or anything?"

She shook her head. "Typically the bus requires payment before entry. Thus it will be assumed we have already paid the appropriate fees."

"And if someone figures out we haven't?"

"Then we pay through the nose for the on-the-spot tickets," Ned explained. "Or they toss us right back off."

Great. I hoped they'd accept my debit card. And that it didn't come to more than $112.57. After tax.

"Do not worry on that score," Mary assured me, resting a hand on my leg. Man, my body temperature rose at least twenty degrees—it's a wonder I didn't scald her! "We will—"

Whatever else she'd meant to say was drowned out by a sound I'd heard too many times in movies not to recognize.

Gunfire.

Well, laser fire.

Or alien attack fire. Whatever the weapon. It had a particular "zing" and whine and beep like nothing else.

"What the hell?" I shouted, sticking my head up to look around—only to have Tall shove it back down as we all dove off the bench and squatted behind it. "Who's shooting? We'll buy tickets, honest!"

"It's not the bus conductor!" Ned whispered near my shoulder. "They don't carry weapons!"

"Who is it, then? And what are the odds of one bus getting boarded twice in less than ten minutes?" I was guessing it was somebody else crashing the party because—as near as I could tell—the rest of the passengers were freaking out just like we were.

Ned fiddled with one of his gadgets, and turned pale. "Temporal raiders!"

"Whosis what now?"

"Temporal raiders!" He was shaking in his boots—yes, he had boots. Big heavy work boots. With Velcro straps, which is just wrong, really. Boots should have laces, unless you're under the age of six. And they should never, NEVER be that shade of yellow.

I turned to Mary. "Who or what is a temporal raider?"

"They are a marauding band from the planet Dilexese 12," she replied quietly. "They believe there are gaps in their race's evolutionary history and so they travel the galaxy, abducting likely candidates and propelling them back through time to fill out the holes in their record."

I glanced around. "They steal people to plug up their own history?" She nodded. "That's impressive. Do you think that would work on my taxes?"

"Shush!" she warned, but of course it was too late. The sounds of shooting came closer, and then a mirror-faced silver-suited alien stood over us. It had a long, bulky purple gun in one hand, and aimed that thing toward our little group and the bench we were using for cover.

"Don't shoot!" I shouted, standing up, hands up by my head. "Look at me! Do you really want me as your ancestor?"

I must have said the wrong thing, though, because next thing I knew it was aiming that long barrel my way, and then there was a flash and a glow and a sizzle and everything spun and danced and disappeared.

When my eyes cleared I was in the middle of a jungle. A big, fluorescent jungle. With insects the size of my head—yes, my head, and not even my original-issue one—fluttering and swooping and zooming around.

And there was a dinosaur—a huge, bright purple dinosaur with blue markings—towering over me.

I think I was about to fill somebody's belly rather than somebody's evolutionary niche.

Chapter Seven
The what effect?

The massive dino opened its jaws. Geez! Ever heard of an orthodontist? It was disgusting in there! I could see whole trees jammed between some of those teeth—of course, it'd take dental floss thicker than me (and I'm not exactly svelte) to work them out, so maybe it wasn't the big guy's fault. Though he might be able to fashion a toothbrush or at least a toothpick out of some redwoods. And breath mints? A city's worth, please. Stat.

But my dismay at his lack of dental hygiene was quickly shoved aside by the more practical side of my brain, which screamed, "He's going to eat us! Run, you idiot!" I turned—and saw a thick batch of bushes to my left, sporting thorns as long as my forearm. I twisted to the right—and discovered we were on a cliff, because there wasn't anything to the right but air and a nasty lack of guardrails. Behind me—more bushes, and trees, and vines thick as my legs all coiled around like a snake after an epileptic fit. Nope, nowhere to go.

Forward, maybe? I considered that as the dino stepped closer, its gargantuan foot creating shockwaves that almost knocked me off my own feet. Could I dive forward, between those massive legs, avoid that mammoth tail, and scoot away to safety before it could turn and come after me? It didn't look good but I was seriously considering it. Too late, though—the dino leaned in over me, its jaws opened even wider, its thick pink tongue lashed out, and—

"Pardon me, but you are obstructing my appreciation of Nature's intrinsic bouquet."

Huh?

I stared up at it. And it spoke again.

"I say, would you mind just shifting a smidge to the side? If it's not too much trouble, of course."

Obstructing his appreciation? Nature's bouquet? Shift to the side? I glanced behind me. Oh. I was blocking his view of some flowers.

I sidled over a step so he could see the blooms clearly.

"Ah, much appreciated," it roared, then leaned over—and sniffed them delicately. "Such a lovely fragrance! Delightful!"

"Yeah, it's a real treat," I muttered. What the hell was going on here? Dinos that liked sniffing flowers instead of gobbling up passers-by? What was the world coming to?

But, I realized, it wasn't coming to anything. Not my world, anyway. Because this wasn't my world, this was the world of those temporal-raider guys. They'd zapped me back here. So apparently in their history dinosaurs were . . . pacifists? Flower-sniffers? Sissies?

It occurred to me that I hadn't seen any sign of meat in the dino's mouth when he'd gaped that maw at me. Just trees and other foliage. I added "vegetarian" to the list and suddenly felt a whole lot better about my chances of surviving this impromptu field trip. Of course, getting back on the bus might be another matter but first things first.

"I say," the dino commented after getting his fill of the prehistoric daisies, "you are not from around these parts, are you?"

"No, I'm new here," I admitted.

"Well, welcome to the neighborhood, old fellow!" The dino waved one of its little tiny arms at me. I waved back. I've never understood that, about massive T-rexes and other dinosaurs having such puny little arms. Was it a cosmic joke? Like "hey, we're making you one of the most dangerous critters ever to walk this earth, but as a tradeoff you only get jokes for arms. No fisticuffs for you but at least you can bite through mountains!"

"Thanks. So," I glanced around. "Any advice? Good places to see? Things to avoid? Tasty burger joints?"

"The land is filled with glory and wonder," the dino answered me, ratcheting up its "sissy" score. "You have but to see to admire. And I know not of these 'burger joints.' But to avoid, yes. Steer clear of the dragonflies if you can."

"The dragonflies? Really? Those pretty little bugs with the glossy wings? Why, they're bad here?"

"Oh, very." He shuddered. Shuddered! A T-rex or Allosaurus or whatever the hell he was, one of the baddest creatures ever, and he was shuddering like a little girly-man over the mention of some dragonflies. Next he'd start shrieking and run off in tears.

"Right, I'll keep an eye out for 'em. Thanks."

"Certainly, happy to help. Ooh, is that a *misticulia beautifica*?

It is!" I left it squealing with delight over some little yellow flower and started walking. I had no idea where, but anywhere away from Little Miss Sunshine the Thunder Lizard was a good start. I walked for a while. This place was huge! I mean, everything in it was enormous—I know it was a whole world and those are big, I'm not an idiot no matter what my high school guidance counselor claimed. I was pushing past ferns taller than most apartment buildings, sidestepping spiders the size of compact cars, and watching out for skyscraper-sized dinos thundering across the plains. It was like SuperSize Me Land, and I was the outsider, the tiny little duckman that didn't belong. If this was some children's fable I wasn't sure I wanted to see how it ended.

I found a nice flat, open plain, no vegetation taller than my waist, with a few small boulders scattered around to break the monotony, and clambered up onto one of them. Ah! It felt good to take the weight off my poor bruised feet for a minute, and from here I could see anything coming a mile away. I leaned back and took a deep breath—

—and yelped as something socked me in the head.

"Hey!" I spun around but there wasn't anybody there and I almost fell off the rock in the process. Checked the other side but still nothing. What the hell? After a second I lay back again—

—and something banged my temple again.

"Knock it off!" I shouted, leaping to my feet. The coast was clear in all directions, but then a shadow flickered past and I glanced up—

—and dove off the boulder to cower behind it.

Okay, for the record? When a big-ass dinosaur—even a

flower-sniffing sissy one—tells you to watch out for dragonflies? You should listen. Because that's exactly what was hovering just above my head right now. A dragonfly. Just as pretty as I remember them, too, with iridescent wings and a long slender body and big glittering faceted eyes.

Only this one? Had a wingspan like a plane. And not a tiny cropduster, either. No, we're talking 747 here. The thing had to be at least twenty feet long! Its eyes were bigger than my head!

And, as I stared up at it, my bill hanging open, it spat a basketball-sized hunk of rock at me. Only a quick stagger backward kept the thing from putting my eye out.

"What's the big idea?" I yelled, brushing myself off and trying to look like I wasn't scared of some gaudy giant-sized insect. I don't think I fooled it. "Why're you spitting rocks at me? Please tell me those are rocks and not eggs or partially digested food or something else equally gross."

It spit another rock but this time I was ready and it missed me completely. "Why not?" it taunted. "What're you gonna do about it?"

Oh great. I'd met the rebellious teens of this prehistoric park. And they were giant dragonflies.

I bent to scoop up two of the rocks it had fired at me, one in each hand, and then straightened. "Oh yeah? Well, two can play at that game!" And I hurled one, then the other at him. They both missed, of course—the dragonfly just darted gracefully back out of range. Then it divebombed me, firing rock after rock after rock. Damn, it must have a lot of room in its mouth!

Crouching behind the boulder wasn't working. I grabbed

up a few more rocks and threw them up, not really trying to hit him but hoping they'd distract him long enough for me to find better cover.

Of course, I had selected a nice flat, open plain. Stupid me.

But I guess it ran out of rocks because after pelting me for a few more minutes it flew away. I swear that sucker was laughing as it took off.

I kept going until I'd reached a small stand of bushes and plants. I didn't want it to come back once it'd reloaded. Then I considered my options.

Okay, this world officially sucked. Giant everything, nasty rock-throwing bugs, wacky hippy dinosaurs—I didn't want to find out what the spiders and grubs and worms were like. I needed to get the hell out of here, and fast.

But how? I didn't have a nifty time-travel device to send me back—where was a snazzy gull-wing car when you needed one?—or any way to signal Mary and Ned. I had my cell phone and I went ahead and checked it but, no surprise, it was out of service. I didn't have any weapons, or any body armor, nor did I have any food. And spaceship? Right out.

I leaned against a daisy—at least I think it was a daisy, I couldn't actually see the flower because it was above my head—to think. A few insects fluttered past me and I waved them away. At least they weren't super-sized! One of them was a butterfly, all delicate purples and pinks, and it circled my bill twice before drifting away to check out some big green and gold flower a little away from the other blooms. I watched it idly, and something nagged at the back of my head.

Butterfly. Butterfly. Why did that mean something to me? Something to do with time travel.

Wait a second! I'd read or heard or seen a movie once about something called the Butterfly Effect—something about how everything was connected and if you went back in time and stepped on a butterfly you'd change the course of history.

Well, here I was back in time. And there was a butterfly. And this was the temporal raiders' homeworld, in their past. So if I stepped on that butterfly I might change their history. And maybe if I changed it enough they'd never exist, which means they'd never attack the bus and send me back here. Which means I wouldn't be here.

Wa-hoo!

It was worth a try, anyway. I walked slowly toward that flower, trying not to scare the butterfly off. No worries there—it was glued to the thing, dancing around the lacy little petals. I'm pretty sure I could hear butterflies this one would have been tittering out of sheer happiness.

"Sorry about this, little guy," I whispered once I was right up by the flower. "But you're my ticket out of here. And I'm apparently the only one who can save the universe. So, in a way, your sacrifice will save the universe. That's not so bad, right?"

The butterfly circled my face, almost like it understood me. Then it fluttered back down and settled on the flower, alighting gently on one of those delicate petals—

—and I stomped on it. Hard. With my enormous webbed feet—size 15 triple-wide, thank you very much. Never mind pontoons—put a few support columns on them and my shoes could be used as those oilrigs you see out in the ocean. It'd probably leak less, too.

"Noooo!!!" I glanced up to see one of the dinos standing there, tiny arms waving, slack-jawed, eyes wide with shock. "Not the millennium lotus! It only blossoms once an epoch! How could you? You, you—you barbarian, you!"

Then everything got all hazy. It was like the world around me was on a dry erase board and somebody was swiping at it with a damp cloth—the dino faded a bit, and parts of him disappeared completely. I could see right through him—

—to the inside of the galactic bus. It'd worked! I'd never scoff at crappy low-budget sci-fi films again!

The Land of the Lost continued to disappear, and finally I was back on the bus completely. I breathed a sigh of relief. Mary was right next to me, which made me feel even better. Ned and Tall were there too, but you can't have everything.

"Hey guys, didya miss me?" I asked. "You won't believe what just—"

"Keep down!" Tall yanked me down by the arm as I tried to stand up, which is when I finally realized we were all crouched behind what I can only charitably refer to as a bus seat. "Do you want to get your head blown off?"

"What?" I looked around, suddenly noticing the loud crackling sounds and the smell of burning dog hair. "What the hell's going on here?"

"I told you already," Ned snapped behind me, using me as a shield. "We're under attack!"

"By the temporal raiders, I know. But I already dealt with that. See, I—"

"The what?" Mary frowned at me, her eyes roaming my impressive forehead—I think she was checking if I'd cracked my noggin, actually. "No, the dinotropic aesthetic elite. Extremely dangerous, particularly to anyone of an avian persuasion. You see, they believe that—"

Just then something crashed through the side of the bus only a few feet ahead of us. It was a spaceship, exactly the kind you imagine when you have nightmares about an alien attack— narrow and sleek and needle-nosed. Okay, maybe the kind you imagine after playing a marathon of Space Invader. It was also really pretty, like one of those high-end exotic sports cars rich men buy to forget about their expanding waistlines and receding hairlines. It had a glassy bubble across the top, tinted dark, and that somehow melted back into the body, exposing a small but neatly arranged cockpit—and the pilot within.

It saw me the same time I saw it, and we were close enough that I could see its eyes widen.

"It's him!" The space invader squawked. "It's him! The Destroyer of Beauty! The Millennium Lotus Murderer! He Who Hates All Things Lovely! He's here!"

I stared back. The guy shouting all this looked exactly like those big purple dinosaurs I'd seen in the Land of the Lost, not two minutes and millions of years before—at least if one of those things was shrunk down to the size of a kindergartner, except for his arms which were now proportionate to the rest, and outfitted in a really snazzy silvery jumpsuit-spacesuit thing.

Those teeth were still mighty impressive, though.

"Oh, come on!" I shouted back. "You've got to be kidding me! It was one lousy flower! And a butterfly!" The dino pulled a nifty-looking ray gun from somewhere and pointed it at me, all while clambering out of his ship. Tall yanked me back just in time, as the ray gun's beam disintegrated the chair and part of the wall behind me. Then, clearly deciding discretion was the better part of valor, he tossed me over his shoulder—I'd love to know the physics that made that possible without me smushing him flat, by the way—and ran for the door, Mary and Ned right behind him.

"I was aiming for the butterfly!" I hollered as the door opened and we charged through. My last glimpse of the dino was him barreling toward us—and four more just like him appearing at his back.

Great. I'm never watching another crappy sci-fi film again. All they do is get you in trouble.

Chapter Eight
Why I hate taking the bus

"We've got to get off this bus!" Tall shouted as he hauled me down what looked to be another train car. It was almost exactly the same as the last one: crazy-looking furniture, crazy-looking passengers, no way to tell the two apart. And, oh yeah, a bunch of small, smartly dressed purple dino-people shooting at everyone. Well, almost everyone—I noticed what looked like a group of flower people huddled in one corner, petals all a-quiver, and the raiders were leaving them well alone. Swell. Where was that daisy costume Ms. Trey made me wear in first grade when I needed it?

"We cannot!" Mary replied from a row or two ahead of us. She'd ducked behind what looked like a rock with pipe-cleaner arms and inflatable-raft legs, though it was blubbering so much I think she was at much at risk of drowning as of getting shot. She motioned us over and we huddled beside her, Tall dropping me to the floor in a heap. Ned was nowhere in sight.

"The bus only makes scheduled stops throughout the galaxy," she explained in a quieter voice. "That is why we were forced to effect such a violent means of entry. The nearest stop to Earth is two-point-nine-five million light-years away."

"And how long does that take without stopping for the lights?" I asked, pulling myself up and dusting myself off. Man, don't they ever clean those floors? Then again, for all I knew those little flecks were paying customers. Or bits from Mr. Sensitive Boulder. Eew.

"One hour, Earth-standard time."

"One hour?" I shook my head. "My time-sense is all out of whack and my cell phone isn't working—how long ago did we crash this party?"

Mary consulted a watch on her wrist—I was amused to see it was a plastic kid's watch with a picture of Betty Boop on it. Good to know she wasn't all business all the time. "Twelve minutes."

"Twelve minutes? So we've got to ride it out for another thirty-eight minutes without getting shot before we can ditch this crazy ride?"

"Forty-eight," Tall corrected.

I glared at him. "Oh great, just add another ten minutes to our death sentence, why don't you? As if thirty-eight minutes wasn't tough enough!" Yeah, math isn't my strong suit. Neither are spelling, grammar, history, geography, science. . . . Well, let's just say my strong suits are more . . . recreational in nature. I rock at Foozball, for example.

"Isn't there an emergency cord?" I asked Mary. I barely even noticed how hot she looked crouched there, which tells you how scared I was. "Can't we make an unscheduled stop?"

She shook her head. "The train is automated, and only the controllers can force it to deviate from its normal schedule."

"Great. How do we get in touch with them?"

She frowned. "There should be an emergency communications device in the front car," she said finally.

"The front car. Right." I glanced out from behind the Weepy Rock. There was still a lot of shooting and screaming going on all around us. "How many cars does this thing have?"

"Four hundred and twenty-four."

"And which one are we in now?"

"Number four hundred and twenty-one."

"So we have four hundred and twenty cars between us and the panic button?"

"Four hundred and nineteen," Tall corrected. "The front car itself doesn't count."

"What are you, a retired Mathlete?" I scowled at him. "Well, at least your math skills are coming in handy this time—you just got us one car closer." He started to say something, stopped, frowned, and shook his head. I have that effect on people a lot. "Okay, so what we waiting for?" I started to pull myself up, using Mr. Sobby Stone for handholds.

"We cannot traverse that many cars without being seen and destroyed by the DAE," Mary warned me. She had a weird expression on her face—if I had to guess I'd say it was a mix of shock, terror . . . and admiration. I didn't see that last one a whole lot, though, so I might have been wrong. It could have been constipation instead. "The distance is too great."

"Not if we go someplace they won't expect us!" Ned slid in beside us. Little beads of purple sweat—at least I hoped it was sweat—stood out all over his face and head, and he mopped

them up with a big pink paisley handkerchief while he grinned
at us. I can honestly say I was happy to see him, broccoli-hair
and all.

"Where the hell have you been?" I demanded. It's a time-
honored tradition, mostly used by parents—cover worry and
relief with irritation.

"Scouting ahead," he replied. "I needed to know what we
were up against."

"And?"

"And there are over three hundred DAE members on this
train, all of them converging on us." He glanced at me. "What'd
you do to piss them off so much?"

"Stepped on a butterfly. Oh, and a flower. A big flower." They
were all looking at me like I was crazy. Maybe I was. Though if
so, I had to give myself props—I had no idea I was this creative.
"Never mind. So where can we go?"

Ned grinned. His teeth were perfect, tiny like a baby's and a
gleaming white. Except for one that had a little ladybug carved
into it. I stared at the tiny design and it winked at me. Then
he opened his mouth, mercifully hiding the flirtatious bug
ornament, and said one word:

"Outside."

"Outside? *Outside* outside? You mean out in space?" Now I
wondered if he was nuts, or if my imagination was just sadistic.
Which would explain all those dreams about the IRS showing
up in my bedroom, along with my mother and my fourth-
grade science teacher. "How the hell are we gonna manage that?
Wouldn't we blow up or something?" Tall started to open his

mouth, no doubt to correct me again on something. "Not a word out of you, Science Boy," I warned him, "or I'll bite your nose off. I'll do it, too!" That shut him up, anyway. Not that I'd really bite his nose off. Can you imagine how disgusting that would taste? Yuck!

Mary was considering Ned's suggestion, which told me either it wasn't as crazy as it sounded or we were in even worse danger than I'd thought. "The shields extend far enough to protect us?" she asked.

"Seventy-five centimeters, all the way around," Ned confirmed. "It'll be a tight squeeze but we should be able to manage it. And they won't think to look for us out there."

I was trying to do the math in my head and failing horribly. "Alright, Mr. Wizard," I turned to Tall, "go ahead and impress me. Seventy-five centimeters is how much to us normal joes?"

"Twenty-nine-point-five inches." He took the opportunity to smirk at me, of course. "That's just under two-and-a-half feet."

"Yeah, that part I got. So we've got two-and-a-half feet of clearance on the roof?" Ned nodded. "And what happens if we go beyond that?"

"Any part that extends past the shields will be instantly exposed to the full rigors of outer space," Mary answered. "Sub-zero temperatures, explosive decompression . . ."

"Don't worry about it, though," Ned assured me. "This train's moving at ridiculous speeds and the shields are all that keeps us from feeling the velocity, so if you do stick your bill out past the shields it'll be ripped away long before it freezes or blows up!" He slapped me on the back.

"Great. Thanks. And is there anything to hold on to out there, or are we supposed to slide our way down?"

"Already taken care of that part," Ned assured me. "Come here." He pulled out one of his weird little vegetable gadgets— this one looked like a wilted piece of celery with circuits in it and a big red clown nose at the bottom—and tapped me with it. "Lift your right foot," he ordered.

I did, or tried to. It didn't want to come off the floor! It was like I was glued there. I finally did manage to raise it about an inch before it got sucked back down again.

"I've magnetized your body," Ned explained. "We'll stick to the hull, no problem. And the shields hold in air as well as heat, so we'll be able to breath just fine, too."

"Nice!" I gave him a friendly pat on the back. "Hey, this just might work! Okay, where's the sunroof? How do we get up there?" Mary and Ned both started to answer, when a sudden flurry of ray gun blasts turned Weepy the Pet Rock into rubble— and blasted a hole through the wall behind him as well. "Never mind."

"Everybody out!" Ned tapped Mary and Tall with the clown-celery wand, then himself, and led the way. "Come on!" Mary was right behind him and I quickly followed her, leaving Tall to bring up the rear again. What am I, stupid?

The dinos were everywhere, shooting everything in sight, but fortunately all the debris from the Teary-eyed Stalagmite made it hard to see anything. Then one of them shot one of the flower-guys by mistake, and they all huddled around sobbing while two of them pulled out what looked like Ceran Wrap and tried to reattach the leaves they'd just shot off. That gave us the distraction we needed, and we beat a hasty retreat for the new side door—if by "hasty" you mean "moving like we're underwater because we could barely lift our feet from the floor." We got there without getting shot, anyway, and without anyone shouting, "Hey, there they go!" which already made this different from most of my nights drinking with the guys.

Ned slipped out through the hole and started climbing up the side, Spider-Man style. Mary was right behind him, and I followed her as closely as I could without getting slapped. Tall was all but breathing down my neck. It was actually pretty easy, thanks to my hands and feet sticking to the surface, and in seconds we were all crouched on the roof.

"Right," Ned called over his shoulder. "Let's go!" And we set off. It only took us a minute to get to the end of the car, and fortunately the next one butted up against it—there was a thin seam marking the break and that was it. I did have a moment of panic while climbing across that seam, with visions of a thousand train-chase action sequences dancing in my head, but nobody showed up to uncouple the cars and laugh maniacally. Must have been the wrong movie. Then I was safely onto the next car.

One down, four hundred and twenty to go. Or four hundred and nineteen. Whatever.

Chapter Nine
Can you get top-forty on this thing?

". . . **his** name is my name, too, and whenever we go out, the people always shout—"

"Will you shut the hell up?!"

"Oh, come on! I was just getting to the good part! You can join in—I don't mind."

"This is not summer camp, and we are not ten years old!"

"Did something horrible happen to you at summer camp when you were ten years old? Because you're getting awfully upset about one little song."

"It's not one little song! It's all the little songs! It's the teapot song and the dreidel song and the cat that never came back song and the man on the MTA song—"

"I never got that one, really." I stopped for a second to scratch my head, but started moving again before Tall could get within swatting range. I'd already learned my lesson. "He's stuck on this train, right? Because he doesn't have enough money to pay the exit fare? And his wife hands him his lunch every morning as the train goes past? Why doesn't she include a nickel or whatever it was so he get off the damned train? Does she secretly hate him, and enjoy seeing him trapped in there? And wouldn't the MTA workers eventually kick him off for riding around and around on one lousy fare?"

Tall didn't respond for a second. Not a word. Not even that jaw-grinding he'd been making for the past half hour or more—I was afraid to see the state of his molars when we finally reached our destination. He'd be lucky to manage gumming Jell-O at this rate. But even that sound stopped. Then he spoke, finally.

"I hate you," he said softly. "I really, really hate you."

"Aw, don't be like that," I told him. "I'm just trying to keep us all entertained and distracted while we make this fun-filled trek across a speeding train hurtling through outer space. I bet you forgot all about the risk of explosive decompression while I was singing, didn't you?" A faint gurgling sound and some more grinding were my only answer.

"Hey Ned," I called ahead, "what car are we on now?"

"Four hundred and twenty," he shouted back. "Only three left and we're at the head car!"

"Nice!" I glanced back at Tall. "See? Doesn't it feel like we only just started crawling?" He glared at me.

"The DAE have been remarkably quiet these past few cars," Mary pointed out. "We must be especially careful. They may have realized we are no longer within the bus proper."

I knew what she meant. For the first hundred or so cars we could hear those crazy little dinos running around shooting at everything—more than once their wild shots pierced the bus roof and we had a peek at the chaos within as we crawled quietly past. We'd also seen plenty of things—and people—get shoved or kicked or shot out the sides. Most of them hit the shields and bounced back in. Some were too big or too heavy or simply going too fast, and slid right through the shields. They were whipped away before I could even really register their shapes. It was like riding in a really quiet car with a really smooth ride going really fast—you completely forgot you were doing two hundred-plus miles an hour until you saw some idiot hitchhiker on the side of the road and they blurred by even before your brain told you they were there. I was trying really hard not to think about just how fast we were going, or what would happen to us if we stuck our heads up too high, which was why I'd started singing. It'd helped calm me down. And hey, it really had distracted Tall. Whether he wanted to admit it or not.

But after a while the shooting had lessened, and recently we hadn't heard any shooting at all. Maybe the dinos had gotten bored, decided I must have jumped or been vaporized by a stray ray gun blast, and gone home. But I doubted it. They still seemed really pissed off about that stupid flower.

"So what do we do?" I asked.

"We keep moving," Mary replied. "There is little else we can do. Just stay alert."

No problem there—the crawl hadn't been hard, though it was tedious and my neck muscles were straining from holding my head above the hull but below the shields. I wasn't likely to lie down and take a nap just now.

Zap! Pow!

"What the hell—?" I shouted, glancing back over my shoulder as Tall cursed and fumbled for his gun. Two streams of colored light or plasma or silly string or whatever the hell they were had just gone past us. And behind Tall I could see the reason why. "Two dinos! They've found us!"

The cold-blooded little bastards—that's a fact, not just an insult, at least not the cold-blooded part—must have found or cut a hole in the last car we'd passed, and they'd pulled themselves out and onto the roof. Now they were laying on their stomachs, their ray guns held in front of them with both hands, and they were shooting at us.

Fortunately, though they had evolved a long way from their big T-rex ancestors, they still had some design flaws to work out. Namely, though their arms were now roughly the right size for their bodies, their heads were still several times too big. I can totally relate. But what it meant was that, laying down like that with their arms in front of them, their own snouts kept interfering with their aim. Which was definitely a positive as far as I was concerned.

Still, they were bound to get lucky sooner or later. And we didn't exactly have anything to hide behind.

Ned had apparently realized that too, though. "Follow me!" he shouted back at us. Then he began crawling at an angle, still going forward but also veering off to the left. Mary swerved after him and I was right behind her. The view hadn't gotten any less appealing for my staring at it repeatedly. I was sure Tall was following us too—and no, I didn't feel the least bit bad for him having to stare at my butt instead for the past however-many minutes—and I could hear the bang as he fired his gun back at the dinos.

We cut a spiral path around the train, like a big loose

corkscrew, and if I could have reached him I'd have kissed Ned on his little green head. He was a genius! We were magnetized, so our hands and feet—and other parts too, I'd discovered to my discomfort—clung to the hull. The dinos didn't have that going for them. They cursed and whined and roared as we slid around the train's side and out of sight, but there was no way they could follow us. Safe!

At least until, halfway down the car, several more dinos cut a hole in the train floor, stuck their arms through, and began firing wildly in all directions.

"Back up!" Ned hollered, and we hurriedly curved back out a bit. Now we were on the side of the train, which seemed like a good plan to me—too low for the roof-climbers and too high up for the floor-gunners.

Too bad the dinos weren't stupid. And too bad they clearly talked amongst themselves. Holes started appearing all down the car at random intervals and random heights. Some were in the ceiling, some in the floor, and some along the walls. And each hole quickly sprouted one or more arms, all wielding ray guns. Bigger holes even had whole dinos popping up to take shots at us. This had quickly become one of my least favorite duck-references ever—those little tin ducks at a shooting arcade.

"We need some kind of cover!" Tall bellowed. He took a few more shots before putting his gun away again. It hadn't helped much.

"Maybe we should climb back inside," I suggested, but Mary shook her head.

"That is what they are hoping," she explained. "Out here

they cannot reach us. Inside they would mob us. We would have no way to escape."

"Well, can we find some way to cover those holes?" I asked. "Or some way to force their hands back inside? Something that makes their guns stop working? Anything?"

Ned paused for a second and scratched his double chin. "There might be a way," he commented, "but it's dangerous, for us as well as them."

"We're not exactly danger-free as it is," I pointed out. "What's the plan?"

"Well," he fiddled with one of his tools, "I can adjust the shields somewhat."

"Okay, and what'll that get us?"

"I can't turn them off, but I can reshape them slightly. Focus them all on one side or another—and pull them right up to the hull everywhere else."

I thought about that one for a second, well aware that Mary and Ned were waiting patiently and Tall was smirking. "So anything stuck out of the train on those other sides would get ripped right off. Which would mean they could only attack us along one side."

"Exactly!"

"It's gotta be better than playing Dodgeball with ray guns. I say we try it!" Mary nodded, and so did Tall.

"Okay," Ned agreed. "The question is, which side?"

"Top," I said right away.

"Why the top?" Tall asked.

"Did you get a good look at those guys?" I asked him.

"They're short. Really short. Like four feet or less. And the train's at least, what, ten feet high? So climbing up that high's gotta be tough for them. Actually," I glanced at Ned, "in space up and down don't matter much, right? I mean, we're on the side of the train but it feels like what's beneath us is a floor because it's below us."

"Sure," Ned agreed. "What about it?"

"So instead of the top, could you do the upper right corner? You know, curve the shield around a bit so we're actually at an angle rather than straight up and down?"

"Not a problem." Ned grinned. "And that'll make it even harder for them to hold themselves up to shoot! Brilliant!"

I don't know that anyone's ever called me brilliant before. That was kind of cool. I enjoyed it while I could—I was sure it wouldn't last.

Ned didn't waste any time, either. Mary took the lead and guided us up a little higher than we were while Ned tapped and twisted and even bit first one and then a second tool. "Got it!" he said after a minute of muttering and spitting out little bits. "We're all set. Don't stray off this path, whatever you do—it's only about six feet wide. Everybody ready?" We all nodded. "Here it goes!" He jabbed one of his tools down against the train and it was like somebody took the world off mute.

Ever open the window of a car when you're going really fast, and then close it again because the sound of the wind rushing by was deafening? That's exactly what happened here. There was a tremendous rushing sound, so loud I thought it was going to tear my head off. There were screams, too, and things flying past, but I tried not to notice those. Then the sound suddenly faded again—I could still hear it whooshing by but it wasn't as close or as loud.

"Come on," Ned said. "We've only got two cars left."

He took the front again and we followed him quietly. I wasn't in a singing mood anymore. Besides I'd run out of camp songs and would have had to start on the drinking songs next. And those are no fun at all when the nearest alcohol is a couple hundred light-years away. Not counting some of those passengers I'd seen earlier.

Dinos were still blasting through the train's hull to try shooting at us, but they quickly realized it wasn't safe to stick their hands out so they contented themselves with glaring at us and trying to zap us as we crawled past. Having a few hundred little purple dinosaur-men all giving you the hairy eyeball isn't a lot of fun, believe me. It was a good thing we didn't have to do much more than crawl in a straight line, because just knowing they were all there, and seeing them every time we passed a hole, made it hard to concentrate properly.

Then something beeped quietly and Ned said the scariest word in the English language:

"Uh-oh."

Actually, is that even English? Or really a word? Is it two words, "uh" and "oh"? Is this why no one ever wants to play me at Scrabble? I thought it was because every time I lean over to see the board clearly my bill knocks all the pieces off.

Regardless, his muttering made my blood turn cold.

Though not as cold as it would if I were on the wrong side of the shields, in the sub-zero of outer space.

Because that would be cold. Really cold. This wasn't like that. I mean, my blood was still flowing normally, but I had one of those little chills that makes your whole body shiver.

You know what I mean.

"What's wrong?" Mary, Tall, and I all asked at the same time. If we'd had one more we could have been a barbershop quartet of queries and concern.

"They've figured out how we're staying out here," Ned muttered. "They're demagnetizing the hull!" I suddenly felt a static charge wash past me along the train's surface—and then my hands and feet started drifting loose. "Hang on!"

"Hang on?" I shouted, scrabbling at the way-too-smooth surface below me. "Hang on to what? There's nothing here to grip! It wouldn't have killed them to put a few little decorative bits along this thing, like door moldings and windowsills and flying buttresses?"

"Just relax!" Ned hollered back.

"Relax? We're on an outer-space train speeding along at millions of miles an hour, inches from instant death by decompression and überfrostbite, being shot at by the dinosaur midgets from Crayolaland, and you want me to relax?"

"Go limp!" Ned corrected. He spread-eagled himself, arms and legs out wide, and let his whole body relax as he floated up off the train's surface, into the shield—and bumped up against it gently before drifting back down.

"Oh. Why didn't you say so?" Limp I could do—I'd had lots of practice at limp. Who knew all those late nights drinking would actually be good for something besides making my credit card company dance for joy?

I let my body go limp, and struggled not to panic as I wafted up off the train. But it worked—I'd seen before that the shields kept things in as long as there wasn't too much velocity involved, and with us completely unresisting we touched it light as a feather, then our own momentum carried us back to the hull. Of course we still couldn't grip it, so we just floated there, touching it but not actually secure.

"Now what?" I yelled up at him.

"I'm working on remagnetizing the hull," Ned assured us. His fingers were a blur as he worked on those devices of his. I bet he was great with a remote, and could flip back and forth between several games without missing a beat. I made a mental note to invite him to my next Superbowl party—assuming we lived that long.

Suddenly a giant hand slammed into my back, flattening me against the train. It was crushing me down onto the flat cool surface, so hard I couldn't breathe. Lights swam before my eyes.

"Too . . . much . . ." I heard Mary gasp ahead of me.

"I . . . know . . ." Ned managed to reply. A second later the pressure eased enough for me to lift my head and gasp for air. "Sorry about that. The initial burst to restore its magnetic charge was a little strong. We'd better hurry before they figure out what I did and erase it again."

We clambered after him as quickly as we could, checking our hands and feet every second to make sure they hadn't started drifting loose again. Halfway down the last car they did exactly that, and again we went limp, bounced, settled back down, and groaned as the new charge slammed us into the train a second time. At least this time we knew enough to take deep breaths first.

Then we were crossing the seam between that car and the front car. We'd made it!

There was only one problem. This car was as featureless as all the others we'd passed. And it looked like the dinos hadn't gotten this far yet, so there weren't any holes.

"How do we get inside?" I asked.

I could see by the panicked look in Ned's eyes—and the matching stares from Mary and even Tall—that they didn't have a clue either.

"There isn't an access door?" I shook my head. "An escape hatch? A trash chute? Something?"

"There's a secure hatch between it and the first passenger car," Ned admitted, "but we'd have to backtrack and cut in through that car to reach it. And even then I'd have to bypass the security to get us through."

"Can we shoot our way in?" Tall asked. He had his gun out and pointed down.

"NO!!!" This time I was the one in chorus with Ned and Mary. "You could kill us all!" I shouted at him. "That bullet would probably just bounce back up and take out one or more of us before it cut through the shield—and who's to say we wouldn't all be sucked out with it before the shield could repair itself?"

"Oh." I hadn't seen Tall look embarrassed before. It made him look almost human. "Right. Sorry." He holstered his gun.

"There's gotta be a way in, right?" I glanced at Ned and Mary again. "Did anybody bring an electric can opener?"

Ned stared at me for a second. Then he grinned. "DuckBob, you're a genius!" That was the second time he'd called me a genius—I was really starting to doubt his intelligence. "That just might work!"

"What might?" Yeah, I'd confused myself. Trust me, it happens a lot.

"If I reconfigure the shields on this car," Ned explained, "I might be able to dip them below the hull's surface for just a second. That'd let the train's own velocity punch a hole right through it." He had three different doodads out and was messing with all of them at once. I had no idea eyebrows could be prehensile. "The trick," he muttered, "is to keep the displacement extremely focused, so it only effects a single spot and not the entire car."

"Oh. Yeah. Because cutting the shields all along the car would be bad." I nodded. I think I'd moved beyond fear and into shock, which at least meant I was calm about the chances of our violent and messy death. Hey, if it happened it'd be kind of like having yourself cremated and your ashes scattered, only it'd be over several galaxies and there wouldn't be any burning or, y'know, peaceful sleep beforehand.

"I think I've got it," Ned announced after a minute. "Hold on!" He kept saying that, but there still wasn't anything to hold onto, so I grabbed Mary's hand. She glanced down at my hand on hers but didn't say anything and didn't pull away. Hey, that was further than I got on most first dates. Then again, we'd gone a lot further for this date, too.

The first of Ned's little devices made a high-pitched squeal, like a pig spotting an especially nice mudhole. Then the second one beeped and the third one chirruped. It was like his own little orchestra there, comprised of electronics and barnyard animals. But it worked. I felt a mild tingle across my back and over my head as the shield shifted, and ducked down to be safe, and then watched as an area a few feet to our right buckled and vanished, torn clean off in an instant. The tingle faded, and Ned beamed.

"We're in! And I've reset the shield so we can approach it safely. Once we're in I'll pull the shields in tight on this car, so the DAE won't be able to follow us."

"You rock, Ned." I meant it, too, as we followed him over to the hole. It was maybe three feet across and roughly circular, so all of us fit through without too much trouble, though I did have to tilt my head way back for my bill and Tall did have to suck in his shoulders a bit. Then we were all inside and looking around.

What a dump!

The walls and ceilings and floors were the same as the train cars we'd seen already, smooth and metallic but brushed instead of shiny, with some kind of faint light coming off them so the whole space had a nice even glow. But there was crap all over.

Okay, not literally crap. Just wires and circuit boards and monitors and other random electronics. It was like an IT department had gone completely *Exorcist* and just started spewing gadgetry across every available surface.

Ned, of course, was in hog heaven. "This is amazing!" he

gasped as he stumbled through the forest of circuitry, running his fingers along this or that bit. "The tech they're using is unbelievable!"

"I'm glad you're happy with it," I told him. "Now can you find this emergency call button we actually risked our lives to reach?"

"Oh, sure." Ned glanced around. "There it is."

The rest of us all made a beeline for the thing he'd gestured toward. It was a small box affixed to the wall just inside the door from the next car, actually, and it had a big red button on it.

"So, what, we just push it?" I stared at the thing suspiciously. It seemed too easy. And too easy usually translated to "completely wrong."

"Yep." Ned was disassembling something that looked like a futuristic neon coffeemaker gone rogue and didn't even glance up.

"You're sure this is it?"

"Absolutely."

"Ned!"

That made him look up, finally. "What?"

"You're sure this is it?" I pointed at the button.

"I'm sure," he confirmed. "What else could it be?" I heard him mutter as he turned back to the space-age Mr. Coffee.

I looked at Mary and Tall but they both shrugged. "Ned is the expert," Mary pointed out. "If he says this is the call button, I must assume he is correct."

"What've we got to lose?" Tall added.

"Okay, fine. Just remember, if something goes wrong, we

all agreed to this," I warned them.

Then I pushed the button.

Squeak!

There was a tremendous scraping noise, like a giant with titanium claws attacking an equally large chalkboard. It set my bill on edge and sent spikes of pain through my head. Then the whole car shuddered and shook, hurling us against the door. The grinding continued—I wanted to tell Tall to knock it off but this time I knew it wasn't him—and the shuddering grew worse.

And then it all stopped.

All the sound. All the noise. All the shaking.

The car was completely quiet.

Oh, and dark. No lights. And no soft "whoosh" of air, either.

I picked myself back up and helped Mary back to her feet as best I could. Hey, I couldn't see—is it my fault my hands may have strayed a bit? A few times? Tall I let get himself up.

"What the hell just happened?" I demanded.

"Um." We heard a cough from the direction Ned had been in before. "Well." Then we saw a faint glow—he had one of his doohickeys up, and it was putting out a soft light. "I may have been a little hasty in my assessment," he admitted, not looking at us.

"Meaning what? What the hell was that?" I shouted. The words were really loud without any other noise.

"It wasn't an emergency call button, that's for sure," Tall commented.

"No, apparently not," Ned agreed. "I think—I think it was actually an emergency brake."

"I thought you said this thing didn't have an emergency brake!"

"Actually, no, I never said that. Though I would have if you'd asked."

"I said it," Mary reminded me. "And I believed it to be true. The train is fully automated and does not make unscheduled stops for any reason."

"Yet here's an emergency brake."

"Yes."

"How do you explain that, then?"

Mary shrugged. "I was mistaken." That one was impossible to argue so I turned back toward Ned.

"So we've stopped?"

"Yep."

"Completely?"

"Yep."

"Why aren't there any lights? Or any air?"

"The train's motion powered everything else," Ned explained. "With it stopped the other systems all shut down."

"The shields?"

"Still active for now, but those'll fade too after a while."

"And then what?"

"Then we freeze to death. If we don't suffocate first."

"I thought we couldn't suffocate," I asked. I glared at Mary. "Isn't that why you jabbed me with that great big horse needle before we left?"

"It is, and under normal conditions it would provide sufficient oxygen," she agreed.

"So what's the problem?"

In answer, she gestured around her. "This room," she said. "It is a vacuum."

"It is?"

Ned looked embarrassed. "Helps keep the equipment running more smoothly," he told me. "Sorry."

"Great." I turned back to the door behind us. "Get this thing open."

"Why? It's just as bad in the other cars."

"Yeah, but the dinos are out there. If they see me they'll shoot me. And at least that way I won't have to sit around and wait for it."

"You're a pessimist," Ned told me. "Look on the bright side."

"What's that?"

"I found the emergency call button." He held up another little silvery box with a big button, but this one was blue.

"Great. Hit it and get us some help."

"I can't." He tossed it aside. "No power."

"Oh. Right." I sank down to the floor and put my head in my hands. "So what now?"

Ned reached into his coveralls and pulled out a small green flask. "Do you know any good drinking songs?"

Chapter Ten

Hello, are you my nine o'clock hallucination?

Don't ask me what Ned had in that flask. I couldn't tell you. Not because I didn't ask him, or he didn't answer, but because every time he did tell me it was apparently really, really funny—not just to him but to me, to Tall, to Mary, and after a while even to the walls and floors and all those cables and things. So funny we couldn't do anything but laugh and laugh about it. Which meant we couldn't remember his answer. Which meant—after handing the flask around again—one of us asked him all over again. Repeat as necessary.

Wow, that little-bitty flask sure held a lot of . . . liquid. Though when I try to remember the exact color or flavor or consistency of its contents I'm utterly stumped. So it's possible it was gas. Or tiny tiny chewable beachballs. Or concentrated solar-whale snot. I'm really not sure.

For a while there I wasn't sure of anything. Including my name, my address, and the general contours of my head. My shoe size I remembered all the way through, though. Some things just stick with you.

So there we were, sprawled out on the floor of the space-train's lead car, sipping or snorting or swallowing or smearing what Ned had in that flask, laughing our butts off. It was cold without the lights and with the shields starting to go, and getting harder to breathe, but drink enough and you don't worry about those little details so much anymore. You're too busy concentrating on grander issues, like why peanut butter only comes in crunchy and smooth. Is it because peanuts are crunchy and butter is smooth? What if you were to add a third ingredient, like chocolate peanut butter? Would you then have additional options, like "sweet" or "sticky"?

So we were bouncing around heavy thoughts like this when the hallucinations started.

First the room turned a cheery light blue. It was very restful, actually, though my eyes hurt a little from the sudden illumination. So I shut them. Ah, better!

Then there were sounds. And not Mary and Ned and Tall, either. These were weird noises, clumps and clanks and thunks and cranks. We'd heard a little bit of thumping from the dinos initially, as they pounded on the door, but after a while that had faded. This car was the last one to lose air and shields, Ned had explained (this was after only one pass of the flask, so coherent thought was still more or less possible for all of us), so the DAE agents had probably collapsed already.

But now there were sounds again. And these were closer than the door, and louder, and more prolonged. It was more like a giant robot had climbed into the cabin with us and was pounding on everything and whirring and ratcheting about between our feet.

I could have opened my eyes to look, I suppose. And I tried,

I really did. But they didn't want to cooperate. I think they were scared. My eyelids have always had a very keen sense of reality.

After the sounds—which lessened and then stopped completely—there were the voices. I had no idea what they were saying but they weren't familiar and that made my eyes open despite themselves—curiosity overcomes fear every time. That's why I stare whenever I'm on a rollercoaster. The fact that the safety bars can't fit over my head doesn't help.

I was looking at . . . cotton candy. Fluffy pink and purple cotton candy. With eyes. And a little mouth. And hands, like little gloved cartoon hands, but without any arms. And little tiny cartoon booted feet without legs.

And it was staring at me.

"Hi," I said. "You look tasty."

"Thank you," it replied. "You don't look half-bad yourself." And sadly no, that's not the first time I've gotten that, and in exactly that way.

"Are you a hallucination?" I asked it.

"I don't know, are you hallucinating?"

"I'm not sure—a lot will depend on your answer."

"So if I say yes you're hallucinating and if I say no you're not?"

I thought about that one for a second. "Well, if you say yes I'm almost certainly hallucinating," I decided. "If you say no I might still be hallucinating and you could be lying."

"Odds are, then, that you're hallucinating," the cotton-candy creature pointed out.

"Odds are, yes. But I've never been one to stick to the

odds. I'm a longshot kinda guy."

"Fair enough." It beamed at me, which made its . . . body turn more pink than purple, like it was blushing. "In that case, no, I am not a hallucination. You win!"

"Awesome!" I blinked. "What did I win?"

"A last-minute rescue," it told me. "And—" it slapped something into my hand. It felt like a pamphlet or a brochure, but it was silvery and the paper, if it was paper, was pebbly and sucked all the moisture from my skin. "—a citation."

"A what?" I stared at the brochure. It had symbols and markings I didn't recognize, though they were an attractive shade of fuchsia. "You mean like a commendation?" Hey, we had stopped those dinos! Sort of.

But it sighed. "No, not that kind of citation. More like an official censure, a warning, a summons."

"Oh." Yeah, that figured. Even my hallucinations gave me bad reviews. "What for?"

"For all this." Its unattached little hands waved around it, and I gaped at all the destruction. It looked like someone had blown up a Radio Shack with us inside.

"Wow! What happened here?"

"You did," it answered. "You and your friends. You activated the emergency brake."

"Oh, right. That. We had to! Those little dino-guys were chasing us!"

"The dinotropic aesthetic elite? Yes. They killed several dozen passengers and caused a significant amount of damage."

"See!"

"So the four of you broke into this control car and hit the emergency brake, stopping the train dead—and, as a result, killing hundreds of passengers and causing *catastrophic damage.*"

"Oh." I tried to smile at it—not easy when my bill felt like its two halves were simultaneously stapled to my skin and clamped shut by bands of razor-barbed iron. "We thought we were hitting the emergency call button."

"Why would you think a button colored bright red—the universal color for "stop"—was a call button, rather than the one labeled calm, communicative blue?" It shook its . . . well, it shook its whole body, really. So basically saying no meant doing a jig. That probably made fights hysterical to watch. "It doesn't matter," it told me. "You and your friends hit the brakes and caused the damage, so you've been cited. The courts will settle the rest."

"The courts?" I tried to sit up and discovered I was already standing. Who knew? Of course that meant the cotton-candy guy was floating five feet off the floor, but I found that easier to believe than the fact that I was already—or still—on my feet.

"Yes, the traffic courts. They will arbitrate the matter."

"Oh. Where's the court? And when are we supposed to see them?"

"The court is located in ultraspace," it told me like I was stupid—and at that moment it wasn't far wrong, "and the time is—now."

Everything blurred around me, turning a lovely but disquieting green paisley pattern. Then the green dimmed to almost black and I was standing with Mary, Ned, and Tall in a huge curtained room. The little cotton-candy creature gone, which made it almost certain he hadn't been one of my hallucinations—they tended to linger unpleasantly for days on end.

The paisleys, it turned out, were real. They were stitched into the curtains.

"Where are we?" Tall slurred. He was swaying on his feet. I was steady on mine, actually—the advantage of feet like mine. I was either steady or falling but never in between.

"Ultraspace," Mary answered. Her words were a little indistinct too, and her hair was mussed. She looked amazing. I can't believe I got drunk with a chick that hot and all we did was laugh and fall about.

Actually, that was pretty cool.

"Whatthehellisultraspace?" Tall must have been worried about using up his word allotment for the day, so he jammed them all into one. Impressive.

"It's a layer of reality atop our own," Ned replied. If the flask's contents had affected him at all I couldn't see it. "Time is extended here—an hour in our reality can be days here. They tried using it for travel—you know, fly for three days here, pop back out and it's only been an hour back home— but for some reason you always show up exactly where you started, no matter how far you went." He shrugged. "Lousy for space travel. Great for meetings, though. Everyone can step through, go to the appointed meeting place, talk for as long as necessary, and when they leave ultraspace they're right back where they started and almost no time has passed."

I could see where that would be handy. I could also see where it would be a nightmare. "Hey, let's have a series of meetings for no real reason on things that don't matter in the least. Each meeting can take days and days—it doesn't matter, because we're not losing any time in the real world."

Now if they could figure out a way to make the boredom disappear too, they'd be golden.

"Let the accused step forth," A voice suddenly echoed out from behind the curtains. It was deep and gravelly and commanding, exactly what you'd expect from a powerful judge. Mary, Ned, Tall, and I all looked at each other.

"Accused of what?" I asked. Yes, I'm that guy who always speaks up when I have a question, even when it's clear they don't really want questions. I try not to talk during movies, though. And I always sit in back. After the first time I got pelted by an entire room full of JuJuBees and MilkDuds and Good&Plenties, I learned. Those suckers hurt!

"Those cited in Traffic Violation E37945FQRT177913-X," the voice replied. I glanced down at my citation but still couldn't read it. I guess Mary and Ned could, though, because they both nodded and gestured Tall and I to step forward with them.

"State your names for the record," the voice stated. We were standing in a rough line now, I noticed, with Ned at one end and Tall at the other, and Ned replied first so we just went down the row:

"Ned."

"MR3971XJKA."

"DuckBob Spinowitz."

"Roger Henry David Thomas."

"You have been charged with activating the emergency brake on Galactic Train 3479E5R3, without permission or authorization, and as a result endangering both the train itself and the passengers and cargo contained therein. How do you plead?"

"Uh," I looked at the others. I was wracking my brain trying to think of excuses or extenuating circumstances, but I didn't think "we thought it was the phone!" would do the trick and there was no way this guy was going to buy the old "my dog made me do it!"

Mary and Ned shook their heads anyway. "Guilty, your honor," both of them replied.

"Guilty," Tall echoed.

"Yeah, I guess," I added.

"Very well," There was a pause. "You have been found guilty by this court. For your crimes you will face the following punishment: you will surrender the color mauve."

"What?" The problem with not having external ears anymore is that you can't clean them out when you're sure you've misheard something. "We have to what?"

Mary laid a hand on my arm. "It's a fair sentence," she whispered to me.

"Could be a lot worse," Ned agreed from her other side. "I knew a guy once, ran a red at Galactic Sector Twelve and jackknifed a fleet of Cotidiar battle cruisers. They took aqua AND tangy from him—they tried taking B-Flat too but he appealed that as cruel and unusual."

"They're taking the color mauve from us?" I repeated. "As in, we can't see it anymore?" Hell, I wasn't sure I'd ever seen it, really, but I still objected on general principle.

"Exactly."

"Prepare for punishment to be carried out," the voice boomed, and Mary and Ned hurried back to their places in line before the curtains. "Three, two, one—sentence completed."

"That's it?" I asked. "No flashing lights, no sharp pointy things, no nothing? Not even a moment of nausea? Just 'click' and it's gone?"

The voice was silent.

"Come on," Mary said, taking my arm again. "We need to get back to the train."

Oh right, the train. I let her guide me back a few paces, till the curtains had disappeared around a corner I hadn't realized was there—maybe it was mauve or something—and then stopped.

"Requesting exit from ultraspace," she called out once we were all grouped around her.

"Request granted," a new voice responded. My vision turned green again, and then we were back on the train. Only the lights were back on, and the heat. And the cords and circuit boards and whatnot were more or less where they'd been when we'd first broken in, which meant it was a controlled mess rather than a completely unhinged one.

The little cotton-candy guy was still there, and he nodded as we reappeared. "Right," he said. "Passenger complement complete—prepare to resume travel." There was a soft whoosh and I could feel a thrum through my feet. The train must have started moving again.

"We'll let you off at the next stop," it told us then. "Sorry, but we can't have troublemakers onboard any longer than necessary."

"We understand," Mary assured it. "Thank you."

The door to the second car slid open and it pointed. "If you'll wait in the passenger section," it requested politely.

"What about the dinos?" I asked it. "Are they still waiting to kill us?"

"The DAE agents have been ejected," it replied. "They had gained entry unlawfully, and we don't tolerate freeloaders."

"Oh. Right. Thanks." I didn't need the panicked looks on my companions' faces to remember we had hitched as well. "We'll wait in the next car." I edged out, and only breathed again when the door closed again behind us.

"Whew!" I glanced around. There was something like a bench nearby, so I went and sat on it. When it squeaked and started cursing me I apologized and found a different one, though this time I asked first. "So we're getting off at the next stop. How bad is that?"

"It's perfect, actually," Ned answered, grinning. "Next stop is Galactic Core Central. It's the closest stop to the quantum fluctuation matrix."

Mary nodded. "We will need to find other transportation to cover the remaining distance," she reminded us, "but that should pose little problem."

I didn't bother pointing out that she'd thought catching the train wouldn't be a problem either. I hoped I didn't ever need the color mauve for anything—I couldn't imagine why I would, but lately my imagination had been forced to admit that it was woefully inadequate, and now it was petitioning to be given a bit more exercise and a whole host of multivitamins. I was letting it have its head for now, with a warning not to overdo it. What would I do if my imagination up and had a heart attack? It was something I didn't want to think about.

"So how did you get mixed up in all of this, anyway?" I asked her instead as she settled herself onto the bench next to me. Not quite as good as when she'd slid into that chair back on in the warehouse, but still pretty amazing. "You get abducted, too?"

She shook her head, which did amazing things to her hair, shoulders, chest . . . I had to stop there and focus if I wanted to even register her answer. "No, I sought out the Grays deliberately."

"You what now?" Was I still drunk from Ned's . . . whatever? "Why the hell would you do something like that?"

That got a smile out of her, but it wasn't a happy one. "I hold two degrees," she explained softly. And yeah, at the mention of her holding two anything, my eyes went there. How could they not. "One in astrophysics and the other in astronomy."

"Ah." Hey, I'm slow sometimes, but not that slow. "So you were already hooked on the stars, and figured you wanted to see them up close and personal."

"Precisely. The Grays were impressed that I had calculated their next location, and agreed to take me on as an intermediary and scout."

"So they signed you up, did whatever to your head, and that was that?"

"Yes." The sad smile faded, and she looked . . . content. "It has proven thus far to have been a more than satisfactory choice."

"Huh." I leaned back. "I guess that's what happens when you're overeducated, right? Not a lot of career options left."

"That is very true." She turned those devastating blues eyes on me. "And you? Did your education also lead to your current life state?"

"Hm? Oh, yeah, sure, I guess." Fortunately, I don't blush anymore. Or if I do the plumage hides it nicely. "I didn't exactly, though—I mean, that is—I don't have a degree." Man, that was tough to admit to her!

"Oh." I was surprised to see sympathy in her eyes, instead of the scorn I'd expected. "Of course. I am sorry." One hand rose to stroke my cheek, and I thought I'd died and gone to little duck heaven. "Attending school in your altered state must have been difficult."

"Right." I didn't bother to correct her. Yeah, so I'm coward, okay? I didn't really want to tell this gorgeous, brainy, brave chick that I'd actually been kicked out of school long before my "alteration." I'd gotten expelled as a seven-year senior, along with the rest of our frat, after a little . . . incident. Hey, how were we to know the chancellor's house would be that flammable? Or that he and his wife were home that weekend? They made it out okay, anyway. I did still feel bad for Fluffy, but the statue they'd erected in her honor was really pretty. Or so I'd been told—after the first time with the cops I hadn't tried to go back.

I didn't really want to think about the past anymore. It always depressed me. And Ned had pulled a little 3-D map out of somewhere—I didn't want to ask, I was just going to assume it had been in a pocket of those overalls and leave it at that—and he and Mary were trying to map out our most likely route. Tall seemed to be asleep—good skill to have, I suppose, if you're on long stakeouts or in boring meetings. Which left me to my own thoughts. I didn't care for that much. They have a tendency to gang up on me when I'm alone.

Instead I turned to the nearest other passenger, which looked a lot like a giant weasel in a pair of sweat socks and a tasseled cap, and struck up a lively conversation about the differences between American baseball and something it called "snout-sack."

They were remarkably similar, it turned out. The biggest difference seemed to be in our insistence that all players wore uniforms.

The rest of the trip passed really, really slowly. I was afraid more than once we'd slipped back into ultraspace and no one had told me. But I didn't see any paisley anywhere.

Chapter Eleven
Christmas at the galactic core

"Okay, so tell me again why it's snowing?"

Ned sighed. "We've been through this already."

"I know, I know. But explain it again."

"It isn't snowing."

"Right. Not snowing." I held up my hands, letting the big, fluffy flakes cling to them before shaking them off to join the drifts piling up all around us. "So all this—"

"Doesn't exist, no."

"Right. But it looks like snow because—"

"Because this environment is filled with tiny supercharged particles of information. Like a billion little microscopic packets, whizzing all around at supersonic speeds. And your brain—"

"Can't process that," Tall added. He sounded both smug and annoyed at the same time, but this time I don't think the second half was aimed at me. "So instead your brain converts the image, the setting, into something you can handle. In this case—"

"Snow. So really, it's only snowing in my head."

"Essentially, yes."

I scooped up some snow, packed it tight, and hurled it at Tall.

It hit him full in the face, hard enough to stagger him backward. "So did I just hit you with a whole bunch of information?"

Tall growled. "No, you idiot, you just smacked me in the face with a snowball!"

"But how, if it's all in my head?" I stared at him, then laughed. "Or is your brain not able to handle it all either?" I knew from the glare he gave me that I was right. "That's it, isn't it? The two of us, the monkey boys—or, in my case, duck-monkey—can't handle it here. Not without a pretty snowscape to protect our fragile little minds." I laughed again. "You're right in here with me."

"Maybe I am," Tall snarled. "So maybe if I cram enough of these particles down your throat you'll finally grow a brain!" He started stalking toward me, gathering snow in his ham-sized hands as he drew closer.

"Enough," Mary warned. "The illusion is a harmless one and allows you to pass through this region without mental damage. Utilize it rather than fighting it or being distressed about it!"

Which was easy for her to say. She didn't perceive the galactic core as looking almost exactly like the wilds of North Dakota. I swear, if even one alien walked up to me and said "Oh, you betcha" or "You don't say?" I was out of here, matrix or no matrix.

But that got me thinking—rare, I know. Mary wasn't seeing the snow. I was sure of it.

"You can see what this place is really like, can't you?" I asked her as Tall and I fell into step behind her and Ned again. She nodded. "Is that because the Grays modified you?"

"Yes. They altered my mind, my senses, so that I could register and utilize a higher consciousness." She didn't sound entirely happy about it, and I had a feeling right now she'd trade it all for a single illusory snowball.

"So what does it look like?"

She glanced around and smiled. "It is . . . indescribable."

"But is it beautiful?"

Her smile widened. "Yes. Oh, yes." She turned that smile on me, warming me so much the snow melted right off me, and I knew she'd gotten over the sadness of a moment before. Hey, I'm not just a jerk—I'm a jerk with a soft spot.

Kind of like one of those cheap chocolates with the too-gooey, too-sweet center.

I think I need to find a better personal analogy.

"Where're we going?"

"We need to find localized transport," Mary reminded me. "The bus placed us in the correct region but there is still a short distance remaining between us and the matrix."

"Define 'short distance.'"

She considered for a second. "Three hundred and twelve-point-seven-three-one light years."

"A half-step and a skip, gotcha." I shook my head and set off a minor flurry. "So we just hail a space cab and we're outta here?"

"It is not that simple."

I sighed. "No, of course not. Why start now? So what's the problem this time? Too much traffic? Or it's all going express and we need the local?"

To my surprise, that got a nod out of her, and a quick smile. "Exactly!"

"Wait, what?" Tall looked surprised too. Ned, who was trailing us now, just looked amused. "I got it right?"

"Essentially, yes," Mary agreed. "Ships in this region tend to operate by way of galactic convection, the flow of particles emanating from the core and moving outward. This is a cheap, quick, easy means of power. We, however, are attempting to make our way farther in. The particles there are too tightly packed for most vehicles to process correctly. They would overload their engines. Only ships specifically intended for travel to and from the core have powerful enough engines and strong enough particle filters to bring us to our destination. Most ships would be unable to accommodate us."

"Everybody here has puny little engines and we need something big enough to cut through all the crap?"

"Correct."

I shook my head. "That doesn't make any sense. What about the ships that come out of the core? They've got big engines, but once they get this far out doesn't that mean they aren't getting enough fuel anymore? How do they get back home afterward? I mean, they can make their way out to the store, but they've got to return with their groceries, don't they?" I had a crazy image of hordes of spacemen wandering the galaxy with bags of groceries and little signs around their necks that read "Help me, I can never go home again!" and "Galactic convection took my house!"

"Most core-equipped ships stay within a certain proximity

to the core," Mary admitted. "There are only a few that travel back and forth, and once they have passed beyond a certain distance they must utilize a supplemental fuel source to yield enough power for them to return. Either that or they rely upon the scoops to ferry them back to their starting points."

"The scoops?" That sounded ominous.

"Yes, the galactic scoops. Great massive ships that scoop up the raw particles and compress them, converting them to fuel for others farther from core, where the flow is too diffuse for direct utilization."

"They're huge," Ned supplied. "Gotta be, since they're scooping up every particle in sight. They're big enough that they've got both core-standard and general galactic engines and can switch back and forth—that way they work fine in either place."

"Right. So we hitch a ride ourselves. Cool. And where do we find one of these scoops?"

We'd been walking this whole time—well, Mary and Ned had been walking, Tall and I had been slipping and sliding because of all the snow and ice we thought was underfoot—but now Mary stopped. And pointed.

"There."

The rest of us stared. Even Ned said, "There? Really? You're sure?"

Which is funny because as far as I know he could see this place for what it really was. Not what I, and probably Tall, were seeing:

A truck stop.

Yeah, a truck stop. Exactly like you see in movies all the time, with the huge diesel gas pumps and the big dirty lot and the eighteen-wheelers and dump trucks and garbage trucks and tow trucks all parked at random angles all over the place—and the greasy-spoon diner right smack in the middle of it all.

"Is that—?" Tall breathed.

"It certainly looks like it," I whispered back.

"Do you think they—?"

"There's only one way to find out, isn't there?"

"Hey, where do you two think you're going?" Ned demanded as Tall and I began making an awkward, shambling beeline toward the diner.

"You sort out the ride!" I shouted back over my shoulder. "We're gonna have breakfast!"

Because I wasn't entirely sure how long we'd been on this crazy trip so far—it was hard to tell, what with the ultraspace court appearance and the faster-than-light travel and, oh yeah, passing out from lack of oxygen!—but it had definitely been way too long since I'd had anything to eat. And greasy-spoon diners were always loud, smelly, crowded, dirty, sticky, cramped—and served the most amazing really-bad-for-you-but-you-just-don't-care food.

"Waffles!" Tall was drooling beside me.

"Flapjacks!" I replied. It's not easy to drool with a duckbill but I managed. I've had practice.

"BACON!!!" we sang together.

"Bacon?" Suddenly Ned was next to us—he plowed right through the snowdrifts as if they weren't there, which for him

I guess they weren't. "Where?"

We pointed in unison. "There!!!"

"There?"

"Yes, there!"

He didn't seem convinced. "You think they'll have bacon?"

"Of course!" I wanted to smack him upside the head but my hands were so cold I was afraid a finger might splinter off if I tried. "What kind of greasy spoon would it be if it didn't serve bacon?"

"And sausage," Tall added.

"And Canadian bacon."

"And toast."

"And COFFEE!!!"

Ned was still studying us like we were weird lab rats that had suddenly gotten up and started dancing the Watusi. "You think that's a greasy spoon?"

"Yes, yes I do," I replied. "And I don't care if it isn't really. That's what I see, and it's what my brain is processing. Which means whatever food they do serve there, my brain will convert it to greasy-spoon diner fare. Right?"

He considered that for a moment, then nodded. "I think so!" And he fell in beside us.

I squinted at him. "But you don't see it as a greasy spoon, do you?"

Ned shook his head.

"So won't the food they serve you seem like whatever it really is, then?"

"Maybe." He grinned. "Or maybe, if you watch me eat and

you think it's greasy-spoon bacon, my mind will be forced to concede that it could in fact be bacon. There're two of you and only one of me, after all—I'm willing to let my consciousness be outnumbered and overpowered for the sake of a tasty breakfast."

"Spoken like a proper blue-collar worker," I agreed, slapping him on the back—but carefully. "Let's go!"

And the three of us sloshed our way through the rest of the snow and around the various rigs, finally pushing the door open and stepping into the diner itself. I was careful to clean my feet on the welcome mat first, though—I didn't want to go tracking metaphorical snow all over everything.

Chapter Twelve
Order up!

"What'll it be, boys?"

We were crowded into one of those tiny little booths you always find at diners—it was either that or shoulder our way in at the counter, and there were all manner of large, smelly, surly truckers covering that stretch of Formica. The waitress was short, heavy, moon-faced, bleached-blonde, and as cheery as one could be working in a place like this. Her nametag, though, read "Delaxicon Ultra 359."

"I'll have the full breakfast," I told her, slapping my menu down on the stained table in front of me. "Eggs over easy, pancakes, toast, bacon, sausage, hash browns, orange juice, and a tanker's worth of coffee. Black, with sugar." I eyed her nametag again. "Thanks, uh, Delaxicon Ult—"

"Oh, you can call me Delia," she cut me off. "Everybody does. What about you, hon?" This was directed at Tall, who looked like he was in love. Maybe he was, too—you never knew with feds. Or maybe he was just as excited as I was about the prospect of a real breakfast.

"Same as he's having," Tall replied, poking a finger toward me, "but eggs scrambled, waffles instead of pancakes, and coffee straight black, no sugar. Thanks."

"Gotcha. And you, sweetie?"

Ned beamed at her. "Make mine the same as both of theirs."

Delia frowned. "Well, which one, hon? You want your eggs over easy or scrambled? Waffles or pancakes? Coffee with or without sugar."

"Yes, please."

She eyed him a second, then laughed. "One of those, huh? Okay, you got it." Coffee'll be right up." And she swept up our menus and somehow disappeared into the throng.

I rubbed my hands together. "I can't wait! When was the last time we ate, anyway?"

"I ate on the train," Ned admitted without even a trace of guilt.

"You what? There was food on that thing?"

"Oh, sure—there's a whole dining car. It's in the middle."

I glared at him. "When did you have time to eat there?" I demanded.

"While I was scouting," he answered.

"You mean while those dinos were shooting at us?"

He shrugged. "There wasn't a line."

"So you ate a few hours ago, basically—not counting however much time we were passed out in the control car?"

"Yep."

"And now you're gonna have a double breakfast."

"Yep." Ned patted his ample belly. "I never pass up a good meal."

"I can see that." He was clearly unapologetic—and I couldn't really blame him, since I wasn't entirely sure I wouldn't have done exactly the same thing in his shoes—so I turned to Tall, who was sitting next to me. Ned had the other side of the booth all to himself. He needed it.

"What about you?" I asked Tall. "When was the last time you ate?"

"I had a PowerBar while we were on our way here," he admitted. "After the whole Ultraspace thing."

"A PowerBar? What, were there vending machines on the train, too?"

Tall shook his head. "I always carry one in my suit jacket," he explained. "Along with a glow-stick, a book of matches, a roll of tape, a pocket knife, a permanent marker, some chewing gum, a few paper clips, several band-aids, a little tube of skin lotion, a travel toothbrush and toothpaste, dental floss, my iPod, and a finger puppet."

I stared at him. "What are you, a Boy Scout?"

"Eagle Scout," he answered proudly.

"You carry all that in your jacket?" He nodded. "I shudder to think what you've got in your pants. Pockets."

"Not much," he admitted. "Coins, cash, credit cards, ID, a pen, a handkerchief."

I shook my head, but couldn't help asking, "What's with the finger puppet?"

"Entertainment on long rides," Tall replied. "That and it's a good ice-breaker."

"Uh-huh." I eyed him closely. "Admit it, you have an entire finger-puppet kingdom at home, don't you? And when no one's around, you get them all out and play with them, have them fight each other and stage little parades and tiny sting operations and all that." The blush that flickered across his face for half a heartbeat told me I was right, but I found I couldn't laugh at him as much as I'd thought. It was nice to know Tall did have some wacky little habits of his own. It made him almost approachable.

Delia broke the awkward silence by reappearing beside our table and plunking down four cups of coffee, three glasses of water, and three place settings. I didn't see a tray anywhere, but I was careful not to look too closely. I didn't want to spoil the illusion.

"Food'll be up in a minute," she told us before sashaying off again. I didn't miss the appreciative glance Tall threw her way. So it wasn't just the food!

"Ah!" I was busy wrapping my hands around my coffee cup, letting the warmth trickle up through my fingers. "Mmmm." I took a deep breath, inhaling the aroma of fresh, hot coffee. Oh, yeah. It had already been too long since my last caffeine fix, and my body was screaming that if it didn't get some soon it was gonna go into full and open revolt. But I overruled it. I wanted to savor this.

Tall and Ned were doing the same thing. Clearly we were all long-time devotees of the coffee god. Finally, our prayers finished, each of us raised a cup, lifted it to our lips, took one last appreciative sniff, and took a long, deep drink.

Ahhhhhh.

I have no idea what we were really drinking. Or where we really were. Hell, for all I knew we were being handed rocks and glowing radioactive sludge. Or nothing at all, and any aliens nearby were laughing their asses or anatomical equivalents off seeing us three crouching on nothing and drinking nothing. But I didn't care. Because as far as I was concerned, this was coffee. Real coffee. Good coffee. I'm not talking gourmet crap, either, with its fancy flavors and delicate aroma. No, this was good strong truck-stop coffee, the kind that you could use to strip paint if necessary. The kind that scalded its way down your throat and into your belly before releasing its caffeine to storm your bloodstream, taking your entire system by force and jolting you with enough juice to power a small city. The kind you could taste in your toes, harsh and heavy and thick as motor oil.

Oh, yeah.

All three of us let out appreciative sighs at the same time. Then we quickly took a second gulp.

"Toast's up," Delia announced, showing up and setting a stack of toast and a handful of butter packets down before us. She laughed at our blissful expressions. "Been a while since you boys had a decent cup, huh?"

"You have no idea," I told her.

"That's a helluva mug you've got there," she noticed, and I knew she wasn't talking about the chipped coffee cup I held, which read "Red's Truck Stop" on the side in faded print. "Where you fellas from?"

"Earth," Tall and I both replied.

"Betelgeuse," Ned answered. "Or thereabouts."

"Oh yeah?" He had Delia's attention now. "Whereabouts, exactly? I've got a cousin over that way."

"Artelusia IX," Ned admitted, then shook his head. "I know, I know—"

But Delia interrupted him. "Get out! That's where my cousin's stationed! She's in the Praetorian Magnate!"

Ned's eyes lit up. Literally. I had to wince at the glare. "Over on Randall Ave.? I grew up right near there!" He leaned forward. "There used to be the most amazing restaurant right near the Magnate, Gus's All-You-Can-Eat Melva Buffet—"

"It's still there!" Delia assured him. "She was raving about it the last time I talked to her, insisted I had to come out there for a visit and try it myself!"

"You do, you do," Ned urged. "Get the warab filet—it's incredible!"

"The warab, huh? I'll keep that in mind." She winked at him, and nodded at Tall and I. "Order's up, sounds like. I'll be right back with the grub." And then she was gone again.

Ned looked the happiest I'd seen him. "Nice to find somebody who actually knows the old homestead, huh?" I asked.

"Yeah." He took another sip of coffee. "It's a really small place, so most people've never even heard of it. I haven't been back there in ages, though. It's good to know Gus's is still around." He leaned toward us. "Once all this is over, you guys've gotta come back there with me. The food will knock you on your rear, it's that good. My treat."

"Thanks!" I never pass up free food, especially when it comes so highly recommended. Hell, I don't even pass up free food that's been rejected. Or condemned. I'm not all that picky.

But it was cool of Ned to invite us back to his hometown. He was okay. For a little alien plumber-dude.

Delia was back, this time balancing four huge trays, one on each shoulder. No, I didn't look twice. I didn't want to know. She expertly slid the food in front of us, stacking it where necessary, then smiled, patted Tall and Ned on the shoulders—I was on the inside so she couldn't reach, but Tall's face turned all kinds of interesting shades and almost expressions at the brief physical contact—and vanished again. I wasn't entirely sure that was just an expression in her case, but right now I really didn't care. I was too fixated on the food.

For the next few minutes there was nothing but chewing, gulping, slurping, cutting, and sighing. With occasional moans of sheer bliss.

It was amazing.

I'm not sure I've ever had bacon that good. Or eggs. Or pancakes. The orange juice tasted fresh-squeezed, and the coffee—well, the coffee defied words and demanded unquestioning homage. Okay, so there was a split-second there at one point where I had a piece of bacon in my hand and it seemed to—well, waver around the edges a bit—and then became something blue and mushy and a bit fuzzy, but I forced that image away. I didn't want to know what was really here right now, thank you very much. I could deal with reality later. For now I was enjoying my food. And man, was I enjoying it! It was probably the best breakfast I've had in my entire life.

This whole trip so far was worth it just for that.

"Oh, yeah," I leaned back and patted my now very full

belly. "That's what I'm talking about!"

"Definitely." Tall burped.

Ned nodded. "This place may just tie with Gus's for my affections," he admitted happily. He'd managed to polish off two full breakfasts and had kept pace with Tall and I while doing it. I guess aliens need a lot of fuel.

"Everything okay, boys?" Delia asked, snatching empty plates and stacking them into a towering, swaying heap. "Y'all need anything else?"

"A little more coffee," I admitted, tapping my almost-empty cup. Ned and Tall both nodded. "But otherwise we're good. Thanks."

"More coffee, coming right up. And I'll bring you your check." The last word came from nowhere because she'd already disappeared again.

The check. Right. I glanced at Ned and Tall—mainly at Ned. There was a sudden blossom of fear in my belly. Though that could have been the coffee consuming the other food and starting to work on my stomach lining.

"What kind of check are we looking at here, Ned?" I asked quietly. "How much is this gonna set us back? And how're we gonna pay? Do they take debit cards?"

"Not Earth debit cards, no," Ned answered, which made the fear or the coffee growl and start chewing more aggressively. "But all kinds of other stuff."

"Like?"

Delia was back, pouring more coffee into each of our cups. Then she tossed a scrap of paper onto the table, where it landed smack-dab in the middle. "There you go, boys," she told us. "Just pay me when you're ready, okay?" She winked at Tall—nearly causing a brief heart-attack, or a sudden attempt to dance the Marengo while still seated, I wasn't sure—and she was gone again.

I glanced at the paper, which looked just like a check from back home—complete with utterly indecipherable scribbles. Tall looked equally baffled and worried by it. Ned didn't seem concerned, though.

"So how much do we owe?" I asked him.

"Seventeen wiglipar," he told us. "Plus tip, of course. Figure twenty."

"And what's a wiglipar when it's at home?"

"One of these." He pulled a few gummy worms out of his pocket and tossed them onto the table atop the check. They really looked like gummy worms. But when I leaned in to stare at one I saw that it had metal traceries within it, and a silvery sheen.

"Okay, that's . . . five. What about the other fifteen?"

He shrugged. "I don't carry a lot of cash," he admitted. "But it's fine. They accept trade here."

"Trade? So we can leave items of appropriate value instead?"

"Absolutely. People do it all the time."

"What do we have that might be worth fifteen willipur?" Tall asked.

"Wiglipar," Ned corrected. "And I have no idea. Let's find out."

We spent the next few minutes emptying our pockets.

Then Tall and I watched as Ned did his impression of Antiques Roadshow on the mishmash before him.

"Worthless," he said, picking up the few bills we'd added and tossing them aside. "Might as well be worthless"—those were the coins. "Too valuable"—he handed Tall back his finger puppet, which looked like a little ghost with an oversized exposed brain. "Too hard to exchange"—that was the book of matches. "These'll do, though." He scooped up two of the Band-aids, the little tube of toothpaste, a stray guitar pick I'd had—no, I don't play—and one of those goofy religious tracts someone had handed me in the subway that morning. I was sorry to see the tract go—I hadn't read it yet.

Delia must have been hovering because she was back the minute Ned gathered everything in his hands. "All set?" she asked. "Need any change?" She held out her hands and Ned transferred the pile to them.

"Nope, we're good," he assured her.

She glanced down at the assortment she was holding, then back up at us—and smiled. "Well, thanks, fellas! Y'all have a real nice day now, y'hear? And stop in again next time you're over this way."

"Oh, we will," I told her. Ned and Tall both nodded enthusiastically. Then we pried ourselves from the booth and lumbered back toward the door and back outside.

"That was incredible," I said as we stepped back out into the cold. There were still flurries but they weren't as heavy as they'd been before.

Tall nodded. "If we ever manage proper space flight of our

own," he muttered, "I'm definitely marking this place as a must." He cast one last, wistful glance back through the door, to where Delia was now tending another table. Poor guy. Long-distance relationships are the worst. Though in my case that tended to mean relationships that quickly became long-distance, as the lady in question moved out of town. And changed her name. And her face.

Ned was looking around. "There's Mary," he said after a second, pointing. "Let's go."

We trudged after him, and caught up with Mary a minute later. She was standing beside a massive garbage truck—and a huge, grossly overweight trucker. He had a long ZZ Top beard, scraggly hair, beady little eyes, acne-scarred cheeks, a red nose, and a battered Minnesota Twins baseball cap pulled down almost to his eyes.

"This is Benenin Li-ong Ack," Mary informed us. "He has agreed to take us to our destination, or near enough that we can make our own way the remaining distance."

The trucker grinned at us. "Call me Benny. How y'all doin'?" His teeth were yellowed where they weren't blackened, and he spat a gob of tobacco on the ground by his feet. "Climb on in and let's get this puppy rollin'!"

I shook my head as he ambled back around to the driver's side—we could hear the grunts as he hoisted himself up and in, then wiggled himself into the driver's seat. "He's the best you could find?" I asked Mary quietly, letting Ned and Tall scoot up into the truck before us.

"His is the first core-equipped vehicle leaving for the center,"

Mary answered just as quietly. "And he agreed to let us travel with him. Why?"

"Never mind." I gave her a hand up, then climbed in myself and pulled the door shut behind me. I was wedged in against the window, but I didn't mind. It put me well away from Benny's breath and tobacco juice, and this way I could watch the snow. I stared out the window as he started up his truck and pulled out of the lot, and craned my neck to see Red's as it disappeared behind us. I was sorry to see the place go.

I'd kept my coffee mug. It was still warm, and I held it tightly in both hands as Benny shifted his garbage truck into a higher gear and we rumbled along our way.

At least, even if I failed to save the universe and we all ceased to exist, I'd had a damned fine breakfast beforehand. And a souvenir—if an imaginary one—to prove it.

Chapter Thirteen
Taking out the trash

"So how long will it take to get there?" I asked. Okay, shouted. Garbage trucks are loud! And apparently there's no soundproofing on the inside—I guess they figure the garbage men are already mostly deaf so why bother?

"Not long!" Bennie shouted back. "Y'all are right on my route!"

"Great!" I considered that for a minute. "On your route? What route?"

That got him laughing so hard he started choking. Tall, who was sitting next to Benny—okay, smushed up against Benny, if you want to get picky about it—wound up having to pound him on the back several times to get him breathing again.

"What kinda route you think I mean, boy?" Benny gasped after he'd recovered. "A paper route?" He looked on the verge of cracking up again. "This is a garbage truck, ain't it?"

"Oh. Right." I glanced around as best I could while sandwiched up against the door. The cab wasn't that big, and behind the bench seat there wasn't a lot of room. Nor had there been anyone holding onto those handles along the back. "So," I ventured after a minute, "you do this route all by yourself?"

"Not usually, no," Benny admitted, hauling on the wheel and sending the truck skittering on two wheels as it cut a sharp turn. I couldn't even see streets out there—the snow had picked up again, and was now at near-blizzard levels—but I guess he could. Or maybe he'd just been swerving to avoid hitting someone. Or just to show that he could. "Got me a partner, Three Blue Alpha, but he took himself sick this morning. Somethin' he ate, no doubt—that boy'll eat anything. And I do mean anything. So I been pullin' the route all on my lonesome all mornin'." He flashed all of us a tobacco-stained grin. "Till y'all showed up. Happy to have the company, and the help."

"Help?" I twisted so I could glare at Mary, who was squeezed up next to me—not that I wasn't enjoying the enforced proximity. "What help?"

"That was the arrangement Benny and I reached," she explained without even a trace of guilt. "He agreed to convey us to our destination, provided we rendered him assistance in performing his appointed tasks."

"You signed us on for garbage duty?"

"Yes." I was pretty sure I saw a glint of amusement in those pretty blue eyes. "The three of you had left me to make the arrangements, and this seemed the quickest and most efficient way."

"I don't suppose you're planning on hauling garbage yourself?" I asked her. I could see from her slow smile that I'd guessed the answer already.

"Why, surely you three big strong men can handle that without me." For an alien-altered intermediary she did a surprisingly good "innocent and helpless little maiden" look. Guess there are some things you just can't take away. "Or would it be too much for you?"

"Yeah yeah, I get it," I grumbled. Still, I couldn't get too angry at her. She had gotten us a ride. And we had stuck her to find that ride while we were indoors, all nice and cozy, and eating enough food to choke a fleet of horses. Fair was fair.

Besides, I had to admit I was curious. Garbage men had always held a fascination for me—as a kid I remembered staring out the window in the morning as they rumbled down the block, riding along the back of the truck like it was nothing, hopping off to lift enormous bags and boxes and bales and toss them effortlessly into the truck's open maw. They'd always seemed unfazed by everything: the weather, the weight, the neighbor's prize pit bulls. I'd thought it'd be cool to be a garbage man. And think of all the stuff you could find! Somebody was tossing it, so clearly anything you found was yours to keep if you wanted it—I'd imagined furnishing whole houses that way. Hell, we'd done our frat house back in school by trolling the dumpsters of the other frats—it was ridiculous what the richer kids threw away just because it wasn't in style anymore or wasn't the latest model. That went double for their girlfriends, but at least those they didn't leave by the dumpster. Just in the parking lot.

And here I was, about to be at least a temporary garbage man! And a space garbage man at that! What kind of cool crap did aliens throw away? And how much of it could I bring with me?

"Get ready," Benny shouted a few seconds later, interrupting my musings. "We're back on my route, and the first stop's comin' up!"

I glanced over at Ned and Tall. "Time to work off those breakfasts, huh?"

Both of them nodded. Ned seemed resigned to helping, but Tall looked as interested as I was. I wondered if he'd dreamed about being a garbage man too, before the Feds had snatched him up and made him one of their own. Or was he just excited about the prospect of finding and confiscating a bunch of broken old alien tech? Maybe both.

"Here we are," Benny announced, slamming on the brakes. The truck slid and swerved and rolled to a jarring stop. "Let's go!"

He wrenched open his door, levered himself out of his seat, and threw himself down out of the cab. I twisted and kicked my own door open and hopped out as well, hopefully a little more gracefully than he had, and then helped Mary out so Ned and Tall could squeeze past her.

"I'll just wait in the cab," she told us with the tiniest little smirk once we were all out. Then she climbed back in, pulled the door shut, and waved at us. Gee, thanks.

But there wasn't anything for it but to shiver a bit, turn up my collar, and trudge toward the back of the truck, where Benny was waiting. At least Tall had a suit jacket! I was in shirtsleeves!

"Right, how's this work?" I asked Benny as we stomped up to him.

"Real easy," he replied, spitting tobacco juice off to the side somewhere. "You lift this lever here," he shoved up a huge lever mounted along the side of the truck's rear end, looking a lot like one of those one-armed bandit machines you see in Vegas, "and that opens the back." Sure enough, the rear split wide, gaping open like a hungry man preparing himself for a huge bite of something tasty. The fact that the two halves had interlocking sections so it looked like big flat teeth didn't do anything to lessen that image. Yeesh! "You toss all the trash in here, then tug the lever back down. The truck does the rest." He indicated the two handlebars mounted on either side of the rear. "Might be easiest and quickest if two of y'all rode back here 'stead of in the cab—that way you can just swing down and toss in the trash each time we stop. I can come back out whenever you need a hand with the really heavy stuff." And with that he turned and waddled back toward the front, spitting more juice as he went.

"Great," I grumbled. "The hillbilly alien gets to sit in the cab with Mary while the three of us handle garbage." But part of me loved the idea of riding the truck like a real garbage man.

"I don't mind," Tall admitted, shrugging. "The sooner we help him the sooner we get to the matrix. Besides—" he grinned at me. Actually grinned! I didn't even know his cheeks could stretch that far! Or that he had teeth! "Didn't you ever want to be a garbage man?"

I couldn't help grinning back, at least the best I could with my bill. "Yeah, I did."

Ned shook his head. "Well, since this is both of your dream come true, why don't I leave you to it?" He laughed and walked back around to the front.

Tall and I looked at each other, then laughed. Yeah, sure,

why not? Then we turned to the garbage.

It must have been the same numbing effect my brain was doing on the particles and the truck and everything else, because what I saw were three large trashcans, filled to the brim with plastic bags of trash. They looked completely ordinary, just like the trash I'd see back home. I admit, I was a little disappointed. I'd been hoping for something more, well, alien.

I could tell from the look on his face that Tall felt the same way. "Hey, maybe as we get more used to it our minds'll relax this illusion a bit and let us see what's really here," I suggested.

"Could be," he agreed, and seemed to brighten a little. "Well, might as well get to it." He grabbed a trashcan, hoisted it up onto the bottom edge of the truck's rear, and tilted it up so the contents all fell into the waiting trash compartment.

"Right." I grabbed a can myself and wrestled it over there, trying to do it as smoothly as he had, but Tall had a good five or six inches on me in height. And he probably weighed about what I did but on him it was all muscle. On me it was fat. And bill—don't forget the bill. I finally managed to get it up and in, only spilling a bag or two in the process, but by that point Tall had already finished the third can.

"Ready?" he asked when I set the empty can back down and grabbed the one fallen trash bag. I nodded, too out of breath to say anything. He did have a smirk on his face but it didn't seem as nasty as the ones I'd seen earlier, back on the train. Maybe he was warming to me. People do that—I'm told I put out a lot of body heat.

Tall yanked on the lever, slamming the two halves back

together. We heard a loud grinding sound as the mechanisms inside crunched up the trash, then a clank as a panel opened somewhere inside and slid all that trash into the truck's main compartment. Tall grabbed the handle on that side and swung himself up onto the wide rear bumper, and I did the same on my side, though not as smoothly. Then he banged on the side of the truck with his fist. Benny was obviously used to that signal, and a second later the truck roared to life and took off down the street again.

And so it went for a bit. It was cold out but not freezing, and the exertion soon warmed me up so the cold actually became refreshing. I got smoother at hopping down, hauling cans, emptying them, and swinging back up. Tall and I started working together better, too, alternating so we weren't in each other's way, grabbing opposite sides of really big cans or massive bags and carrying them over and in together. It was fun. I was starting to wish I'd become a garbage man, after all. Hell, maybe when this was all over I still could. I wondered what their veterinary insurance was like? I'd found it easier to go to vets than to regular doctors—they seemed less freaked out by me, were nicer, had better hours, used smaller needles, and usually had tastier treats. And cooler stickers.

Then things started to get weird.

"What d'ya think that is?" I asked, gesturing toward something sticking out of one of the cans we were approaching.

"No idea," Tall admitted. "Probably best not to ask." He hadn't shown much interest in the garbage we'd tossed so far, though that wasn't too surprising considering it had all looked completely Earth-normal, down to spilled contents exactly matching what you might see on any New York street on garbage day—who knew moldy potato salad and rotten tomatoes and dog-eared *TV Guides* looked the same throughout the universe? But this one was different. It was tall and cylindrical and iridescent even with the overcast and the snow, and it had sections that gave off a faint glow of their own. And it hummed. At first I thought the noise was coming from Tall, or the truck, or even me, but the closer we got the more obvious it was that the sound was coming from the thing itself. Was it an outer space broomstick? A galactic vacuum cleaner? A death-ray bazooka? A cheap telescope? A wireless TV antenna? I had no idea, but for some reason handling it made me nervous, maybe because it was the first trash we'd seen that definitely hadn't come from our world.

The truck ate it just fine, of course. I'm convinced you could shove a black hole or an exploding sun into the back of a garbage truck and its grinders would make short work of the astronomical wonder. It might even work better afterward, like greasing the gears.

When we went to climb back onto the truck afterward, though, I noticed something else. The handles were different. They were flaring out more, curving more—they had been standard towel-rack-style handles before, plain and simple and squared, but now they were more delicate and more artsy. And the rear bumper was wider but thinner and swept out more at the corners, so it was like we were standing on little mini-platforms instead of just part of the bumper.

"Did you—?" I started to ask Tall, gesturing at our feet and our hands as Benny revved the truck and took off for the next stop.

"Yeah," Tall cut me off. He shrugged. "Like you said before, must be our minds adapting to all this weirdness, letting a little of it start seeping through."

I'd said that? Really? It sounded almost like it made sense. But yeah, I guess I had. Wild.

After that we started noticing other little changes. More and more of the garbage had odd shapes or textures or smells or sounds—or all of the above. The bags became silvery mesh things, or shimmering energy webs, or plated metal sacks. I emptied one of the energy webs out and kept the thing itself, which squashed down into a ball the size of my cell phone and fit neatly in my pocket. Hey, you never know when you might need an extra garbage bag, and I had a feeling this one wouldn't leak no matter what you put in it. I'm pretty sure I saw Tall pocket one of the mesh ones, too. And a few of the smaller metallic items we ran across, probably to investigate later and possibly add to his Boy Scout Wardrobe stash.

The truck's outline was shifting a bit as well, becoming less blocky and more streamlined, though its surface was still gray and pockmarked with dings and scrapes and dents. It was bigger, too—a lot bigger, or at least a lot wider, and seemed to spread out and then angle back sharply in front, like a spearhead or an arrow. The compactor in back curved in on itself, as if the mouth were opening in surprise, until it became a circular hole that irised open and had some kind of crackling blue energy within it. The big lever shifted into the truck, recessing into its side, and became a sleek silvery handle that you reached in, tugged out, and twisted to the side—to reset it you reversed the process.

Our little nooks on the rear bumper had changed, too. They weren't really part of the truck, for one thing. Not exactly. They were little disks now, connected to the truck by glowing strands of some sort, and there was a faint sheen all around them that extended up over our heads and all the way under the disks as well. When we "hopped off" to pick up the trash, the disks actually separated from the rest of the truck and zoomed us over to the right spot, apparently controlled by our thoughts or the twitches we were sending to our leg muscles or something. The sheen stretched to envelop the trash, too, so it stayed around us the whole time. "Gotta be some kind of protective field," Tall commented when I asked him what he thought that was. "We're actually moving at faster than light speed, and dropping out of that all of a sudden, then accelerating back up again? No way we'd be able to withstand that normally. This field is keeping us from going splat." That made sense, but it did take some of the fun out of the job for a little bit—every time we sped up or slowed down I kept picturing the field failing and me becoming nothing but a DuckBob-shaped smear across a dozen star systems.

And we were traveling from star to star and system to system. Whereas before it'd looked like we were stopping along the driveways or at the front doors of normal, ordinary Earth houses, now I could see that really we were stopping at asteroids, space stations, tiny moons—one time we even grabbed trash from a comet, matching its speed so we could reach out and snag the energy-bags it was trailing behind it! That was wild.

What was even stranger was that I was still seeing houses, just in weird locations. So the comet? Had a fancy, ultramodern high-rise parked atop it, all glass and steel and straight edges. Yeah, I suppose living on a comet would be pretty high-rent, but it was still weird to see the familiar mixed in with the utterly strange.

Then, at one stop where what looked like a fuzzy green rug overflowed a row of five trash receptacles and spilled out into the space around it, I got the biggest shock yet.

"Here, I'll give ya a hand with this one."

"Aaahhhh!" I nearly jumped out of my skin—which would have been mighty embarrassing, not to mention cold—when the thing shambled around the corner of the truck. It was . . . it was . . . well, you know Jell-O? The red kind? With the fruit in it? This looked like that—if that was a crude artist's rendering of somebody's nightmare. It was reddish-brown and jiggly and you could sort of see through it, enough to make out the organs and spine and other stuff floating within. It had little shiny eyes on long stalks, and a bunch of thin tendrils like noodles hanging from its face where its mouth should be, and a glowing red ember right in the middle.

The Minnesota Twins cap, though, hadn't changed a bit.

"B-Benny?" I asked.

"Yeah?" It had gotten past us, and now its eyes swiveled back. "You comin' or what? We don't got all day—I'm already behind schedule!"

I looked at Tall, who was pale but looked back at me and shrugged. So we joined Benny and together we heaved the thing around—his arms were more like tapioca than Jell-O-O but they were strong and apparently he could stretch them way out when he wanted—and managed to feed its front end into the trash compactor. Then some kind of suction took over because the truck literally sucked the thing in, chewed it up, and that was that. Benny oozed back to the cab and Tall and I maneuvered our little disks back over to their resting places by the back of the truck.

"That was—" I started as the truck jolted into motion again.

"Yeah," Tall agreed.

"So that's how he really—"

"Must be."

"Whoa." I thought about that, trying to mentally overlay the two images of Benny, the before and the after. It kinda fit, actually—I could see where the beard had come from, and the beady eyes, and the red nose.

"What about the tobacco?" I wondered aloud after a minute.

"What?"

"The tobacco. Benny's tobacco. If it's not really tobacco, what is it he keeps sucking and chewing and spitting?"

Tall and I exchanged a glance and shuddered at the exact same time.

"Right. Never mind." I looked around, desperate for any other thought or image, anything at all. Illusory or not, I didn't want to lose my breakfast. "Hey, the snow's letting up."

We both stared out at the world around us. Only it wasn't

a world anymore. The last mental suggestions of streets and houses and trees were completely gone along with the snow.

Instead we were looking at streams of tiny golden particles, whizzing by in all directions and at all angles, like we were caught in the world's biggest confetti storm. It was amazing. And through the particles I could make out the stars—so many stars! It was like the ones we saw at night were only the brightest ones and now we could see all of them, so many they looked like a solid glowing mass in places. It was amazing. And beautiful. And kind of terrifying.

I missed North Dakota. At least that I could understand.

But at least I didn't feel cold anymore.

Chapter Fourteen
Can I take your order?

We gotta pull in soon!" Benny shouted out his window as Tall and I walked back from the most recent stop, a floating space station shaped like a glittering star pendant. "Gotta weigh in!"

"Weigh in? What, you mean a weigh station?" Tall asked. "Figures," he muttered when Benny nodded. "Rules and regs no matter where you go."

"What's a weigh station?" I asked as we hopped on our platforms, grabbed hold, and the ship—I couldn't really call it a truck anymore, not since the wheels had disappeared and what looked like giant neon tubes appeared below the sides and apparently supported the ship's bulk—took off.

"Back home, trucks have to pull into weigh stations at regular intervals," Tall explained over the ship's noise. "Every type of truck has a maximum weight allowance, and you can't drive on the highway if you're over that limit—too much risk of overturning, blowing out a tire, and other problems. So you pull in, your truck gets weighed, you get it cleared for its current cargo load, and you move on."

"Oh." I'd passed those signs for Weigh Stations a hundred times along the highway and never really known what they were about—I'd sometimes wondered if it was a free service for people on vacation, so they could weigh themselves and see whether they needed to stop sampling quite so much of the local cuisine. I guess this made more sense, but I still liked the image of overweight tourists standing in long lines and calling out to each other, "Hey, Marge! Twenty pounds over! Guess I'd better lay off the meatloaf, huh?"

"Doesn't sound like it'll take too long," I said after a minute. "I mean, they can probably just scan this thing from a distance and know everything about its contents, right?"

"Maybe." Tall didn't sound convinced. "But if there's one thing I know, it's that no matter how easy it might be to do something, if it involves a bureaucracy they'll find a way to make it take forever."

We zipped along in silence for a while, and then Benny pulled off to one side—not that there were lanes here, and we saw very little other traffic, but the colors around us were a consistent shade of golden-green-brown, and on either side they were redder and more blue, which made me think we were in the equivalent of a space lane. Now we were on the "curb," and Benny hopped out. Ned and Mary piled out after him—I'm guessing he told them to—and all three of them converged on Tall and I.

"Weigh station's just up ahead," Benny told us once we were all gathered. "Shouldn't take too long, but best if y'all wait just the other side of it."

"Why, afraid we'll throw off the weight?" I asked. I wasn't sure how that could work—even in his real, Jell-O body form, I suspected Benny weighed more than the rest of us put together. Even counting Ned. And Tall. And the crap in his pockets.

"It's not just weight they check," Benny answered, shaking his head, which caused it to jiggle alarmingly. "They check everything about your ship, your licenses, your clearances, your route and destination."

"So what does that have to do with us?" I scratched at my bill. "You said we were on your route!"

"Y'all are," Benny agreed. "But my cab's only rated for two occupants total, including me. And the whole rig's got a maximum of three allowed. Most a' the time I'm the only one inside and TBA's on the back. For big jobs we might grab an extra pair of hands. But there're four a' y'all, and there's no way I'm cleared for that." He shuffled his "feet," leaving little gelatinous trails. "Sorry. But like I said, it shouldn't take long. Y'all just mosey on past the weigh station and wait for me there—soon's I'm cleared I'll drive out and pull off and y'all can hop back in and climb back on, then away we go again."

I wasn't too happy about it, and it didn't look like Tall was either, but Mary nodded. "Of course," she told Benny. "We appreciate your providing us with transport, and we have no desire to jeopardize your occupation. We will meet you past the station, as you suggest."

"Great! Won't be long. See y'all there!" Benny nodded to the rest of us, grinned at Mary, and waddled back to his cab, spitting as he went. I shuddered and looked away quickly.

"Okay," I said once he'd pulled away. "So now what?"

That got a frown from Mary. "Now we walk past the station

and then wait, as we agreed."

"That won't work," I warned her. "We've got a schedule to keep, remember? And we're already out of time. We can't afford to wait the hours or days it's gonna take for him to get his truck cleared."

"From the way he was talking, I figured it'd be less than an hour, myself," Ned offered.

"Not likely," I told him. "How many times did he say it wouldn't take long?" The three of them stopped to replay the conversation in their head. "I counted at least three times. And you know how that works." Mary and Ned both gave me blank stares and I sighed. "Say it once and something that should have taken ten minutes will suddenly take you twenty. Say it twice and you're looking at at least an hour. Three times? We could be sitting out there all day, maybe even several days! He might never come out at all!"

Ned snorted. "That's ridiculous!"

Surprisingly, it was Tall who came to my rescue. "No, he's right, actually." The way he shook his head, I think he was as surprised by that sentence as I was. "I've seen it happen way too many times not to know it's true."

"That every time you say something won't take long it winds up taking longer?" Ned snorted again. "You've both been breathing in truck exhaust for way too long. You've gone loopy."

"Come on, you've never noticed this?" That surprised me. Mary was your typical egghead type, though admittedly way hotter than most and of course the whole alien-alteration thing, but it made perfect sense she didn't know about something like this. Ned, though? He was a worldly guy. "Look, you've seen the sports announcer thing, right? He looked even more baffled. "You know, how they can change the results of a single toss or throw or kick by talking about how likely it is the player'll make it? Every time a sportscaster says how the player on the free throw line never misses, the ball bounces off the rim. And every time they say he's lousy at free throws he makes it, nothing but net."

Ned nodded. "Yeah, that one I know," he admitted. "Damn sportscasters! It's like they do it on purpose!"

"Of course they do! What'd you think, it was an accident— every time? They control the outcome of a game by deciding when to talk up some poor kid's throwing arm or laugh about some poor shmoe's inability to pull off a safety. What, you didn't know that?" I had to laugh. "Dude, where I grew up there was only one rule when betting on games. You can bet against a team's record, or a coach's history, or a player's trophies. But never never NEVER bet against a sportscaster! You'll lose every time." I shook my head. "But anyway, this is like that. The more time you claim something'll take, the less time it takes unless it's important, in which case it really does take that long. And the more you say something'll be easy the harder it becomes, while the more you say it'll be quick the longer it takes." That made me think of something, and I whirled to face Mary. "When you first told me what we needed to do, did you ever say it was easy? Did you?"

She shook her head. "I do not remember," she admitted. "I may have. Why?"

But I was thinking. "Who else said it would be easy, and how many times?" I muttered to myself. "How many times? And did it matter that it was different people each time?" Because I was pretty sure she hadn't been the only one—a lot of people had been encouraging me to accept this crazy mission, and it felt like all of them had comforted me by saying how easy it should be to get the thing done. Great. If it really had been as many people as I thought, I'd be lucky if I didn't spontaneously implode right before reaching the darned thing.

"We can discuss that later," Mary urged, putting a hand on my shoulder. "For now, if we accept your . . . theory we may need to find an alternate method of travel. But regardless we will need to pass by the weigh station and find a strategic location at which to wait." She gestured in that direction. "Shall we?"

I couldn't think of any reason why not, and plenty of reasons why, so I followed her. Closely. We trotted up a small rise—I asked Ned why there were hills and valleys and things if this wasn't really a road or really ground or really solid. He only shrugged and said, "space is curved," as if that explained everything—and paused at the top to get a better look at this weigh station.

Wow.

It was like looking at the Death Star, that was my first thought—the Death Star if it was merged with the Fisher-Price Weeble-Wobble Garage I'd had when I was a kid. It was big and bristly and covered in scanners and radar dishes and massive laser cannons. It was also cheery and brightly colored and had big colorful signs pointing out useful things like airlocks, docking bays, command center, and dead bodies. And there were bright shiny ramps everywhere, going every which way.

"That," I whispered, "is amazing! That's what every Philips 66 and Shell and BP wants to be when it grows up—a massive angry station, loaded for bear, and with smiley-faces imbedded in the floor."

Ned, who was next to me, nodded. "They figured out a long time ago that there was no reason to make places like this grim and ugly," he explained. "Better to make them happy and cheerful, to at least mask the pain and suffering within."

"Who's they?" I asked.

He shrugged. "The governments. The bureaucracy. You know, the men in charge."

I noticed Tall was taking notes. That didn't bode well. Still, I had wondered earlier why the Feds didn't use happy, cheerful cars for rounding up suspects. Maybe this would finally get that ball rolling.

In the meantime, we had a Happy Funland O' Misery to bypass.

"So can we just walk past it?" I asked. We hadn't moved from the top of the "hill" yet, and I took that as a bad sign.

Sure enough, Mary shook her head. "The weigh station is equipped with sensors," she told us. "It registers every vehicle that passes through the surrounding spacelanes, and will act to intercept any it feels must be weighed, catalogued, or otherwise inspected."

"But we're not vehicles!" I argued. "We're people!"

"That's the problem." Ned sighed. "This is a major thorough-fare, the equivalent of your superhighways." He gestured in either direction. "Look around. Whaddya see?"

I looked. "Tons of those particles," I answered after a second. "A few ships." And there were a few, in a variety of sizes and shapes—I saw a classic-SF-movie flying saucer whiz past, and something that looked like a salad bar with tentacles sprouting out the bottom, and what I was sure was a World War II Sherman tank. I tried to forget about the middle one. I had a feeling I'd never be able to look at buffets the same way again, especially if they included both lettuce and calamari. Ugh.

"And what don't you see?"

Tall was ahead of me again, as usual. It's just 'cause he's taller.

"People," he growled. "There aren't any people. No pedestrians."

"Exactly. No pedestrians. They're not allowed on or even in proximity to the superhighway. Too much risk of getting sucked into intakes or caught up in RAM scoops or otherwise mucking with the various ships' engines. If the weigh station spots us, it'll grab us and hold us, probably charge us with vagrancy and jaywalking and all sorts of other things. Then it'll throw us in a small, wet cell somewhere and toss away the key."

He was talking like the station itself was alive, and given what we'd seen so far I couldn't help thinking it wasn't just a colorful turn of phrase. "So can we just detour?" I asked instead. "Give it a wide berth, so we won't be within range of its sensors?"

But Ned shook his head. "Two problems with that plan," he explained. "First, that thing's sensors are stellar—and I mean that literally. It can read anything within a few light-years of it, no problem."

That sounded a bit farther than I was prepared to walk. "What's the second problem?"

He gestured at the superhighway again. "See how the particles thin out big-time once you get past the outer lanes?" I did, too. It really was like a highway, a broad ribbon gleaming in an otherwise empty expanse. "That's because they concentrate them through here to make it easier for travel—and for control. We venture away from the lanes and we're floating in space, nothing to grab onto."

"Got it—we stick to the road, or close by it, or we're sunk." I knew I was mixing my metaphors, but I figured what the hell. Mixed drinks were good, right? And mixed-match tennis? Why not mixed metaphors? As long as they weren't mixed signals, we should be fine.

Thinking about signals brought me back to the problem at hand, though, and I studied the place again, half expecting to see eyes and a big fanged grin this time. Nope, it still looked like Ronald McDonald's idea of a truck stop.

And that gave me an idea.

"Listen," I said. "I think I know a way we can sneak past it."

"This," Tall said for probably the hundredth time, "is insane. Completely cracked. There's no way this'll work."

"Shut up," I warned him. "And make vroom-vroom sounds."

He grumbled something else under his breath, but started putt-putting anyway. I nodded and glanced over at Ned. "You doin' okay there?"

Ned grinned back at me. It was, I'd already figured out,

his favorite expression. "Absolutely! I've always worried about being a fifth wheel—now I'm the first one instead!"

"Quiet, all of you," Mary warned. "We are approaching scanning range!"

We shut up. All except Tall, who kept making engine noises.

We'd done this trick back in college, during my frat days. It'd be late at night and we'd all be hungry, jonesing for fast food, but after midnight most of the burger joints and taco joints and such shut their front doors.

But they kept their drive-thrus open.

The only problem was, none of us had had cars. Well, okay, a few of us did. But those kept getting wrecked, or impounded—something about driving under the influence. And about wrapping them around trees.

But that wasn't going to stop us. No sirree. We figured, "They're open, and we're paying customers. Why should we have to have a car just to pay them for food?"

Some of them were stricter about it than others. Some you could literally walk up, place your order, walk around to the window, hand them your money, get your food, and leave. They might look at you funny, but they'd let you get away with it. Others were like "Hey, this is a drive-thru, not a walk-thru!" So we'd beep at them, make car noises, say things like "What, you don't see my car? What's wrong with you?" and "Sure, I'm in my car. It's a cousin to Wonder Woman's plane. You got a problem with that?", and brazen our way through.

Of course, none of those places had the kind of scanners and sensors this psychedelic Fort Knox did. That's why we had to be a little more creative here.

I was the front, of course. With my bill, I made a perfect hood. I was also the front left wheel. Ned was the front right wheel. Tall was the rear wheels, and the engine. Mary? Mary was both cockpit and driver. Car had to have a driver, right?

We were moving pretty slowly—hard to move fast when you're crawling on your hands and knees, and even harder when you're four people trying to hold onto each other and stay in formation—but Ned and Mary had assured us that wouldn't be a problem. "There are minimum speeds out here, sure," Ned had said, "but you're supposed to slow down when you're passing the weigh station, in case it decides it needs to pull you in. So crawling past here is fine."

We even had a license plate, courtesy of Tall's Sharpie and one of Ned's little gizmos. It hung from the back of Tall's belt. I'd resisted the urge to tell him he should make it his new badge afterward, but it had taken a lot of willpower. Judging by the glare he gave me, he'd known what I was thinking anyway.

"Almost there," Mary whispered. "It should be scanning us soon. Keep going!"

I inched forward and so did Ned. Mary and Tall were right behind us. I'm sure we looked like one of the craziest cars ever— we had no roof, no doors, our "wheels" were hands and feet— but I figured out here that couldn't make a lot of difference. And Ned had pulled some kind of little metallic square from his pocket, then opened it into a silvery tarp that he'd spread over the two of us, wrapped around Mary, and then spread over Tall as well. So you couldn't actually see that we were just three guys and one hot chick pretending to be a car. Instead we looked like a weird, lumpy car with funny tires.

I hoped.

Something beeped near my head. "They're scanning us!" Ned warned. The beeping continued, then stopped. Then started again.

We kept going.

Then I heard something else. A weird whooshing sound. And something like a scream, if blenders and saxophones could scream together. There was only one thing that noise could be, even out here.

A siren.

"Oh, great," I whispered. "They're onto us!"

"Not necessarily," Ned whispered back. "Stay cool! And don't move out of position!"

The siren drew closer, then alongside us.

"Pull over!" A mechanical voice announced. I couldn't peek but I felt like I was being chased by my neighborhood ATM.

"Yes, officers!" Mary replied. "To the right," she whispered. "Gradually."

Ned and I shuffled to the right, and I could feel the tarp tugging across me as Mary and Tall followed.

"Slow down," Mary whispered again. "And—stop!" We came to a halt, and I let out a little sigh of relief. The surface of the superhighway, whatever it was, was a bit springy and not too hard and surprisingly warm. It was like crawling across a water balloon if it weren't slick and sticky—there were other comparisons springing to mind but I was steadfastly ignoring them. Even so, this car stuff was rough on the hands. And my knees were killing me.

"Is there a problem, officers?" I heard Mary ask.

"License and registration, please," the mechanical voice replied. Great, the ATM had gotten out of its car. Or maybe it was the car. Who was I to point fingers?

"License and registration," Mary repeated. "Yes. I have it here somewhere. Hold on one moment while I find it." Ned was frantically twiddling and clicking and adjusting some of his gizmos, and after a few seconds he shoved two little cubes back behind him. "Ah, here they are," Mary announced, taking them from him. Part of me really loved the idea of a glove compartment that could hand you what you were looking for. The rest of me never wanted to put my hand in any sort of box or compartment or briefcase ever again.

"I am unfamiliar with this make and model vehicle," Officer ATM stated. "What is it, please, that I may update my database."

"Oh, it's a Duckbill Nedthomas 450Z," Mary replied smoothly. "It's a prototype, actually."

"Fascinating. What manner of fuel does it use?" Was this thing a car enthusiast, or trying to hit on her? Either way, I hoped she could speed things up. I was starting to get a crick in my neck.

"It runs on standard hydrocarbons," Mary answered. "Plus certain base elements. And the occasional insertion of biomatter." Food, air, and water. Cute.

"Impressive. You will need appropriate warning lights, however. I am writing you a warning citation, but due to its experimental nature I will not issue a full ticket." I heard a sound like a bee buzzing, mixed with the clicking of an old electric typewriter and then the ratchet of what I'd swear was an early dot-matrix printer.

"Thank you, officer. We will of course have the lights added before we go to production."

"Excellent." Officer ATM paused a second. "I have included my name and badge number at the bottom of the citation," it informed her. "With those you can contact me easily. If you have a mailing list for this vehicle, please add me to it. I have a large collection of vehicles and would very much like to add one of these when they become commercially available."

"I certainly will, officer," Mary told it. "Thank you again. You have a good day."

"You as well." A minute later there was a whooshing sound again, and then I heard Mary give a big sigh of relief. I wish I could have seen it.

"It's gone," she informed us quietly. "That was close."

"Too close," Tall agreed from the rear.

"Hey, look at the bright side," I told them. "It scanned us and the only problem was our lack of headlights. So we should be in the clear." I could feel the others nodding. "And besides," I added, "you heard the officer. We're a collectible!"

Chapter Fifteen
Take me to Havana!

Fifteen harrowing minutes later, we veered off the road once more and did our best imitation of rolling to a stop. I was soaked in sweat, my hands and knees were raw, I couldn't move my neck, my back was a mass of pain, and my entire body was shaking. But we'd done it! We were safely out of scanning range from the weigh station, but now on its far side. We'd gotten through!

And, in the process, we'd heard a wider variety of horns—and curses—than I'd even imagined possible. Who knew some races screamed by bursting into full symphonies? And harmonizing with themselves? Pretty impressive, and it certainly would make fights at the local bar a lot more pleasant.

Ned crawled under the tarp and pulled it free, releasing us, and I sprawled backward on the grass. Okay, no grass—no ground at all, really, just a slightly different texture, color, and smell to the near-invisible surface beneath our feet—but I was too wrung out to be picky. The others collapsed beside me, though Mary actually sat cross-legged instead of lying down.

Then again, she hadn't had to play any of the wheels.

We just lay there for several minutes, catching our breath and letting our limbs slowly return to normal. Man, playing car had been a lot more fun when I was a kid, and a lot less painful. Then again, we'd mainly just run around making noises and pretending to hold a steering wheel, so it hadn't required as much acrobatics. And I was a lot more limber then. Plus I hadn't been lugging a ten-pound duckbill on the front of my face.

"Okay," I said after I thought my arms and legs were solid again. "So what now?"

"Now we wait for Benny to finish inspection and pick us up," Mary reminded me.

"Yeah. Right. He's either trapped in that Playschool hellhole for the next decade or long gone," I groused. "I say if he doesn't show in the next hour, two tops, we move on."

"How?" Tall asked. He groaned. "I am not doing that car thing again!" To prove his point he yanked the "license plate" off his butt and threw it down on the ground behind him.

"No, we'd never be able to maintain it," Ned agreed. "Or go any faster than we were already." He was folding the tarp back up into its little tiny square. It was like one of those wet-naps, only a thousand times bigger and silvery. And, well, not wet. "We'll need to hitch a ride again," he concluded.

"Will anyone else stop for us, d'ya think?" I tried lifting my head up to look at him but the strain was too much and I collapsed again. "I mean, last time it was Mary getting us a ride at the truck stop. This time we're on the side of the highway. Is hitching even legal out here?"

"It is not technically illegal." I could tell Mary was frowning without even seeing her, just from the tone of her voice. "But it is not encouraged. We might have a difficult time convincing anyone to stop for us this close to the highway, and this close to the weigh station."

"Then there's the whole 'going my way' thing," Ned pointed out. "Benny was heading to the core, same as we were. Here, everybody's going every which way. There's no telling which ships are going coreward—if any."

"So what do we do?" I asked again. "If we can't find somebody going the right direction, how do we get there? Do we hijack a car, or what?"

Dead silence.

After a minute I forced my head up and glanced around. "You've gotta be kidding me!"

"We're trying to save the universe," Ned replied. "I think a little grand theft auto is a small price to pay for all that."

"Yeah? Tell it to the cops when they arrest us and throw our butts in the outer space equivalent of a hoosegow!" I shot back. "Tall, back me up here, man! You're a federal agent! You've gotta uphold the law, right?"

But Tall was shaking his head. "I'm authorized to break certain laws in the pursuit of my duties," he argued. "And this would definitely be for the purpose of our mission. Ned's right—we can't let something as minor as car theft prevent us from saving the universe!"

"Mary?" I looked at her. "Mary, tell me you're not seriously considering going along with this? We're talking about stealing a car!"

"We have no choice," she answered. I couldn't pull away from her eyes. "As you yourself said, it is unlikely Benny will return for us in sufficient time. And if that is the case, we must make our way to the matrix by any means necessary. I am sure, once we explain the situation, any driver would understand our pressing need."

I tried to think of something to say to that, but I couldn't. They were right, really. What was stealing a car versus saving everything? And why did I care, anyway? It's not like I'd get my license revoked—out here I didn't even have a license.

"Okay." I lay back down. "So we're gonna steal a car. A ship. How?"

Ned chuckled, which sent shivers down my spine. "Leave that to me."

"This," I muttered, "is insane."

"Hey," Tall countered, "you're the one who suggested we pose as a car."

"I know, I know." I ground my beak. "But that was only to get us past the weigh station! Not for this! No one's gonna fall for this!"

"You wanna bet?" Ned laughed. "Universal truth—most people are idiots."

"And that's supposed to make me feel better? Some of my best friends are idiots!" And I'm sure most of them said the same thing about me.

"Which is exactly my point," Ned argued. "Would your friends be dumb enough to fall for this?"

I started to say no, then stopped and thought about it. Well, maybe—okay, definitely for at least two of them. Three. Five—

no, wait, not since that last thing with that one chick. Okay, four. Oh, right—seven. And of course if we were talking about my old frat buddies . . .

"Yeah, okay, fine." I would've glared at him if I could've moved my head. "Let's just hope somebody takes the bait quickly. My back may start spasming otherwise."

"That's fine," Ned assured me. "It'll just add to the realism."

Great.

We were saying all of this in hushed tones, of course—wouldn't do to have the car talking to itself. At least not if we weren't just saying "Check your oil" and "door is ajar" and "please fasten seatbelts" over and over again. Mary wasn't involved in the conversation, either. She couldn't be. Not and still play her part in this little charade.

I was starting to wish I'd never suggested the car idea in the first place.

One of Ned's little gadgets began beeping. "Somebody's coming!" I could hear him tapping out some kind of command. "Nope," he said a second later. "It's an Artusian roadster. Only seats three, and that's if they're triplets. No good." He pressed a button on another doodad and it gave out a short squawk.

That was Mary's signal to let the car pass us by.

"No, I am fine, thank you," we heard her telling someone. "My engine overheated but it will be fine in a few moments." I could have sworn I heard a cat meowing, and then nothing. I wasn't sure if that had been the car or its driver.

Another vehicle stopped to offer its assistance—funny how that works when it's an incredibly hot chick standing there looking all helpless—but Ned said it didn't have the range we needed to get all the way to the core. A few minutes later a third slowed down, but it was the equivalent of a space jalopy—according to Ned it would take us over a year to reach the matrix in that thing. So we threw both of those guppies back and waited for a bigger fish to take the bait.

And boy, did it!

Ned's toy was beeping so fast it was one continuous whine. Then that blended with a sound like a bell ringing, overlaid with the hiss of compressed air.

"Need some help, little lady?" we heard a voice say.

A big voice.

A big, deep voice.

A voice like John Wayne's if the Duke had been twelve feet tall and carved of solid stone.

"A Ratavari sonic glider," Ned whispered beside me. "It's one of the fastest things on the road, it's built for long-distance travel, and it could fit ten of us and have room to spare! It's perfect!" His signal device gave a chirp, and we could almost hear Mary turning on the charm.

"Why thank you, yes," she all but purred. "I do not know what is wrong with my vehicle. It just sputtered to a stop. I was lucky to get to the side of the road."

"Hm, I don't recognize it," the mysterious Good Samaritan rumbled. "Is it new?"

"Brand-new, yes," Mary told him. I was assuming anything with a voice that macho had to be male. "That is probably why it malfunctioned."

Well, let me just take a peek under the hood," her savior announced, "and I'll soon figure out what's what." Earthshaking footsteps signaled his approach, and then two massive feet parked themselves right in front of my face. Which was also the hood.

Then two massive hands reached out, gripped the edge of my bill, and lifted.

Which is when Ned slid out from beside me, raised one of his ever-present technosticks, and said, "Gotcha!"

There was a bright light, and a second later he called back, "Okay, you can come out now."

I wasn't sure what I'd been expecting. No, scratch that—I'd been expecting a towering figure, all machismo and chromed steel, a cross between the Marlboro Man and a Transformer. What I saw instead was—

—a bunny rabbit.

No, not a real one. A cartoon one, with the oversized eyes, the cute little nose, the great big front teeth, the little tuft tail. Only real.

I know, that doesn't make a lot of sense. But that's what was standing in front of me, and that's whose oversized mitts I had to pry off my face.

Because this guy was maybe five feet tall, tops. Long, lanky limbs, just like Bugs. But his hands and feet were ENORMOUS!

So were his ears. And they stood straight up, like they had wire in them. Maybe they did. Or maybe it was just a result of whatever Ned had done to him, because he was stiff as a board, and his eyes were completely glazed over.

"He'll be fine," Ned assured us. "Temporary paralysis, light-induced. He'll wake up in a few minutes with a mild headache." He grabbed a little green pouch hanging from the bunny's neck—he wasn't wearing any clothes, and I guess why would you if you were covered in rabbit fur? It was a lot more concealing than duck feathers, I'll tell you that for nothing!—and rummaged in it for a second before producing something that looked a lot like a miniature flattened Rubik's cube. "Got 'em! Let's go!"

Which is when I finally turned around and saw the car.

Oh.

My.

God.

I must have started hallucinating again, or masking reality, or whatever. But I didn't care. It was a Corvette. "It's a Corvette," I said. At least I think I said it. I must have, because Ned frowned.

"No, it's a Ratavari sonic glider," he corrected me. "Look at the dorsal fins, the emitter array, the subsonic housing." I could almost see the little hearts in his eyes as he turned back to stare at it. "She's beautiful."

"Oh, yeah," I agreed softly. "But you're wrong about what she is. She's a Corvette, no question. And not just any Corvette, either—that's a 1963 Corvette Sting Ray. Just look at the split rear window—they discontinued that the following year." Yeah, so I know a lot about Corvettes, okay? My friends and I were into muscle cars when I was in high school and early college, and this was one of the great classic American muscle cars. She was in perfect condition, too, from what I could see."

"You're both high," Tall interrupted us. "That's not a Sting Ray—are you blind?" A look of sheer adoration claimed his face. "She's a 1968 Ford Mustang GT fastback. Which means she's got a solid V-8 under that hood." He sneered at me. "She'd run one of those little sissy Sting Rays right off the road."

"Oh yeah?" Figures he'd be into Mustangs. Gearheads always seem to divide into three camps when it comes to the great American muscle car: Sting Ray, Mustang, and Charger. I was half-surprised he wasn't a Charger enthusiast, since they were monstrous, heavy road hogs. Which didn't mind I'd turn one down if someone offered me one.

Mary shook her head. "I do not know why you are unable to see it properly," she informed all three of us, "but you are all mistaken in your identification of this vehicle. It is a Ya'atum Transwarp Jumper, which is precisely what we need to complete our travel with the utmost speed." She was already walking toward it. "Shall we?"

"Okay, hold on a second here." I stepped in front of her and put up a hand, forcing her to stop short before she bumped right into me. She managed it, more's the pity. "You're seeing some kind of jumper thing?" she nodded. "Ned's seeing a glider?"

"Ratavari sonic glider," Ned corrected.

"Right, that." I glanced at Tall. "You're seeing a Mustang—I know, I know, '68 GT fastback. Which is an awesome car, by the way. Just not as good as the '63 Sting Ray I see." I scratched my head. "So each of us is seeing something completely different. What's up with that?"

We all stared at the car—or cars—for a second. Then Ned

burst out laughing. "Not just different," he explained after he caught his breath again, "but exactly what we want. We're each seeing our perfect vehicle!"

I nodded. "Okay, yeah. So?"

"So," Ned replied, still chuckling, "it's gotta be a Get Lucky."

"A what?"

"A Get Lucky. It's a device some people use to pick up chicks . . . or guys, or whatever," he explained. "It basically taps into the viewer's thoughts and makes them think you're the person of their dreams. And this guy's got one installed in his car!"

"So whoever looks at it sees whatever they really want to see? Nice!" I wondered how I could get one of those, and whether it was strictly visual—looking like Hugh Jackman wouldn't help me a whole lot if the first time some chick leaned in to kiss me I accidentally crushed her nose with my bill. Hey, there's an art to it, you know. And the learning curve was pretty steep—let's just say when I mentioned how disgusting a nose would taste I was speaking from experience.

"So what is it really?" Tall asked.

"Does it matter?" I gestured toward it. "We can each take our dream car to the prom! How sweet is that?"

But Tall was giving me that you're-so-stupid-it's-a-wonder-you-can-talk look again. Or maybe that was just his default expression. "Think about it, genius," he sneered. "The Mustang's got a back seat. The Sting Ray doesn't. So how many seats does this thing really have? And how much head room? And where do the doors open?"

Oh. Right. Okay. I glanced at Ned. "So how do we turn it off and get a look at the real car underneath?"

"There's gotta be a control here on the key," Ned replied, studying the thing he'd taken from the bunny rabbit. "I just have to find—ah, here we go!" He pressed two different spots on the shape and it squeaked like a deflating balloon.

And the car behind him changed.

"Oh, you've gotta be kidding me!" I stared at it, then at Ned, then back at it again. "Can we make it go back to looking like a Sting Ray? Please? Or a Mustang? Hell, I'd settle for a Ford Pinto!"

Because the real shape, the actual vehicle we were in the process of stealing, was . . .

. . . a bridge.

Okay, no, not really. But that was my first impression, was a suspension bridge like the Brooklyn Bridge or the RFK. Steel girders and arches and linking it all like somebody with twelve hands trying to do Cat's Cradle using four sets of string.

On second glance—well, it still looked like a bridge. Just not one I'd ever seen before. It had weird curves and the angles didn't seem to add up right and the planes kept twisting when I studied them, like they were shy.

So it was more like an alien bridge. And only a model of one at that, seeing as how it was only ten to twelve feet long and about eight feet wide. Or maybe it was an alien bridge for little tiny aliens. I didn't see any of them around, though.

What I also didn't see was a seat. Or a steering wheel. Or wheels of any sort.

"That's not a car," I pointed out. "It's what cars drive across to get from Point A to Point B."

"It's not a car, no," Ned agreed, "but it is a vehicle. A Dreymar Suspension Cluster, to be precise." He glanced over at Mary and shrugged. "It can get us where we're going, and it is fast enough to get us there in a hurry," he admitted.

"Fine." She tossed me a disapproving frown like I used to get from old Aunt Mildred (and that was before the duck thing! If Aunt Mildred had still been around after my little unelective cosmetic surgery she'd have hit me with a frown so hard my bill might have snapped!), then threw one at Tall and at Ned for good measure. "The vehicle's appearance is unimportant. We must reach the matrix in time, and if this vehicle can accomplish that goal we will use it. Quickly." And she stepped around me and walked to the bridge-cluster-thingy.

"Okay, okay." I hurried after her. "So how do we use it, exactly?" I looked for anything to indicate a start button, a gearshift, a control panel. Or seats. "And where do we sit?"

Mary had clambered up onto the part that would have been the roadway on a real bridge, and sat herself cross-legged just behind the central spar. Guess that answered that question. I pulled myself up and sat next to her. Tall grumbled a bit more before settling himself behind us, and Ned took up a position in front, leaning back against the spar like it was a backrest. Which maybe it was.

"Everybody on?" he asked. "All strapped in?" He laughed when I started frantically searching for a seatbelt. "Just kidding—it's got an inertial dampener, of course. Okay, hold on to something. I'm about to start her up."

He played with the flattened Rubik's cube—any second I was expecting a Hasbro version of that guy from *Hellraiser* to pop out—and I heard that humming bell tone we'd heard before. And the bridge-cluster-thingy began to glow. And to raise itself up off the ground. We were hovering a few inches above the roadway, and I started to believe this could actually do the trick. Ned said it could get us there, and fast—maybe in a few minutes or hours or however long this ride took we'd be at the matrix finally, and then I could realign it and get back to my old life, such as it was, before it shriveled up and blew away.

I should know better by now.

"Here we go!" Ned shouted. He jabbed the key into the front of the bridge-cluster-thingy and it . . . extended. It was like a glowing walkway suddenly burst forth from its front edge, shooting off ahead of us into infinity. Then there was a small click, and a pop, and the rest of the bridge-cluster-thingy took off after it, hurtling along like we were the back end of a rubber band that'd just been stretched way too far and let go.

Or like we were the rock in a giant cosmic slingshot.

I wanted that Sting Ray back. Badly.

Chapter Sixteen
Did we take a left at Albuquerque again?

"Ow."

That was about all I had to say for that.

For the first few minutes.

Repeatedly.

"Ow."

"Yes, ow, we got it," Tall growled. "Trust me, we're all feeling it."

I had my head between my knees and didn't bother to look up. Actually, I wasn't sure I could. I think somebody may have removed my spine in there at some point, and replaced it with a spastic porcupine.

"Why the hell," I moaned when I was able to form coherent sentences again, "would anyone voluntarily drive this thing? It should be some form of punishment for violating galactic traffic laws—"Oh, you've got twenty speeding tickets and four major collisions, if you want any sort of vehicle you'll have to use the Manic Slingshot Deathbridge." Okay, mostly coherent. I groaned again.

"I pushed it to its maximum speed," Ned managed to whisper between his own groans. "Normally it wouldn't be that . . . abrupt."

"Abrupt?" I'd have glared at him if I could have moved. "I'm pretty sure the left half of my body is still back there somewhere. I only hope it catches up before the right half falls apart or something else wanders in and replaces it." The idea of having only half a duckhead was even worse than the reality of having a whole one, and I quickly shook that idea off, then wished I hadn't. Shaking hurt.

"We have arrived," Mary reminded us, though her voice was tight with pain too. "That is all that matters. This discomfort will soon pass." It sounded like she was trying to convince herself as much as us, so I didn't bother to ask for her definition of "soon." I just hoped it wasn't being measured in geologic epochs.

Several more minutes passed that way, with groans and whines and curses interspersed with occasional grousing. But finally I managed to bully my neck muscles into getting back to work. They didn't have much choice—I was starting to get lightheaded.

So I lifted my head, slowly and carefully, and looked around.

Then I looked around again.

"Say," I asked no one in particular, "what's this matrix thingy supposed to look like, anyway?"

"It's a grand confluence of universal truths, all coalesced into a single coherent structure," Ned replied. "Kinda like one of your Earth power plant's control stations, with levers and buttons and monitors everywhere."

"Oh." I blinked a few times. "So it doesn't look anything like a small desert island, then?"

"Not even remotely. Why?"

"Because I think we made a wrong turn somewhere. Or took the wrong bridge."

Ned grunted and let out a string of curses I couldn't decipher as he hoisted himself into a sitting position and peered about, squinting. Then his curses got louder. There were a few in there I did recognize, and I wished I hadn't.

Tall levered himself up as well, and I gave Mary a hand. All four of us stared.

"Definitely an island," Tall agreed after a few seconds.

"Thanks for confirming that," I snapped. "What gave it away, the sand under our butts or the water all around us?"

Because it wasn't just an island, it was the kind of island you see in movies and commercials. Perfect white sand, a few brave palm trees or coconut trees or something—and nothing else.

Nothing but water. Clear blue water, a few shades deeper than the clear blue sky.

And all around us. Like, not more than ten feet from us at any point. By craning my neck—and I regretted that immediately—I could see the other side of the island. Hell, if I'd been able to stand up I could have walked to it. Or possibly just fallen over onto it.

"This," Mary summed up for all of us, "is not the matrix."

"Yeah, I figured that much." I glared at Ned. "What'd you do, decide we needed a little tropical getaway first?"

Ned glared right back at me. "Do you see pretty island girls in grass skirts bringing us fruity drinks in coconuts? Do you? No? Then this isn't my idea of a tropical getaway!" He had the Rubik's cube pancake out again and was fiddling with it.

"I don't know what happened," he muttered as he tinkered. "I programmed it to bring us straight to the matrix."

"Maybe it moved," I suggested. "When was the last time you visited it?"

"One does not simply visit the quantum fluctuation matrix," Mary scolded. "It is off-limits to all but its caretakers except in times of significant crisis."

"Like now, you mean?"

"Yes."

"So you've never been there?"

Mary frowned. "No."

"Ned?"

He shook his head, still not looking up from the key. "Never had a reason to go," he admitted.

"So we don't actually know for certain that you had the right address for this thing?"

"Not for certain, no," he reluctantly agreed. "But it's the one they gave me."

"Okay. So we should find somebody to ask, somebody who can confirm if they screwed up somehow or if it moved or something."

Ned finally looked up. "That could be a problem."

Tall sighed. "What's wrong now?"

"Look around," Ned told him.

He did. So did I. I saw the same stuff I'd seen already: water, sky, and sand. Plus three trees.

And nothing else.

It took a second for that to sink in. "Where's the bridge-cluster-thingy?" I demanded when it did.

"Yeah. That's the problem."

"Whaddya mean, 'that's the problem'? Where'd you park the damn thing?"

Ned looked really embarrassed. "I, uh, didn't."

"You didn't what?"

"I didn't park it."

"What does that mean, exactly?" All three of us were glaring at him now. So were the three suns overhead, but they were glaring at all of us equally so that didn't really count.

Ned took a deep breath. "I set the Dreymar Suspension Cluster to bring us to the matrix," he explained slowly. "I disabled a few of the safeties so we could get the maximum speed out of it." He mumbled something.

"What was that?"

"I forgot to reset the inertial dampener to compensate," he repeated just loud enough for me to make out.

"Which means what?"

"We, ah—slid off."

"We slid off."

"Yes."

"Off a hyperspeed bridge-cluster-thingy."

"Yes."

"That was aimed at the matrix."

"Yes."

"Where we need to be going."

"Yes."

I glanced around quickly before focusing my ire on him

again. "So this place—we basically fell out of the car while it was hurtling down the superhighway, and this is where we rolled to a stop?"

"That's pretty accurate, yeah," Ned agreed. "Fortunately the Cluster has built-in gravitic displacement chutes, so in case of an accident its passengers are ejected but at sub-relativistic speeds which then reduce further until they've normalized with the local velocity." He saw the utter confusion battling anger in my eyes. "We landed intact, instead of becoming galactic roadkill."

"Depends upon your definition of 'intact,'" I argued, "but yes, at least that's something. So we fell out and wound up here. And the car kept on going?"

"I certainly hope so."

"So we're stuck here. On this little tiny island. On some wacky world with"—I glanced up to confirm it—"three suns. Without a ride. While the universe is under attack."

He sifted sand through his fingers and stared at it. "That's about it, yeah."

I collapsed back on the sand. "Nice. Well, at least we can get a tan while we WAIT FOR THE UNIVERSE TO END!" I'd have tried to throttle him but I wasn't sure I could raise my arms properly yet. Hopefully there'd be time enough for that later.

"Look on the bright side," Ned offered weakly. "We're a lot closer to our destination now."

"Yeah? How close?"

"I'm not exactly sure," he admitted. "I'd need a better reading on our current location to be sure of that. But definitely closer."

"Is it behind those trees?" I managed to jerk my head in their direction.

"Uh, no."

"Is it floating just offshore?"

"Probably not."

"Is it buried in the sand beneath us?"

"Not even a little bit."

"So being closer DOESN'T EXACTLY HELP US, DOES IT?"

Ned hung his head.

"Okay, enough—stop yelling at him." I was surprised enough by Tall's interruption that I stopped. At least long enough to glare at him instead.

"Why should I?" I demanded. "He screwed up! And now we're stuck here!"

"Maybe we are," Tall agreed. "And yeah, he screwed up. Big-time. But we all agreed to take that weird-ass bridge thing. And we all agreed we needed to reach the matrix as soon as possible. Ned was just trying to accomplish that. So he made a mistake. We all make mistakes. Cut him some slack, and let's focus on what we do next."

It was the longest I'd ever heard him talk. The longest any of us had. I'd actually started to think he couldn't say more than ten words at a time, due to some obscure government regulation somewhere. And I had to admit, what he said make sense. Even if I didn't want to hear it.

"Agent Thomas is correct," Mary said. Figures she'd be quicker to forgive than I was. "Ned did his best, and we have all made errors along this journey. The important thing now is to figure out how to leave this place and continue toward the matrix as soon as possible."

"Yeah yeah, all right." I gave Ned one last glare before relenting. "I guess it's no worse than making an entire race spend centuries wanting to kill you."

"Thanks." Ned gave me a half-smile. "You'll have to tell me the rest of that story at some point."

"I will," I promised, heaving myself back up to a sitting position. "Over lots and lots of beer. Provided we survive all this." I looked around us. "Okay, so we're on a tiny little island somewhere in the middle of an ocean on a planet with three suns. What do we do now?"

"Swim?" I tried giving Tall the stink-eye but he played innocent. And given that this may have been the first time on this entire whacked-out trip that he cracked wise like that, I figured he ought to get away with it.

"Works for me," I agreed. "Hell, I'm built for it." I deliberately rubbed the tip of my bill. "No wings, of course, but I'm a damn good swimmer now. The only problem is, you bozos'd never be able to keep up. And where would I be going, anyway?" I surveyed our surroundings. "There's nothing out there as far as the eye can see. So going for a dip might be refreshing for the first hour or two, but then we'd be floating with no land to come back to, and no closer to getting off this waterworld."

"Our first step should be establishing this planet's coordinates," Mary suggested. "Once we know those we will have a better idea of our general location, our distance to the matrix, and what steps must be taken to bridge that gap."

"Fair enough." I frowned at the sand below us. "So how do we figure that out? There isn't anyone here to ask, and it's not like we've got a map."

"I may be able to figure out what planet we're on," Ned offered. "I'll need to know everything we can about this place first, though. So examine everything with all your senses and tell me whatever you learn, even if it seems obvious."

"Uh, okay." I crouched down and ran my fingers through the sand. "There's sand here. It's really fine, not coarse at all, and almost white."

"The sky's blue, lighter than Earth's but a comparable hue," Tall commented. "And we've got three suns here, one big and two small. The big one"—he squinted up at it— "looks like a typical red, probably a Class-C like ours. The two smaller ones are paler, almost white—I doubt they're white dwarfs, though, so just standard dwarf stars."

Okay, that was way more impressive than my observations about the sand. Ned nodded, too. "That'll definitely help narrow it down." He fiddled with one of his doodads. "There aren't that many triple-star systems, even in the core. What else?"

"The water's a deep blue," I said quickly. "But clear. No major waves, no whitecaps. A gentle rolling motion. Looks deep, too."

"There is no major technology within one hundred miles," Mary announced. The three of us stared at her, and she smiled. "The air is crisp and clean, with no trace of ionization," she explained. "Almost every technology involves some form of burning to release energy, and that would produce a particular odor. It is absent here, completely so."

"Right, so no heavy tech." Ned was twisting and tapping his toy. It looked a lot like a man playing the spoons. And sounded suspiciously like "She'll Be Comin' Round the Mountain When She Comes." "Mostly water, three suns—yeah, only a few dozen planets like that between that weigh station and the matrix." None of us wanted to bring up the chance that we had wound up overshooting our target, or veering off in the wrong direction.

"There's trees," I pointed out, gesturing behind us. "I wouldn't know a palm from a birch if they walked up to me and handed me their astrological charts, but those look tropical to me. They look a lot like ones we'd see on Earth, actually."

Tall took two long steps and was next to the nearest tree. "Coconut," he stated, resting one hand on its trunk. "Definitely." He squinted up at the top. "And there are even coconuts up there now."

"Really?" I grinned. "Great, I'm starving!" Hey, that breakfast was a long time ago! And we'd been through a lot of stress since then.

Tall wrapped his arms and then his legs around the trunk and shimmied up it, graceful as a snake. When he was high enough he reached out and plucked one of the nice big green coconuts from its stem. He dropped it down onto the sand, repeated that with a second one, and then lowered himself back down after them.

"Smells like a coconut," he informed us after a quick sniff of one. The tree's trunk was rough and even had what looked like overlapping shingles all the way and all the way around.

Tall eyed one of those, then took the coconut in his hand and slammed it against the trunk, right on the top ridge of one of those shingles. We all heard a loud crack, and saw that he'd split the coconut partway through on both sides. Then Tall gripped the two sides, one in each hand, and twisted. I heard a louder pop and a tear, and then Tall was handing Mary and I each a half of a coconut.

"Thanks!" I took my half eagerly and studied it for a second. Inside the green outer shell was the wrinkled brown inner shell I'm more used to, and inside that was a thick slab of milky white coconut meat, and cradled by that maybe three ounces of almost clear coconut milk. It looked just like the ones I'd seen as a kid when my uncle used to sometimes bring back real wild coconuts, and smelled exactly the same, too. Sure, I realized there was a chance it would be some kind of alien fruit that could have nasty effects on me, or even kill me.

But right now I didn't care. I tilted the whole thing up to my lips and drank down the coconut milk, then used my fingernails to dig out pieces of coconut meat and toss them down my throat. It wasn't as sweet as I'm used to from coconut, but it was also extremely fresh and very thirst-quenching and really tasty.

Tall had already split the second coconut and given half to Ned, and for a minute all you could hear over the gentle waves was slurping and chewing and swallowing.

"Ah, I feel better!" I said after I'd dug the last of the meat from mine. "Thanks, man." Tall nodded and continued consuming the last of his. "So, Ned, learn anything from the coconut you just ate?"

Ned wiped his face with the back of his sleeve. "I did, actually." He checked his gadget. "Fourteen of the possible planets couldn't support this kind of plant life. Which leaves twenty-three others."

Okay. Time to get serious about this. I walked over to the edge of the water, squatted down, and thrust my bill into it. After a second I swallowed, then straightened up again. "The water tastes funny," I told him. "Almost sweet, like fluorinated water. Warm, of course. No salt, either."

"No salt? Hmmm." Ned twiddled the technostick a bit more. "Of those twenty-three, eight have fresh-water oceans."

"Down to eight? Nice!" I wiped my bill with the back of my hand. So drinking the water had helped. Excellent. And we'd tried the coconut, too. What else was there around here? Water, trees, sky—

—and sand.

I eyed the sand dubiously. Who knew where it'd been, how many others had walked across it, and how many had peed on it or let their pets do the same? I shuddered. I had to stop scaring myself all the time! It was ridiculous, not to mention mean. What'd I ever had against me, anyway? Instead, before I could think of more reasons not to do it, I bent down and stuck my bill into the sand, then sucked some into my mouth.

"Okay, that's weird," I commented after a few seconds.

"What's weird?" Tall asked. I could tell from his face that he wished he'd thought of eating sand. Well, ha ha!

"It's almost . . . sweet," I told him. I tried a little more, and actually now that I wasn't so worried and could study the taste better it really was a little sweet. "Less like sand and more like . . . sugar."

Tall clearly didn't believe me, because he scooped up a big handful and nibbled some before offering the rest to Mary and Ned. Both refused, Mary apparently not wanting to eat something we'd just been walking on and Ned preferring to hunt and gather his own food. But Tall nodded once he's swallowed a little bit.

"It is sweet!" I wasn't sure why that blew his mind but clearly it did.

"Sugar-sand," Ned said, licking the last of it off his chin. Whoa. "Excellent! Only two planets match all the other details and have sugar-sand." Then he frowned. "Uh oh."

"Uh oh? Why 'uh oh'?" I asked. "What's wrong?"

He lowered his little toy. "Well, there are only two planets it could be, really. One of them's way off the elliptical from our projected path—we'd be almost as far away as we were before. The other's a lot closer—only a star system or two off, actually. But . . ."

I waited, but he'd trailed off. "But what? Come on, tell me!" I demanded. "What's so bad if it's that one?"

Ned sighed. "That planet's under Galactic Interdict."

"Okay, and that means what, exactly? No pay channels on late-night cable?"

"No visitors." Ned shook his head. "Not ever."

"A planet is placed under Galactic Interdict," Mary explained, "when its population is considered either too primitive for contact with the spacefaring population—or too dangerous."

Too dangerous. Great. "So which one is this? Are they too scared of us creepy spacemen, or do they like to nosh on a few spacemen for breakfast?"

"I don't know," Ned admitted. "I've got a galactic database programmed into this scanner but only with the most basic details—I've got the planet listed as under interdict but not how long ago or why."

"Well, if it is for being too dangerous, maybe that's somewhere else," I mentioned. "I mean, look around. What exactly would we be worried about here? The coconut trees?"

"Maybe," Tall answered. He glanced up at the tree he'd climbed a minute before and shuddered slightly. "Imagine if that tree was alive? I basically just cut off its nuts so we could have a light snack."

I put up a hand to stop him from talking any further. "Boy, that was an image I didn't need, thanks very much." It was a good thing coconut meat wasn't heavy or I'd be heaving it back up right now. "So how do we find out which it is? And does it really matter?"

"It might." Ned sighed. "At least it'd tell us whether we should be worrying for our lives."

Which is, of course, when something erupted out of the water and came charging straight toward us.

It was a shark. A massive one, just like the one from Jaws. Except that it was a deep purple, and kind of pebbly all over, like that rubber covering you get on flashlights and such.

Oh, and it had legs. Big, strong, muscular legs. I realized

that when it burst from the ocean and ran, not flew, across the sand.

Swell, I thought as we all threw ourselves to the sides in the hope of avoiding its mad rush. An honest-to-god land shark. No wonder this place is under Edict or whatever.

I'd thrown my hands over my head and held my breath, waiting for the thing to gobble us up. I remember reading once that great white sharks can eat pretty much forever, and I figured this rough-skinned purple version would have a similar appetite. The four of us probably wouldn't be much more than an appetizer before it went on to consume an ocean liner or something. Sure enough, it skidded to a stop in our midst, opened that gigantic mouth wide, revealing row upon row of razor-sharp teeth—

—and sobbed, "Don't let it get me!"

Then it dove behind the coconut trees and cowered there, whimpering.

Oh, great.

Chapter Seventeen
Who ordered the shrimp Fra Diablo?

It took a few seconds before what'd just happened sank in. Then I pushed myself back to my feet and dusted myself off. The others did the same.

"What the hell?" I finally asked.

"I have no idea," Ned admitted. "Maybe the sharks of this world are cowardly vegetarians?"

"Oh, come on," Tall told him. "Did you see those teeth? I've hunted great whites off the Barrier Reef, and that thing could be their bigger, uglier cousin! There's no way it's not an omnivore like they are!"

"A talking one, with legs," I pointed out. "But yeah, I agree." Of course the closest I'd gotten to hunting great white sharks was watching one of those treasure-hunt adventure movies where the heroes went up against sharks, but I figured it was much the same thing.

"The great white shark is one of Earth's dominant aquatic lifeforms," Mary mentioned. "If this creature holds a similar prowess, what could scare it enough to force it to take cover on this tiny island?"

I heard a weird hissing sound, and turned back toward the

water to see bubbles of steam rising from a small patch—a patch that was growing steadily closer to our little refuge. "I have a feeling we're about to find out."

We all watched the bubbles approach. All except Sharky, who was still sobbing behind the trees.

"Anything we can do to defend ourselves?" I asked Ned over my shoulder.

"I might be able to rig a temporary forcefield," he answered, extracting two of his technowands and rubbing them together. "It'd only last a few seconds, though. At best." He checked the wands. "And it'd only be a foot across."

Tall pulled out his pistol and checked the clip. "I've still got about six shots," he offered.

"I have neither offensive nor defensive capabilities, I am sorry to say," Mary admitted. Even so, her voice didn't wobble at all. She had guts, that's for sure.

"Yeah, well, all I've got is the head of a duck, so we're even," I assured her. "Okay, here it comes, so let's look alive. And hope that shark's just got some kind of weird phobia for harmless little fish."

The bubbles had reached the shore. They stopped there, hissing and steaming. And then they grew larger, bursting angrily and filling the air with a curtain of steam. And something rose within that wave of heat.

Rose and stepped onto the beach, only a few feet from us.

It was hard to make out more than a menacing shadow, all tentacles and waving limbs. The four of us shrank back together for protection, retreating until the trees were at our backs.

Behind us Sharky was making little horrified squeaking noises.

Then the steam dispersed and the air cleared, and we could finally see the owner of that shadow—

It was a shrimp.

No, not a really short man. A shrimp. An actual shrimp. The kind you get stuck around a big cup filled with cocktail sauce, or skewered and buttered and grilled. A shrimp.

It was maybe six inches tall. Which, when you think about it, is actually huge for a shrimp. Like it was a giant shrimp.

And it was red. Candy-apple red. Fire-engine red. I thought shrimp were a blue-gray before they were cooked, but then again sharks were usually white so what did I know? This one was definitely red. And hot. I could still see steam rising off it. Where it stood on its little tiny feet, the sand was turning to glass from the heat.

Oh, and its eyes were glowing black.

"Okay, what exactly are you, then?" I asked it, crouching so I could see it better. "The killer shrimp from hell?"

The shrimp bristled—literally, as little spines sprang out all across its back and sides—and its antennae waved. "Mock me at your own peril," it replied darkly. Its voice was surprisingly deep for such a tiny thing, and had a weird echo to it like someone was sampling the words and running them back on a sub-bass line. Yeah, I worked for a band one summer. Nellie and the Hackeysacks. Death-metal group, big in Weehawken and in Osaka.

"What're you gonna do?" I replied. "Jump down my throat and choke me?" I know, bad idea, but I couldn't help it. I'd been all freaked out because here we were on this island on this waterworld and then this giant shark shows up and then it's terrified and it turns out the thing terrifying it is Wally the Wonder Shrimp! I just couldn't bring myself to be scared of the thing.

I never did know what was good for me.

"You insult the honor of the Herenga," the shrimp intoned. "For that you must pay with your lives, your consciousnesses, and your very souls."

"Uh huh. Do you take checks?" But it didn't reply again. Not in words, anyway. Instead it pulled out a gun.

Okay, that's not fair. Calling this thing a gun would be like calling the Sting Ray I'd seen earlier a car, or the amazing meal at the truck stop a snack. This wasn't a gun. It was a death machine with a handle. It was an Armageddon device with a pistol grip. It was the fury of the universe, packaged in chrome and equipped with a laser sight and a trigger.

It was massive. Easily as big as I am, if not bigger. Barrels and sights and flanges and cables growing out of each other, all heaped and mounded together like a mass of eels devouring one another—and it was all pointed at my head.

"Ned!" I shouted as the devil-shrimp glared at me and the gun began to pulse and whine like an attack dog begging to be let off its leash.

"On it!" he shouted back. Then the shrimp fired. I saw a blue fireball emerge from the gun's main barrel, merge with lightning bolts from several sides, pick up steam and laser fire from above and below, and become one massive smoking, snarling, writhing, crackling, steaming sphere of doom. All leaping right toward me. It zoomed straight for the spot between my eyes, closing the gap before I could blink—

—and then it rebounded.

And engulfed the crazy killer shrimp instead.

"NO!!!" It screamed, then its voice vanished as that fireball consumed it. The gun clattered to the ground, parts of it charred and smoking. All that was left of the shrimp was the miniature glass plain where it had stood.

"Well, that went well," I muttered. Then I fainted.

When I came to, I found Mary looking down at me. She was right above me, and I was laying on something soft. It didn't take a brain surgeon to realize I had my head in her lap. I wanted to close my eyes and pretend to still be unconscious—for the next fifty years—but she noticed me staring at her.

"You are awake," she stated. 'Have you recovered sufficiently?"

"I'm okay, yeah." I sat up, slowly so I didn't flatten her with my bill in the process, and rubbed the back of my head. "What happened?"

"You fainted."

"I did?"

"You sure did," Tall said from where he was sitting a few feet away. "Dropped like a little girl."

"What little girls do you know?" I countered. "Cause the ones I've met'd tear you apart without breaking a sweat." I blinked. "Besides, I just narrowly escaped being vaporized by the Scampi of Satan. Excuse me of I was overwhelmed by my near-death experience."

Tall started to snap back at me, then shut his mouth and nodded. "Smart move," he said instead after a second. "Getting that thing to aim its gun at you so Ned could focus the forcefield there and bounce the shot straight back on the shooter instead."

"Oh. Thanks." I hadn't actually planned it like that. I'd been stupidly taunting the seafood from hell, and called for help when it pulled the cosmos' largest handgun on me. But it had worked out, so I wasn't going to complain about it. Or admit to my own stupidity. Hey, that's how I've kept my day job so long.

"How long was I out?" I asked instead, shifting over to give Mary more room. Not too much room, though.

"One hour," she told me. "Ned has been disassembling the weapon of the Herenga." She glanced past me and I turned to see Ned with what looked like an entire garage worth of parts spread out before him. "He hopes to find something there which might aid us."

"Cool." I staggered to my feet and lurched the couple of steps over to him before dropping back down again. "Hey, Ned, how's it going? Didja find a lifepod stashed in that thing?"

"I wish," he replied without looking up. "No, this entire thing is designed for one thing and one thing only—to destroy its target utterly. You're lucky my forcefield held."

"Yep, that's me. Lucky. So it's just made for killing and vaporizing. What good does that do us?"

"More than you'd think." He grinned at me before returning to his work. "I think I may be able to cobble something together out of the parts, something that could get us off-planet."

"Really? Wow. So there really was an emergency lifepod in

there!" I scratched at my bill. "But what happens once we get off-planet?"

"We can worry about that then," Ned pointed out. "Being off-planet is at least back in outer space, which is better than being stuck here."

"Fair enough." I suddenly realized that it was quiet. No blubbering. "Hey, what happened to the Great Purple Whiney-tail?"

That actually got a laugh out of him. "Once he saw the shrimp-thing was dead, he jumped up, started thanking us frantically, and ran back into the water." He gestured up ahead and to the left. "He tossed those up here a few minutes later, I'm guessing as a thank-you. He hasn't been back since."

I looked where Ned had pointed. A large pile of fish, clams, mussels, eels, and seabirds lay mounded together near the water's edge. It was more than the four of us could eat in a week, assuming we weren't too picky. A part of me wondered whether Sharky had caught these for us or simply coughed up whatever he'd eaten lately, but the rest of me ambushed that part, knocked him out, bound and gagged him, and stuffed him in a trunk somewhere. Pesky rational thoughts.

"Okay." I stood up again, a little less shakily than before. "So we've got food. But it's raw. Have we got any way to cook it?"

In answer Ned picked up a gun component and held it out for me. "Be careful," he warned as I took it.

It looked like a super-soaker, a long tube inside another long tube with a handle and a trigger mounted on the outer one. I wasn't sure how that was going to help—we could already drown our food, and it's not like it wasn't all dead already—but I took it anyway and trudged over to the mound.

"Right." I looked at the tube-thing again, then at the mound. "Well, let's give it a whirl." I started to aim it at the pile, but then my common sense pulled loose its gag and levered the trunk open long enough to shout at me "hey stupid, try it on one piece first!" Fine, whatever. I grabbed a random fish, tossed it a few feet away, and aimed the tube at that. Then I pulled the trigger.

There was a soft splat sound, and a rush of hot air knocked me off my feet. I landed right beside the mound of dead things. And the fish? Nothing but a smoking cinder.

Okay, I'd have to dial it down a bit. No problem. I looked at the tube, then looked again, more closely. Big problem. No dial. No lever, no buttons, no scale, no thing except the trigger.

And the tube within a tube.

Hm.

I thought about that for a second. Then I tugged the inner tube until it was almost completely out of the outer one. And I tried again, this time with a clam I set up beyond the remains of the first fish.

There was only a warm breeze this time, and the clam wasn't even hot to the touch.

Bingo!

I experimented with the tubes, sliding them in and out like a pro trombone player until I got just the right amount of heat to cook the food without burning it. Then I spread the mound's contents out in a long row and walked up and down it, grilling each piece as I went.

"Lunch!" I called out when I was done. "Come and get it while it's hot!" Though I doubted that would be a problem.

We feasted on seafood, drank warm clear water using the empty clamshells, and sat back to enjoy having a full belly and a nice sunny sky overhead.

"I think I've got this thing worked out," Ned said after a while. "It'll take me a few more hours to build it, but then we should be able to get off-planet."

"Awesome." I'd have patted him on the back but I had my hands behind my head. "Anything we can do to help?"

"I'll let you know, but not right now."

"Okay." I yawned. "Well, if there isn't anything else we can or should do I suggest the rest of us get some shut-eye while we can."

"That is a wise suggestion," Mary agreed. She stretched out on the sand not far from me. "We do not know what will happen once we leave this place, and we should all be alert and rested so we may adapt to any situation that arises."

"Right." Her face was maybe a foot from mine. "That's what I said." She gave me a lazy half-smile, sweet and totally unalien, and then closed her eyes and was asleep. Just like that.

"Works for me," Tall agreed, and I heard him shifting and then a few seconds later he was snoring. Damn! Aliens and feds had it easy!

I thought I'd be awake forever, what with everything that'd happened that day, but amazingly I closed my eyes and the next thing I knew it was night and Ned was nudging my shoulder.

"It's done," he said. "Get everybody up."

"How long did we sleep?" I asked as I rolled over and got to my knees, still yawning.

"Six hours."

"Six hours! You said it'd be three!"

He shrugged. "I ran into a few complications. Got 'em all sorted now, though."

"Oh." I shook my head to clear it, then reached out and laid a hand on Mary's shoulder. She was sleeping so peacefully, and you'd never know she wasn't your average gorgeous full-figured supermodel asleep on a desert island somewhere.

"Mary?" I whispered. "Time to get up. Ned's finished and we're outta here."

Her eyes snapped open and fixed on me. There wasn't any confusion in there, none of the bleariness most people have when they first wake up. "I am glad to hear it." She sat up, then rose gracefully to her feet. "Wake Agent Thomas and we will prepare for our imminent departure."

I watched her walk over to Ned, then turned to Tall. He got a slightly rougher shoulder-shake, but he also snapped awake in an instant. Must be the training. Or the mind-control chip. I was still a little woozy myself, and Tall wound up having to give me a hand to get me standing again, but finally we joined Ned and Mary over by the trees.

And saw Ned's latest creation for the first time.

It looked like an oven rack. That was my first thought. It was basically a grid of thin metal beams I recognized as gun barrels, all criss-crossing each other here there and everywhere. Along the front there were several more little devices, and in back were what looked like silvery space-age rockets.

"What exactly is this thing?" I asked once I'd glanced around to make sure there weren't more pieces—or a small spaceship—hidden somewhere nearby.

"This," Ned answered proudly, "is our ticket out of here."

"It's an oven rack. With rockets on the back."

Tall gave me a look, like saying mean things about this contraption might prevent it from working, but Ned nodded.

"That's not a bad comparison," he admitted. "I didn't really have a lot to work with, and it's not like there were seats and a cockpit on that thing, so this was the best I could do."

'How does it work?" Tall asked him.

"Simple." Ned gestured at the rack. "We lay down next to each other and all grab hold along that top bar. I'll be in the middle where I can work the controls. I've connected my forcefield generator and amped up its power so it'll create a protective bubble around us. I've been sucking oxygen into that container there, which we'll use to keep us breathing properly."

"And the rockets?"

He grinned again. "How else are we gonna get off this pond?"

"So we're strapping ourselves to this thing and shooting ourselves into space?"

"Exactly!" He rubbed his hands together. "Help me stand it up!"

Tall and I did, and then Ned gestured for us to step up and grab hold.

"Wait!" I shouted, remembering something. I sprinted

down the beach, found what I was looking for, and scooped it up. Then I rejoined them.

"The rest of the food," I explained, showing them the grilled seafood clasped in my arms. "We might need it."

"Good point." Ned rummaged through his pockets and came up with a crumpled plastic bag, which turned out to be bigger than it had looked. We shoved the food into it and tied it shut, then I tied the bag to my belt.

We took our usual order along the grid: Mary, me, Ned, and Tall. Each of us grabbed the top tightly. "Get ready," Ned shouted, and hit a button on the frame above him. A soft hum filled my head, and a faint blue-green light sprang up all around us. "Now hold on!" He tapped another button, and the rockets below our feet roared in response.

Then Ned hit a third button, and the ground exploded out from under us.

I've been in fast cars with the tops down. I've been on motorboats cutting across the waves. I've been on motorcycles barreling down the road.

None of those compare to this. Not a one. The ride in Tall's car when we'd broken onto the bus seemed mellow by comparison. I thought my whole body might shake apart as we shot up into the sky, and I could feel the air whistling past as we rose like—well, like a rocket. Even with the forcefield I was warm, and the pressure on our bodies was intense. It was a challenge just to draw a breath, and the air smelled of something burning.

Then the sky burst above us and dropped below us, and we

were beyond that planet's atmosphere. The warmth vanished, to be replaced by a mild chill like a bracing fall day. The stars were brighter and more numerous, no longer hidden by the atmosphere. We'd done it!

"Way to go, Ned!" I shouted. I wanted to slap him on the back but he shook his head as I started to loosen one hand from its deathgrip, so I decided to pass on the manly signs of affection and respect for now.

"Thanks!"

The rockets had cut out once we'd left the atmosphere behind—no air for ignition, even I knew that much—but we were still moving from sheer inertia. We drifted for several minutes, just enjoying being free of the Deathcage Waterworld at last. Then I cleared my throat.

"So, uh, what now?" I asked. "We're off that planet, sure, but we're floating through space on a glorified closet rack, and we can't control where we going. Plus the air and the forcefield each have, what, a few hours left? A day? At most?" Ned nodded. "So now what?"

Turned out none of us had an answer.

Also turned out we didn't need one.

Someone else took care of that for us.

Chapter Eighteen
Interdict Humperdink

It's interesting. I didn't think you could hear anything in space.

I mean, every science fiction movie I've ever seen—well, not counting the really crappy ones that only run on network television late at night or on pay cable channels REALLY late at night—has said that. You can't hear in space. There's no air, nothing to carry sound, so you can't hear. You always see all these shots of astronauts and space cowboys and star travelers banging on the window of some spaceship or space station and mouthing something because the people inside can't hear them, and of playing Charades with each other because they can't hear each other either. Then there are those shots of people resting their spacesuit helmets against each other so the sound will carry, in that sort of I'm-in-a-fishbowl-you're-in-the-next-fishbowl-over sort of way.

So. No sound in space.

Which is why I don't understand how I heard the sirens.

But I definitely did. And they were loud, too. Not much point in a quiet siren, really. I could just see that—probably in Britain, where they're always so darned polite. "Weo, weo, weo. Excuse me, sir, would you mind terribly lowering that chainsaw and ending your reign of crazed destruction? And, please, no more of those wild screams of rage? Oh, jolly good. Thanks ever so much."

Yeah, whoever had these sirens blaring, they weren't British.

"Ow! Mother—" I would've clapped my hands to my ears if 1. I hadn't been busy holding onto the interstellar closet rack for dear life, and 2. I'd still had ears. As it was, I wished somebody would hurry up and answer my head so it'd stop ringing.

"Is that a cop?" Tall shouted to be heard over the din. "Are we being pulled over?"

Mary and Ned didn't get a chance to answer. Somebody else did.

"This is the Galactic Authority Border Patrol, Ship Designation X-3 Niner Blue-Six Alpha," a voice declared. It was, if anything, even louder than the sirens—I guess it had to be, since they were still going and I could hear the announcer clearly anyway. "You have violated a Galactic Interdict. Prepare to be hauled in for questioning, sentencing, and punishment."

"Oh, goody," I muttered. "More punishment. I wonder which color I'll lose this time. Maybe brown—I've never much liked brown." Then my brain registered the rest of what it had said. "Hauled in? Yes, please!"

I craned my neck, trying to see a ship anywhere, but all I could see was us, our rack, the planet we'd just fled, and the stars all around.

"Where are they?" I demanded. "This isn't gonna be one of those 'we leave you sitting to make you sweat' sort of things, is it? Because we don't really have time for that!"

"No, the Galactic Authority prides itself on its prompt handling," Mary replied. "I am sure they will transfer us to their ship very quickly."

"Yeah, but—" I peered about again. "What ship?"

Then there was shimmer to our left, and suddenly an entire swathe of stars blanked out, replaced by something black, bulky, and very, very BIG.

"That ship," Ned offered.

I was gonna say something clever in reply—I don't know what but it would've been really clever, I'm sure of it—when my vision went all blue and hazy. I shook my head and everything cleared, but since I found myself in some kind of holding cell I wasn't sure that was an improvement.

It was definitely a holding cell, too. I get the feeling they look the same throughout the universe. Plain grey walls, plain grey floor, plain grey ceiling, plain wooden benches mounted on three of the walls, a plain metal toilet and sink mounted in one corner, and bars across the fourth wall. Okay, sure, the bars were some kind of crackling green energy, and the lighting was seeping from the edge where the walls met the ceiling, like there was a huge light right behind each wall and we were only getting whatever slipped through to us, and the floor was bouncy like rubber even though it looked like concrete, but it was still the same. I'd been in a few holding cells before—back in college, and again right after my incident, when I was still adjusting and indulged myself in a few "violent antisocial outbursts," and this could have been any of them.

Minus the crazy outer space tech, that is.

"Okay, so we got picked up crossing the border," I said. I found myself a seat on one of the benches—there wasn't anybody else in the cell with us, so I had my pick. "Now what? They haul us in, we tell 'em what we're doing and why, Mary flashes a badge, and they give us an armed escort to the matrix, right? Right?"

"It's not that easy," Ned answered. He dropped onto one of the other benches, and Mary took the third. Tall was pacing back and forth, which didn't surprise me—I've seen a few lawmen get on the wrong side of a law before, and they're always the worst about being locked up.

"Why not? We are on official business, right?" The fact that Mary hadn't answered yet was making me pretty nervous. "Mary? Right?"

"Matters are more complicated than that," she finally replied. "Our mission is of dire importance to the universe as a whole. We must reach the quantum fluctuation matrix and realign it before the invasion is complete."

"Yeah, you told me all that when you signed me up for this crazy escapade. But are we official or not?"

"The Grays do not answer to most galactic authorities," Mary said slowly. "They have an awareness that transcends most other races, and have positioned themselves to shield this reality from threats its other residents may not understand or even register."

"So you're saying nobody else knows about this threat?" Tall asked her. Sharply.

Mary hesitated, then nodded. "That is correct."

"And the Grays are working on their own, without cooperating with other galactic authorities?"

"Also correct."

"So we can't expect anything from these guys except to be treated like the criminals we are?" Man, I thought Tall's head was gonna explode, with his face that red. Either that or he was gonna pick up the closet rack—it had been teleported in here with us—and beat Mary to death with it. This is what happens when lawmen discover they're actually operating outside the law. It ain't pretty."

"Hey, we're not criminals," Ned objected. "We're just doing something they don't understand to stop a threat they don't realize exists."

"But we did violate that Interdict," Tall countered. "We broke the law."

"It was an accident."

"An accident?" Tall was sneering now. "Oh, sure, that'll satisfy them—'I'm sorry, officers, we only broke the law by accident. We tripped and wound up on that little planet no one's ever supposed to touch. Oh, and we killed one of the natives and confiscated its weapons while we were there. That's not a problem, though, is it?'"

Man, I think I liked Tall better before he discovered sarcasm.

"Wait, what about the whole invasion thing?" I asked, both because I really wanted to know and to stop Ned and Tall from hurling themselves at each other in some kind of weird cage match. Tall had the edge in size and strength but Ned was sturdy and probably fought dirty. "They're aware of that, right?

So won't that lend some weight to our story?"

But Mary shook her head. "The invasion is occurring on a quantum level," she explained. "Few beings are even equipped to register such planes of reality, let alone note the discrepancies already occurring. The Galactic Authority remains unaware of the danger, and if we succeed they will never know the peril they and the rest of the universe faced."

"Great, we get to be unsung heroes." I studied the bars. "Unless of course we get locked away for the rest of our lives first.'

Tall was seriously pissed. "You should have told us all this when you first contacted us!" he raged at Mary. He marched across the cell and towered over her, glaring. "You should have told us this was unsanctioned!"

"Would you have refused your aid then?" she demanded back, rising from her seat to confront him. "We had no time to waste! Every hour the matrix remains breached allows the invaders a greater foothold in this reality!" I hadn't seen her angry before. It was glorious. And Tall backed down, too.

"No, of course not," he claimed, backing up a few steps and raising his hands in surrender. I don't blame him—the heat Mary was throwing off could've melted an icecap. "But we could have been more circumspect, sent representatives to the authorities to request their cooperation, handled things a little differently . . ."

"How much of what's happened so far was handled the way you would've wanted, anyway?" I asked. "Seems to me we've been flying by the seat of our pants this whole time regardless."

"I don't know." Tall turned away and banged a fist on the nearest wall, then shook his hand. I could've told him not to try that. They're used to people trying to break out of holding cells, and I'm sure these guys get customers a whole lot bigger, stronger, and meaner than he is. "I just—I'm a federal agent! I'm supposed to be the one upholding the law, not the one breaking it!"

Really? Which agency do you work for, then, because that doesn't sound like any of the ones I've heard of, I really wanted to ask. But I didn't. No point deliberately antagonizing him. At least, not right now. I'd save that for later, in case I got bored.

"We'll figure something out," Ned assured us. "We'll explain how we got there and maybe we can at least get a reduced sentence."

Great. Maybe they'd only take half a color this time. Or a shade. Like Burnt Umber. I've never understood why that was a crayon color. What little kid sits there coloring some picture of Barney or Kermit and says, "would someone pass me the Burnt Umber, please?" And what does Umber look like, anyway, and how did it get burnt in the first place?

We were all sitting there looking glum when we heard a door open somewhere nearby. A big heavy door, by the sound of it. At least there was a lot of whooshing and clanking. Then a shadow slid into view on the other side of the bars. It was growing longer and longer, and finally came to a stop in front of our cell, covering the entire section of floor in darkness. I was waiting for whoever cast that shadow, but the footsteps had stopped. Were they standing just on the other side, out of view?

Was this some kind of weird intimidation tactic? "Ooh, look, you can see my shadow but you can't see me?" If so, it wasn't working. I was curious, not frightened.

"You will follow me," a voice whispered. The bars glowed brighter, then vanished, leaving an afterimage. And in the empty space where they'd been, that shadow rose up and filled the gap. A trio of little purple lights winked out from it. Like eyes.

Okay, now I was frightened.

"Do as it says," Ned urged the rest of us quietly, hopping up from his bench. "Ungoli shadowmen aren't known for their patience."

Like I was gonna refuse a walking, talking shadow-creature. Right. We all filed out after it. I heard something scrape behind us and glanced back, then wished I hadn't. A . . . tendril of shadow had crept around us and scooped up the rack-ship like it was a Tinker Toy, and was carrying it along in our wake.

The shadow didn't make any sound—it didn't have feet or anything, so no footsteps—so the only sound as we walked were our own feet and our breathing. And the whoosh of each door we passed through. There were a lot of them. This ship was as big as it had seemed from the outside, and I'm guessing we were in its bowels. Twice we were herded into small rooms that turned out to be elevators, so it seemed wherever we were going was on a higher level. I wasn't sure if that was good or bad.

Finally the shadow ushered us into a big room. Big may not really cover it. Auditorium-sized would be more accurate. The corners were completely covered in shadow, and I wasn't sure at first if those were more of our captors or just because the light didn't reach that far. Then I spotted a few pinpricks of light in one corner and shivered. That answered that.

The floor of this room wasn't concrete or gray. It looked like hardwood, only in a variety of colors, and it was done in an elaborate pattern. At the center was a seal of some sort—I've been in too many courthouses and to too many ball games not to realize that right off. I didn't need Ned's whisper to figure out that it was the symbol of the Galactic Authority.

On the far side of that seal was a raised platform that hovered a foot or two off the ground. And standing on that was—

Silly string.

It looked like silly string. Like someone had taken several cans of the stuff and sprayed somebody with it, then pulled the person out without disturbing the mess and left it there on its own. It was like a stick figure but swirled rather than straight, and in Technicolor. And I knew it was alive because it turned toward us as we were brought to a stop right on that seal. It had no eyes that I could see—no features at all, and no flesh except the day-glo surface of those strings—but I could feel it glaring at us.

And then it spoke.

"You have violated Galactic Interdict five-seven-three-nine-four-six-Q-B-twelve-seven-Alpha," it intoned. The voice was the same one we'd heard back on the closet rack. "This is a serious crime, subject to the strictest of punishments." It leaned forward. "State your names for the record."

"Ned."

"MR3971XJKA."

"DuckBob Spinowitz."

"Roger Henry David Thomas."

Judge Silly-string stared at us some more. "You four were recently found guilty of Traffic Violation E37945FQRT177913-X," it announced. Wow, these guys have a good intranet!

"Yes, sir," Ned admitted for us. "We pled guilty and received our punishment accordingly." It was funny how he seemed to always take point when talking to the authorities, but I guess even though Mary was the one in charge of the job Ned was the only full alien among us so in a way he had a better connection to these guys and a better understanding of how things worked. Or maybe it was just that everybody respected plumbers. Given how much they charge per hour, you kinda have to.

"So I see." The string-thing paused. "Two crimes within the space of three galactic days. But thirty-three million, seven hundred and eighteen thousand, five hundred and forty-seven-point-six-five light-years apart. Explain."

"We have an urgent mission to complete in the core," Ned answered. "We disabled the train by accident while trying to avoid attack from the Dinotropic Aesthetic Elite, and after leaving the train we found other transportation to our destination. But there was a problem and we found ourselves flung onto the planet, with no ship and no way back off."

"The device you were using when you were picked up," Señor String interrupted. "That was not your ship?"

"It was something we cobbled together out of native technology," Ned told him. "It was enough to get us out of the atmosphere but not much farther." He tried a weak grin. "Lucky for us you picked us up when you did or we might've died."

"Hm. I see." If it'd had a chin I'm sure the thing would've been scratching it by now. "And how did you acquire this native technology?"

Ned shuffled his feet. "We encountered a hostile native and were forced to defend ourselves. It . . . blew itself up. We took its gun and used that to make the device."

"It blew itself up?"

"Yes, sir. Shot at us but the shot rebounded and struck it instead."

I hadn't noticed before this that the seal we were standing on was vibrating slightly. And the air around us seemed, I dunno, thicker than elsewhere in the room? But now that air thickened even more, so it was like we were staring at the officer and its platform through a haze, and the floor vibrations increased. Then they cleared and died down again.

"You are telling the truth," Mr. String-man confirmed. "The creature attacked you and you merely deflected its attack. This is good—you are not guilty of murder, only self-defense." I swear it was frowning, though I couldn't see any change except that maybe some of its strings shifted color from bright red to bright blue. "And your arrival on that planet was unplanned and undesired." It sighed—yeah, actually sighed. "Very well. You did violate the Interdict, and must be punished for that. But you did so unintentionally, and departed the planet as quickly as possible and with as little native contact as possible." I tried not to think of the Cowardly Purple Shark. "Thus I will grant you a reduced sentence." Nice, I thought. Maybe it really would only take Burnt Umber! "You will perform hard labor for two hundred galactic years," it declared.

That got my attention. "Wait, what?"

It ignored me. "This sentence will be carried out immediately," it announced, and shadow-creatures flowed in from all sides, each one grabbing one of us by the arm and leading us away.

"Wait, where're you taking us?" I demanded. "You can't do this! The universe is at stake! I have a medical condition that prohibits hard labor! I want a lawyer!"

But the silly-string guy didn't respond, and neither did my shadow-captor except to tighten its grip.

"What the hell?" I demanded as they marched us back out of the room and down more long corridors. "Ned! Mary! What'd we do now?"

"We serve our time," Ned answered from somewhere in front of me. "There's nothing else we can do. It's a fair sentence, actually—he was pretty lenient."

"Lenient? Lenient? Two hundred years, Ned!" I shouted. "I probably won't live that long!"

"You will," Mary assured me. "All criminal sentences are carried out in intraspace."

"Intraspace? Is that like ultraspace?"

"Similar, yes," she answered. "Only the time dilation is even greater between intraspace and here. Two hundred galactic years will be less than a month here, perhaps even as little as a day or two."

"Oh." Well, that helped—it meant I could still get back home in time for my weekly poker game. "What about the whole aging thing, though? Won't I still be two hundred years older?" Instant aging might actually be a good racket—I could see high school kids and college students shelling out big bucks to suddenly be legal drinking age.

"Naw," Ned replied. "There's a sort of null barrier around intraspace. Information can be brought back and forth, but any physical changes there are reset somehow when you cross the barrier back to this plane. We'll age there—though really slowly—but the minute our sentence ends and we're brought back we'll snap back to our current ages. We'll remember the entire thing, though."

"Nice." I thought about that a bit. "So why don't they use intraspace to get around? You said they couldn't use ultraspace because you pop back in the same place as you left—is intraspace the same way?"

"Not exactly," Ned admitted. "Intraspace has its own . . . peculiarities. It wouldn't work for travel."

"Why not? What kind of peculiarities?" He didn't answer. "Ned? Ned!" But by then the shadows were guiding us into a big room with some kind of glowing purple disk mounted on the far wall, and a circular platform below that. I had a feeling this was the entry to intraspace.

Whatever those peculiarities were, I was about to find them out for myself.

Chapter Nineteen
Working on the chain (letter), gang

"**Okay, in** what world is this considered hard labor?"

"Shhh!"

"What, you afraid they'll revoke our lounging privileges if they catch us talking?"

"No, I'm afraid they'll hear you and give us something worse!"

"Worse? What, you mean like last month?"

"That was worse!"

"For you, maybe. I worked at a call center back in college, to earn extra money during the holidays. That was nothing."

"It was horrible! All those calls! And all those angry people!"

"Well, what'd you expect? We were calling them during dinner. Or sex. Or their favorite movie. Actually, that part was pretty impressive. Back at the call center we used to just guess when the worst time to call would be. They actually have monitors for it here! Talk about pinpoint targeting!"

"Just shut up."

"What? I'm not doing anything wrong. I'm just making conversation to keep things moving. You know, make time fly by more quickly and all that."

"Shut up."

"Fine."

"Fine."

"Good."

"Great!"

"___"

"Um . . ."

"What?"

"Can you—?"

"Say something? Anything? To fill this terrible conversational void?"

"No! Can you . . . pass the stamps?"

"Oh. Here."

"Thanks."

"___"

"___"

"So what do you think of these stamps, anyway? I really like this one, the one that looks like a cat's head and tries to bite you every time you hold it. Feisty little bugger! But I've got its number now—you grab it by the top, like its the scruff, and it can't reach your fingers or wrist. See?"

"Shut up. Just shut up."

We'd been in prison for, as near as I could tell, eleven months. At least we'd changed work details eleven times, and if they really were feeding us three squares a day—literally squares, these flat things like Jell-O sheets but flavored and somehow textured like all sorts of other foods—and letting us sleep each night we were at each job for thirty days. Time flies.

Tall and I were still arguing about how this counted as "heavy labor." Our last job, for example, had been making calls for some universal credit card. I hadn't minded too much—like I said, I've done this work before, and they were actually a lot more lenient about it here than they were back at my old job. They gave us wireless earpieces and throat-mikes, a free-floating monitor to show who we were calling, where they were, their occupation, their annual income, all manner of personal preferences, and what they were doing when we called. A second window showed the duration of the call, the listener's stress level (we got extra points if it hit the red zone, and a bonus cookie if it actually made it to the black circle at top), and the call result. We weren't limited to how long we could stay on any one call, either—I spent a solid five hours on the phone with this beam-miner from Arcturus V one day, comparing baseball and some sport he called "chasing the portable centrifuge." The most important thing was to sell them on the card, using any means necessary. I had a really good sales rating at that. I'd always been good at talking, and knowing so much about each person beforehand made it easy—with a monitoring system like that I'd probably never lack for dates back home. Of course, it didn't hurt that I figured out at one point during a really boring call (dung librarian on Syncopade 429) that I could approve the card but change the recipient's name and address.

I'd have about twenty of those things waiting for me when I got back home.

Anyway, our current job was folding, sealing, addressing,

and stamping chain letters. Something about "if you pass this along to four to the tenth power people within the next thirty-nine galactic hours, your luck will take a dramatic turn for the better." We were assembling maybe a thousand of those things every hour.

I figured my luck was about to become phenomenal.

They'd divided us up once we'd arrived at the prison, been registered, been searched, and been issued prison garb (a weird paisley poncho and a pair of baggy drawstring pants. Oh, and fuzzy bunny slippers. I wasn't sure if we were in an interstellar prison or some sort of cosmic children's hospital.). Mary'd been taken away, apparently to a women's wing, and Ned had been placed with another guy already here. Tall and I were paired together. Lucky us.

Ever seen that movie with the futuristic prison, where they pair prisoners up and stick collars on their necks? And if you ever get more than a certain distance from your partner both your collars explode, killing you instantly?

Yeah, they didn't do that here.

Which is too bad, really. I think they were missing a golden opportunity. Not to mention some sleek silvery collars would have helped offset the rest of our wardrobe.

No, when we got here they just stuck ankle cuffs on each of us. Mine and Tall's were linked together, as were Ned's and his new buddy Gwarmesh, by a stream of glittering emerald dust. "Ionized pharmeons," Ned informed me as they were marching us to our new digs. He actually looked excited about it, bless his geeky little hearts (apparently he has six). "They're stretchable, indestructible, and can pass through almost any solid matter. The Galactic military developed them in the hopes of building warships out of the stuff." Yeah, I could see that—a ship that can't be broken and can ghost its way through any obstacle.

"What went wrong?" I could tell by the way he'd said it that something had gone wrong.

"They're stretchable," Ned repeated. He reached down, grabbed the glowing strand connecting Tall and I, held it in both hands—and shoved it over his head. It stretched around him, so it looked like his head and shoulders had suddenly been molded in bright green plastic. "Not rigid enough to support anything," he explained as he lifted it back off and let the energy-rope fall again. "They couldn't walk on it or rest any weight on it, which meant they'd need other materials for a frame and floors, walls, etc. And those wouldn't be immaterial."

"So whatever it's coating is still solid?"

"Yep."

Darn. So much for the idea of wrapping it around us and just passing through the walls to get out of this place.

Of course, that'd be hard anyway, seeing as how there weren't many walls.

"They don't need them," Ned said when I asked him about that at dinner that first day. "We're in intraspace, remember? Where're we gonna go?"

"Couldn't we just run off in any direction, and eventually get far enough away that they can't come after us?" I was poking experimentally at my dinner square.

Ned had already rolled his up and popped the whole thing

in his mouth—he was still chewing it as he shook his head. "Nope. Remember I said intraspace has some peculiarities?"

"Sure." I peeled a corner off my square and stuck it in my mouth, then chewed tentatively. Hey! It tasted just like a roast beef hoagie! I gobbled up the rest happily, gesturing at him with the plastic fork and knife they'd given me to show I was still listening.

"Well, the biggest problem with intraspace in terms of travel is that it's both spatially isolated and geographically locked." I'm sure Ned could see from my expression that he'd just given me gobbledygook, and to his credit he didn't even sigh. Clearly I was wearing him down. It's a specialty of mine. "In the base reality, space extends in all directions," he explained. "It's all connected, all one big piece." I nodded to show I was getting this. Tall was listening too, and I could feel him nodding behind me. "Okay. Intraspace works differently. When anything is inserted into intraspace from our plane, it draws some of the local spatial material to it like metal to magnet. Space coalesces around the object."

"So space isn't continuous here," Tall asked over my shoulder. Show-off.

"Exactly. It forms in bits and pieces, wherever it's needed." Ned laughed. "There're whole schools of thought dedicated to the question of what this place would look like with no one and nothing from our plane in it, but of course we'll never know because the minute we enter to observe it we change the dynamic. Even energy does that, so scanning won't do the trick either."

"Okay." I was struggling to grasp what he was saying. "So we can't run off into the sunset because there is no sunset—we're basically on an island of intraspace, and around us is a big sea of nothingness."

Ned looked surprised. "That's right on the money," he admitted.

"Gotcha. But then," I scratched at my bill, "why wouldn't it work for space travel? Sounds perfect—you pop a ship in here, some intraspace gathers around it, and you fly to the equivalent location of wherever you wanted to go back in our reality." I could feel Tall staring at me in disbelief. "What?" I demanded over my shoulder. "I'm a little slow, but I'm not completely stupid!"

"No, you're not," Ned agreed. "And that's exactly what they hoped when they first found this plane. But it doesn't work that way. Once enough intraspace gathers in any one spot, it becomes fixed in that location. So you can't move and take it with you—if you tried to move you wouldn't get anywhere because there's nowhere else to get. You'd just keep bumping up against the edge of this particular location."

"Can't you build a bridge, though?" Tall asked. "The prison's an island, sure, but if we stuck a pole out past its edge, wouldn't that extend the island's shape far enough for us to walk out along that new ramp? Then we could keep extending it further and further."

But Ned shook his head again. "We could, sure, except that intraspace seems to be infinite. You'd never hit another object, no matter how far you extended the pole, because each separate bit of matter is fixed to its own starting point, no matter how big it gets."

"Well, what about throwing the pole, then?" I offered. "That'd be its own island, right?"

"It would," Ned admitted, "except that you can't throw something out there. Intraspace itself won't let you. It sort of forms a protective layer around the matter within it, like a bubble. Keeps any air and pressure and local gravity within, which is why we can breathe and walk without floating and all that. But it also keeps matter within each discrete space unless there's another bubble somewhere nearby."

"And you can't get another bubble without more matter, which it won't let out because there isn't a bubble there already." I swallowed the last of my square. "Got it. Well, that sucks."

"Perfect for a prison, though," Tall pointed out quietly. "They can make it as big as they need it, because the more people they add the bigger it gets. And as long as at least one person or object remains it's permanently fixed in one location. Plus you never have to worry about anyone escaping."

That didn't exactly sound encouraging.

We'd quickly gotten into the routine here, which wasn't hard considering they treated us like we were on some intergalactic cruise. Every morning they woke us up around nine, local time, and we showered, got dressed, and gathered in the mess hall for breakfast. Then we worked until one, when it was time for lunch. After lunch we went back to work until six, then quit for the day. We had dinner and then we were allowed "light recreational time." We could read, play cards, take a walk, build something in the crafts room, exercise, watch a video, or just talk. We weren't allowed to nap, since that could throw off our sleep schedule, but that was fine because they sent us to bed at eleven anyway. Ten hours of sleep a night, three solid meals a day, plenty of leisure time in the evening, and work that I personally didn't find particularly taxing. It was like a holiday. Complete with bunny slippers.

We saw Mary at meals and in the evening—women and men (and "other") were housed separately and worked separately but ate and relaxed together. She'd been paired with another newbie, a cute little gal named Tansy. Tansy was from Yaha'tan E-59, and she'd been sentenced to fifty years after she'd gotten into an argument with some guy over a traffic signal and had reduced him to a wet noodle. Literally. She'd changed him into a big pile of Ramen. Soy sauce-flavored, she assured me—the sentence would've been higher if it'd been shrimp, and nearly double if she'd gone for mushroom. Apparently she could have but she hadn't felt it was worth it. She was tiny, maybe three feet tall, and built like a cartoon pixie, with a cute triangular face and big eyes and blond hair and golden skin and a bright smile. She also had butterfly wings on her back, antennae on her head, and row upon row of sharp, triangular ivory teeth. But she was cool, and we hit it off right away.

Ned's ankle-mate Gwarmesh was another story. He was a furball—he said Feharb'lanek—from some place called O59-cubed. He looked like a walking shag carpet from the 70s. Smelled like one too, all stale beer and stale Cheetos and old bubble gum. He was taller than Tall by a good foot, broader than Ned by as much or more, and his hands were big enough to engulf Tansy's entire head. He had beady black eyes buried in that fur, and a cute little pink nose like you'd find on a kitten, and when he opened his mouth—which wasn't often—there were a lot of big barbed teeth bent at all sorts of angles. He wasn't very friendly, and he almost never talked. Most of the time he just grunted. We had no idea what he was in for—all he said was "mayhem" and we didn't want to push it—or for how long, but at least he'd come here on his own so he didn't have any pals to hang out with. He grudgingly sat with us so Ned could.

"So what exactly're we gonna do?" I asked after the third week. We were still on "pack marshmallows into bags" detail, which would have been a lot easier if they didn't insist we fit the squares against each other perfectly and would have been a lot worse if I didn't keep eating all the marshmallows. I kept hoping they'd give us chocolate-covered ones at some point, but no such luck.

"What do you mean?" Ned replied. We'd finished our meal—lasagna and garlic bread! Those little squares were amazing!—and were playing cards at one of the little card tables spaced around the recreation area.

"Well, it's been three weeks already," I pointed out. "We can't just sit here much longer, right?"

"Only another one hundred and ninety-nine years, eleven months, and one week to go," Tall answered. "Gin!" He laid down his cards.

"What, again? I swear, they teach you Feds how to cheat." I threw my cards down. "But seriously," I lowered my voice to a whisper, "how're we gonna get outta here?"

Mary frowned. "We are not. We will serve our time and then will be free to return to our mission." She was already collecting all the cards and stacking them neatly for Ned to shuffle.

"But two hundred years?" I held up a hand. "I know, intraspace and all that, it'll seem like a lot less on the outside. But how much less? And can we afford to lose however long it is?"

Now Ned was frowning, but not at me. "We don't know exactly how much time it'll wind up being in our reality," he admitted. "Time's a bit . . . elastic here. It could be a day, it could be a week. It probably won't be more than two or three weeks, but there's no guarantee."

"Three weeks? But what about the invasion?" Tansy was listening intently—she'd already picked up a bit about our mission from previous conversations, and I didn't see any point in excluding her or lying to her. Gwarmesh didn't seem interested in the least. "Won't it all be over by then?"

"It might," Mary replied. Her frown deepened, but after a second she shook her head. "There is little we can do about it, however. There is no escape from a Galactic Authority prison, and even if there was the idea of violating our sentence and bringing the weight of the galactic government down upon us is not one I wish to contemplate." She shivered slightly, which told me it really was that bad of an idea. "No, we must simply make the best of matters."

"There is one bit of good news," Ned offered. "The officer who tried us said we'd covered over thirty-three million light-years since the problem on the train—thirty-three million, seven hundred and eighteen thousand, five hundred and forty-seven-point-six-five light-years, to be exact. The train would have reached its first stop past Earth, two-point-seven million light-years away, in one hour, so it was traveling at a speed of point-four-five light-years a minute. We stopped the train," he took a second to look slightly guilty before pressing on with his math word problem from hell, "about twenty minutes in. Which means we'd covered roughly nine million light-years, and had thirty-four million to go."

I rested my head in my hands. "And this is a good thing how?" I don't think I'd ever realized just how far from home we were until then.

"We had forty-three million light-years to cross to reach the matrix," Ned reminded me. "The train dropped us within three hundred light-years of it, but we had no idea how far we'd gone before we crashed onto that planet. But if his math was right—and the Galactic Authority doesn't make mistakes when figuring distances—we've actually covered forty-two million, seven hundred and eighteen thousand and change light-years total. Which means we're within three hundred light-years of the matrix, or will be once we're returned to our own plane after serving our time. We haven't lost any distance at all!"

I stared at him. Tall stared at him. Mary stared at him. Tansy stared at him. Hell, even Gwarmesh stared at him, and I wasn't completely convinced he knew what any of those words meant.

"You're excited," I said slowly, "because after all this time and all this trouble, we haven't lost any distance since we got off the bus?"

Ned had the decency to look a little embarrassed. "Well, silver linings and all that, right? Gotta look at the bright side."

"And that's bright for you? The fact that we still have three hundred light-years to go?"

"Sure. Three hundred light-years is nothing."

"Yeah? Look what happened the last time we thought that." Now he looked a little more embarrassed. But something else had occurred to me. "Wait a second. You said intraspace is 'geometrically fixed,' right?"

"Geographically fixed," he corrected. "Yeah."

"So this prison was already here before we arrived."

"Exactly."

"But that ship picked us up by the planet, didn't it? Why would they put a big-ass prison like this right near a planet that's under Interdict, even if it is on another plane of reality?" Ned was starting to look a little concerned, and I don't think it was because he was bending the cards. "It makes more sense that the prison'd be in some other location, and they'd beam us to that spot before sending us through, right?" I could tell from the look on his face that I was on to something, though I devoutly wished I wasn't. "Which means we actually have no idea where we are right now. And when we do finish serving our sentence, they'll probably just drop us at the nearest bus depot to the prison exit, rather than returning us to that planet we were never supposed to be near anyway. So we could wind up anywhere in the universe, including even farther from the matrix than we'd been when we started this ridiculous journey!"

I had to stop because I was out of breath, but I'd gotten my point across. Ned looked at me, then at Mary. Mary looked at Ned and then at me. Tall looked at me, at Mary, and at Ned. I looked at Mary—hey, I've got my preferences here. Tansy's head was moving back and forth so fast I thought it was just gonna spin off and shoot across the room. Gwarmesh was studying those enormous gnarled claws protruding from his fingers.

Tall was the first one to break the silence, and he said the one thing I never thought I'd hear him say:

"We've got to break out of this place. Right now."

Chapter Twenty
Immovable Object meets Irrefutable Farce

"**Ooh, really?**" Tansy started bouncing up and down so fast she was practically vibrating. "You're gonna break outta here? Can I come too?"

"You have to," Ned answered. "Without my tools I can't get these anklets off, and that means if Mary goes you go." He glanced up at Gwarmesh. "And you too, big guy."

Gwarmesh grunted. He might have nodded his head, too—either that or there was a brief hair avalanche from his forehead down—so I guess that meant he was in.

"Okay, so how do we do this?" I asked.

"No idea," Ned admitted. "We need to get out of intraspace first. That's the biggest problem. Then we have to get these manacles off."

"And," Tall added, "we've got to find a way to keep the Galactic Authority from figuring out where we've gone and tracking us down. Ideally, we'd keep them from ever realizing we've left." He frowned. "I've no idea how to do that, though."

"Heh. Leave that part to me." Surprisingly, that rumbling statement came from Gwarmesh. He grinned down at the rest of us, revealing teeth that would've done a nettle patch proud.

"Just give me a week's warning."

I waited for him to explain, but he'd gone back to admiring those scythes he called nails. "I don't even want to know," I muttered, though of course that wasn't true. "But anyway, great. So we won't tip them off when we leave, and there won't be any cosmic manhunts. Excellent. And, Ned, you think you can get these things off us once we're back in our own space?" I shook my leg so the anklet and its green cord jangled against the chair leg.

"No problem," Ned assured me. "I just need a few tools—I'd like to get my own back, of course, but if I can't do that I'm sure I can improvise from whatever I find. These things aren't too complicated—they only work because we can't get to anything to remove them."

"Great. So that just leaves getting out of this prison and out of intraspace. Anybody got any ideas?" There was suddenly a whole lot of headshaking going on. "Right. Well, let's all think on it a while, okay? I'm sure we'll come up with something."

That had been over ten months ago.

"Still nothing?" I asked when we'd gathered for lunch that day. More headshaking. We were all getting really strong neck muscles. But not a whole lot else.

"There's got to be a way," Tall griped for the ten thousandth time—I had been trying to keep track but gave up when we hit two hundred. It just wasn't worth it. "Every prison has a weak point. We just need to—"

"Yeah, we know, find it and exploit it," I cut in. "Great. When we see the big sign saying 'hey, prison weak point over here!' we'll let you know."

"I don't see you doing any better," he snapped at me. "What've you contributed to all this lately?"

"Hey, I'm the one who suggested we start stockpiling food," I pointed out. And it was true. For the past few months we'd been cutting the corners off our meal squares, pushing them back together into a smaller square, and then rolling that up and sliding it into our bunny slippers. Turns out whatever these squares are made of, they stay fresh for two or three days. Then they dry out, which means they become like fruit-leather. They still taste just as good—better, actually—and once in that state they don't seem to age or decay or anything. So we each had a supply of food now for whenever we finally managed our escape. Hey, no point being on the run if you're gonna starve to death, right?

But Tall wasn't impressed. "Yeah, that's great," he sneered at me. "So we have food. We're still stuck here!"

"So find us a way out!" I snapped back at him. All our tempers were short. It didn't help that I'd gotten a nasty papercut that morning, so I was a little irritable already.

"You find one," he retorted, "and I'll happily throw you out of it!"

"Yeah, good luck with that, brainiac," I countered. "You'll just come flying out right behind me, remember?" I raised my leg and shook it slightly to illustrate the point. Then I stopped in mid-shake.

Ever have one of those "Eureka!" moments you always see in cartoons? The one where the light bulb goes off over your head because the most perfect idea in the world has just leaped into your brain and brought its own spotlights and back-up band? This was a light bulb the size of a planet, and there was an entire symphony orchestra in there providing the swelling background music. For a second I was so impressed with the delivery I almost forgot the idea itself. Fortunately it was pretty insistent.

"What?" Tall had noticed my glazed look. "What's wrong?" Aw, he did care! I guess those heart-to-hearts late at night in our cell had meant something to him after all. I'd thought his "shut the hell up before I strangle you with your own tail feathers" had been sounding less genuine the last month or so!

"Nothing," I managed to reply finally when I got my mouth and throat working again. "Nothing at all. Except that you're a genius and you may have found us a way out of here."

"I did?" Now he looked even more confused. "How?"

"I don't know yet. It's just an idea, and it may not work. But if the soundtrack is any indication, it just might at that." He was looking more puzzled by the second but I didn't have time for that. I turned to Ned. "Ned, you said you'd need your tools to get these anklets off us. Any chance you can cobble something together from what we've got here?"

Ned thought about that a second, then nodded. "Yeah, they're not too careful at guarding the automatic tape dispensers or the stamp holders. I could get my hands on some of those, take 'em apart, and probably get something that'll work. It won't be pretty, and I might need three of 'em because they'll fall apart—or blow up—during use, but they should work." He was studying me. "Why?"

"Don't worry about the why just yet," I warned him. "Just work on cutting us loose. We also need a way out of intraspace."

"I thought—" Tall started to say, but I cut him off.

"No, I don't have a way back to our reality," I explained. "I do have a way out of this prison though. I think. So the question is, if we can get out of here, can we get out of intraspace itself?"

"Oh, that's easy," Tansy said. She gave us a bell-like little laugh. "I can get us back to our reality, no problem."

"Really?"

"Sure!" She fluttered her wings and her eyelashes at the same time. I'll tell ya, if she wasn't less than half my height and if I wasn't already stuck on Mary I could probably fall hard for that little space-pixie. "I'm a bender—it's what I do. I bend the laws of physics, though usually just for a few seconds and in a very small area."

"You mean like with the guy who became a walking Box O'Noodles?"

"Yeah, like that." She pouted. "He would've changed back in a few minutes. Is it my fault we were near a schoolyard during lunch hour?" Ick. "But anyway, if you can get us out of here I can warp things enough to get us back."

I scratched my bill. "Wait, if you can do that, why're you still here at all?"

"I can't affect anything in this place," she explained. "They've got the differentials all locked down—I'm guessing they've had benders here before. But if we're outside the prison? Done deal."

"Great!" I glanced up at Gwarmesh. "What about you, big

guy? You still up for creating our stand-ins or alibis or whatever it is?"

He nodded. "Been workin' on it a while, actually," he admitted. "Just need another day or two to finish up."

"Perfect. Ned, you get to work on your release gizmos. Gwarmesh, you finish up your thing. Mary, Tansy, Tall, just be ready. As soon as everything's in place we'll test my idea. And if it works? We're outta here."

It was three more days before Ned said he was ready. It was after dinner, and we all decided to take a little walk. The guards watched us go but they didn't bother to follow us. After all, where we going to go?

Once we were out of sight from everyone, we ran back to the guys' barracks and to the sleeping cell Ned and Gwarmesh shared. Each cell was the same—a little room, maybe eight by eight, with a bed against each side wall. The back wall had a toilet, a sink, a shower, and shelves for clothes, slippers, and the few personal items we were allowed, like toothbrushes and towels and squeaky toys. The front wall didn't exist—after lights-out a mesh of energy covered it, to make sure we stayed in our rooms all night, but until then it was open. Inmates often returned to their rooms to get cards or books or something, then headed back to the rec room for the rest of their leisure time.

"Okay, Gwarmesh—time to knock our socks off," I said as we gathered between the two beds there.

He nodded. "Strip," he barked.

"What?" I stared at him. "It's an expression, about the

socks—I didn't mean it literally."

He gave me his big snaggle-toothed grin. "Strip. All of you. Now."

We looked at each other, then Ned shrugged, kicked off his bunny slippers, and started to shuck his poncho. The rest of us quickly followed suit—good thing those emerald bands passed through matter or we'd never have gotten our pants off.

In a few seconds we were all standing there, completely nude, at least pretending not to look at each other. I especially tried not to stare too much at Mary—this wasn't the time or the place, and I'd gotten the sense during our travels that she might even like me a little bit so I didn't want to jinx that. But damn! Either the aliens had picked her because she was both brainy and built like a goddess or she'd lied and they had in fact enhanced her appearance a bit during all the other modifications. All I can say is, they'd made a great choice.

So there we were, all of us in the one cell. Nude. I just hoped no one else walked by. This might be a little hard to explain. Not impossible, mind, and not all that unheard of in here—hey, you had to amuse yourself somehow!—but tricky.

"Right." Gwarmesh had knelt down by his bed while the rest of us were disrobing, and now he hauled out—

—dust bunnies.

No, that wasn't right. These were more like . . . hairballs. Great big hairballs. Six of them.

"Is now really the time for spring cleaning?" I asked him, but he ignored me. Instead he grabbed my poncho and pulled it on over one of these hairballs. Then he shoved the thing on top of my pajama bottoms, and the whole mess onto my bunny slippers. Ew. I wondered if I could requisition new clothing?

"I don't see—" Tall started to say from behind me, but he stopped and stared. So did the rest of us.

Because the bundle that had been my clothes and some of Gwarmesh's stray fur was . . . rising. And expanding. He wasn't doing anything that I could see, just leaning back with his arms crossed and a smug smile on his face, but the hairball was growing somehow, like a balloon being inflated. It filled out the pajama bottoms and the poncho, slid into the bunny slippers, and rose above the poncho in a distinctly duck-like head. After only a few seconds I was looking at an exact copy of myself.

Only, y'know, made out of yeti fur.

"That's . . . amazing," I whispered. And damn near shed my feathers when it opened its matted-hair bill and echoed me perfectly. "What the hell?"

"Talk to it," Gwarmesh urged. "It needs to absorb the sound of your voice to get it right." He moved on to Tall's clothes and inserted the next hairball. And so on.

In less than a minute the cell was really really crowded. There were two of each of us, and our doubles looked and sounded exactly like us, except for the whole "made of fur" thing.

"Do you really think these'll fool anyone?" I asked. "I mean, the resemblance is uncanny but they are, well, a bit hairy."

"Nobody'll notice," Gwarmesh assured me. "Nobody ever does." He pulled a stack of clothes out from under Ned's bed and started tossing garments at each of us. I was happy to pull mine on, and relieved that I could stop pretending not to notice

Mary's unclothed state, but it did make me wonder.

"If you had these spare clothes all along," I asked Gwarmesh, "why'd you make us strip?"

"Needed the DNA," he answered. "To complete the doubles."

Oh. That made sense. "And how long'll these things last?" It would suck to have them collapse into scattered mounds of hair after a few days or a week. Especially since, back in the real world, that'd mean only seconds from when we left.

But Gwarmesh chuckled. "Long as they get food and water? Indefinitely."

"Nice." I turned to Ned. "Okay, your turn."

"We'll need a little more elbow room," he replied. "And we should send our doubles back to the rec room now, before anyone notices we're gone."

"Fair enough." I looked at my double one last time, then held out my hand. "Good to know you, hair-me. And good luck."

"Same to you," it replied in my voice, and shook my hand. Man, I've got to work on my grip! Then we all left the sleep cell and the doubles turned left to head back to the rec room while the real us turned right and proceeded toward the prison "wall."

"Okay, this is good," Ned said when we'd stepped behind a low wall that marked off one of the work areas. He pulled what looked like a staple-remover from under his cap—they'd let him keep his baseball cap—and bent down to apply it to his own ankle cuff. There was a muffled pop and a quick flash of light and the anklet burst open. "Hey, it worked!" Ned said softly, rubbing at his now-bare ankle. "Whaddyaknow?"

Tansy stared at him. "You didn't know if it would work?"

"It's not like I could test it beforehand," he retorted. "But I figured it should, and I was right. Who's next?" he shattered each ankle cuff, and then we were all free and unencumbered. And had three sets of anklets with pharmeon streams between them.

"Your turn," Tall said, nudging me with his foot. "We've got an alibi and no chains. Now get us out of here."

"Working on it," I assured him. I scooped up one of the anklet sets and studied it. Just as I'd hoped, Ned's little gizmos had cracked the things enough that I was able to pull the pharmeon stream free at both ends. I did the same with the other two sets, so now I had three glowing strands of emerald glitter in my hands. "Come on."

I led the others to the edge of the prison's "land." Beyond it was nothing but gray void. Intraspace, or at least the space between the little intraspace islands.

"Okay, this is going to be a little tricky," I warned the others. I knotted the three strands together, forming a loop of pharmeon particles. "So get ready. On the count of three I'm gonna throw this, and Gwarmesh, you're gonna leap on it— but only once it clears the prison wall. Tall, you hold onto him with one hand and Ned with the other. Then me, then Mary, then Tansy—you've got wings so it makes sense to put you last. Ready?" I cocked my arm back.

"Wait!" Tall put up a hand to stop me. "What?"

But Ned was staring at the loop I held. "That's ingenious," he whispered, glancing up at me. "Amazing! How'd you come up with that?"

"Something Tall said, actually," I admitted. "When we were bickering that one time and he said if he found an exit he'd throw me through it, and I replied that he'd just get pulled out after me."

"Of course!" Ned beamed. "This really should work! Fantastic!"

Now Tall looked really annoyed. "Right, does someone want to explain it to me?" he demanded. Beside him Gwarmesh rumbled his agreement. Even Mary looked a little confused. Tansy didn't seem to care one way or the other.

But I shook my head, enjoying the role-reversal for once. "No time for that now," I claimed. "We've got to move before anyone spots us—if they see us those doubles won't be worth a damn. Ready? Let's go!"

I turned back toward the prison's edge and pulled back my arm, but this time Gwarmesh stopped me. "Let me," he rumbled, and held out one massive clawed hand. Well, yeah, that made sense—it's not like I was a champion discus hurler or anything. So I gave it him and took my place between Ned and Mary.

Gwarmesh nodded, hefted the pharmeon loop once, then flicked it away with a quick, practiced motion. The second it was out of his hand he was leaping after it. The loop flew toward the invisible prison boundary—

—and sliced right through it. Because it was nothing but pharmeons, and they could pass through anything.

Gwarmesh's jump carried him past the boundary as well, and it didn't stop him, because now there was something else out in intraspace besides the prison. The loop. Matter was already collecting around it, and when his huge foot finally touched down in the center of the loop it was more of a disc, solid below the glowing rim. Tall had leaped right after him, and the rest of us had half jumped and half been pulled but it worked, especially since more intraspace was forming below us as we passed out of the prison's influence. Gwarmesh shuffled forward to the very front edge of the new space, and we all squeezed in behind him. I glanced back. We were maybe two hundred feet from the prison wall.

"Right," I said once I'd caught my breath. I picked up the loop—because it was just pharmeons it came out of the collected matter around it without a problem. "That worked well. Let's do it again."

And we did.

And again.

And again.

We jumped a half dozen times, each leap carrying us a hundred feet farther away. The great thing was that, as soon as we'd left one island behind, it dissipated because it no longer had anything from our world to hold it together. And the in-between space here, the null or void or whatever it was, actually had a faint haze to it, like a thin fog. So by the time we were four hundred feet away we couldn't see the prison at all.

And hopefully that meant they couldn't see us, either.

Finally, after the sixth jump, we stopped. "That should be far enough away," Ned judged. "Tansy?"

"On it," she replied. Her wings flapped and she rose into the air in front of us. Then her antennae twitched, as did her nose. And a small spot of color appeared between us and her. It grew rapidly, twisting around itself as it did, and before long we were looking at a circular portal of the same purplish energy we'd seen back on the Galactic Authority ship. The portal that'd brought us here.

"Free!" Gwarmesh shouted as soon as the portal was big enough, and dove through it. Tall shrugged and followed him. Ned went next, and I ushered Mary through and stooped to scoop up the pharmeon loop before taking the plunge myself. Tansy brought up the rear, since it was her portal.

I stumbled through, colliding with Mary—strange how that keeps happening—and fumbling a bit before collapsing on the ground beside her. Tansy was right behind me, and the portal winked out the second she was clear, making a sound like a water droplet as it went.

"Wow." I took a deep breath and glanced around. "We did it!"

"We really did," Ned agreed. "Hell, you did it! That was incredible!"

"I still don't understand how you did it," Tall grumbled.

"It was the pharmeons," I explained, holding up the loop. "They aren't solid, and they can pass through any material, so I figured if anything could cut through the barrier around each intraspace island it was them. And once they were past it and into the gap between, they started collecting matter themselves, forming their own island. But we could remove the pharmeons from there and toss them before the island dissolved, and jump to the next one as it formed. Which meant we could then make the leap from one island to the next."

Tall stared at me for a second. "Wow," he said finally. "That's actually . . . brilliant."

"It truly is," Mary agreed. She gave me a smile that almost made my head explode. "Your solution may well be the answer to travel through intraspace—ships could be equipped to shoot pharmeon disks ahead of them, skipping from one to the next, and thus could travel across intraspace with impunity." She shook her head. "In freeing us from prison you may have singlehandedly revolutionized space travel."

"Really?" I tried to wrap my brain around that but couldn't. "Cool." Then I finally looked at our surroundings. "We can talk about making money off this idea later, though. Right now, where are we?"

The others looked as well. We were lying on a sidewalk, though it was the same particles as the superhighway we'd used earlier. There was a road alongside it, not the superhighway but a smaller thoroughfare, and as I watched some kind of ship slid past, followed by two others. So we were back in the world, and not in the middle of traffic. Nice.

"This should be the path to Proximi Garn," Tansy told us after a few seconds. "I aimed for it because I know it, I thought it'd be near where the prison was in our world, and I figured it was a good crossroads no matter where everyone was going."

"Proximi Garn?" Mary actually looked excited as she picked herself up and dusted herself off. I bit back an offer to help. "That is only a few light-years from the matrix! We are almost to our destination!"

"And I doubt we lost much time," Ned added as he got to his own feet. "We were in intraspace less than a year. That's maybe a few hours out here."

"We need to get some real clothes," Tall pointed out as he stood up. "These stand out, and some people might know they're prison garb."

"Proximi Garn is a reasonably large population center," Mary assured him. "We will be able to find more suitable attire there, and to arrange for transportation the rest of the way." She turned to me, and so did Ned and Tall. "Shall we?" When she offered me a hand, how could I say no?

"Thanks," I told her as I straightened up and reluctantly let go. "And thanks to you guys as well," I added to Tansy and Gwarmesh. "Where'll you two go now?"

Tansy shrugged. "I don't have any plans," she admitted. "Could I come with you guys? At least for a little while? I can help!"

I glanced at Mary, who nodded. "We welcome your company, and your aid," she assured her former bunkmate.

"What about you, big guy?" I asked Gwarmesh. "You heading our way?"

"For now," he replied. Back to short responses, apparently.

"Right." I lifted the pharmeon loop and eyed it for a second before untying one of the knots and retying the whole thing around my waist like a makeshift belt made out of glow strips. "Okay, let's go."

Ned led the way, and the rest of us fell in behind him. It was weird to think that we'd been in prison for almost a year and only a few hours had passed here. Also weird to realize we'd almost reached our goal. I had no idea what'd happen once we did, or after that. But if the events so far were any indication, it was probably best not to think about it too long or too hard. Otherwise I might wish I was back in that cell.

I wondered if any of my new credit cards had reached my apartment yet. And how the "chasing the portable centrifuge" championships had turned out. I'd have to find a paper somewhere—I was rooting for the Three-sided Wallopgawkers. What can I say? I'm a sucker for underdogs.

Chapter Twenty-one
Does that come in a size-mology?

"Okay," I said slowly, "this is one of those 'your brain can't handle the truth' things again, isn't it?"

"What do you mean?" Tansy asked. She was fluttering in place beside me.

"This is Proximi Garn, right?"

"Yep," Ned answered on my other side. Mary was in front of me, just where I liked her.

"So what does it really look like?"

"What do you see?"

I blinked a few times, but the image in front of me didn't change. "Uh . . . a Wild West frontier town."

"That's it, then," Ned agreed.

"What?" I rubbed at my eyes, and considered rubbing at his too. With a cheese grater. "Oh, come on! This is outer space! Not just that, we're in the heart of the Galactic Core! The densest part of the entire universe, the center of everything! And you're telling me your 'reasonably large population center' comes equipped with a dirt road, horse rails, a whorehouse, a small bank, and a saloon?"

Ned shrugged. "Why not?" Then he laughed at my

expression. "What, not high-tech enough for you?"

"Not even remotely!"

"People do not need to cluster together in large numbers," Mary informed me over her shoulder. "There is all of space to inhabit, and even though there are millions of different races and trillions upon trillions of individuals, compared to the vastness of space there is less than one being per ten square light-years. Most live alone or with immediate family only. This," she gestured in front of her, "has at least three dozen residents, perhaps even as many as one hundred. For space that is a reasonably large population center."

I shook my head. "I hear what you're saying, but I still can't buy it. This isn't even a podunk town back home—it's too small! Not to mention it's from the wrong century! I was expecting gleaming skyscrapers, floating fortresses, glittering transport tubes, and a huge number of beings from all different races, all zooming about on their daily business."

Ned laughed again. "You've been watching too many science fiction movies."

"Apparently so. But why does it look like something from the Wild West? Specifically *our* Wild West?" I gestured at Tall and myself, and at Mary as well—she was human too, even if nobody I'd ever met before could look half as good. "Explain that one!"

Tall answered before Ned could. "Transmissions." Ned nodded. So did Mary. Even Tansy did. Gwarmesh just grunted.

"Transmissions?" I didn't get it. "What, you mean car parts? What does that have to do with anything? Are you still pissed about the whole Corvette vs. Mustang thing?"

"Not that kind of transmission!" It still amazes me how clearly he can talk through grinding his teeth. He must practice a lot. Actually, I was his cellmate for months—I know he does. "Television transmissions!"

"Oh." And then I got it. "Oh! You mean all that hooey about us beaming *I Love Lucy* out into space is real?" Everyone else—except Gwarmesh—nodded again. "And so this is based on, what, *Gunsmoke*? *Maverick*?"

"Something like that," Ned agreed. "You have to admit, it's a great visual."

"Personally, I'd have preferred *Hawaii Five-O*," I argued. "Beaches, bikinis, drinks with little umbrellas in them." That reminded me of our last little sojourn on a desert island, though, and the Shrimp From Hell, and what that had led to, so I quickly tabled that notion. "Okay, fine," I sighed. "So where're we going? The saloon? Do you think they have a decent sarsaparilla?"

"First things first," Mary replied. "We need suitable attire."

"Non-prison clothes, right. Which means what, the general store?"

She gave me a smile over her shoulder. "Precisely." Then she led us into the town itself.

There wasn't anybody about, which was probably a good thing given our appearance. It did surprise me, though. I'd thought there'd at least be some irascible old coot perched on the rail outside the saloon, spitting tobacco and swigging from a jug of rotgut. Hey, I love all those old westerns!

I was relieved, however, to not see one familiar Western

staple—the steely-eyed lawman, leaning calmly on the porch beam outside the sheriff's office. There was a sheriff's office, but if he was in he stayed in. Which was fine by me. I didn't want to wind up staring down the barrel of the outer space equivalent to a Winchester.

I amused myself on the walk through town—the general store was on the other end of Main Street—by cataloging the differences between Proximi Garn and the typical town setting of an old Western movie. For example:

- There were tying rails but no horses. I did see what looked a lot like a mechanical kangaroo, with a cross between a saddle and a gazebo on its back. There was also some sort of space-cycle, which was actually pretty cool-looking—it was a lot like a Harley touring bike, the low-slung kind with the huge chopper handlebars, but instead of wheels it had circular pads almost like flattened bells, which glowed purple and blue and floated the bike a few feet off the ground.
- The road—which picked up from the space-particle superhighway about a hundred yards past the town in both directions, the two of them nestled up against each other like high school sweethearts meeting up again at the twenty-year reunion and deciding to make up for lost time—was dirt but it wasn't old Earth dirt. It was a glittering black and more like finely ground crystal, or really coarse black sand. Or Folgers crystals. I resisted the urge to lick it.
- The buildings all had signs in English—except they weren't. When I glanced away I could see the signs flicker out of the

corner of my eye, the text changing to something totally unreadable. But as soon as I looked back it was English again. "Neurempathic signage," Ned answered when I asked him about that. "It beams its content directly into your brain, which then translates it into your native language. What you're seeing when you're not looking at it directly is the base language, which is whatever the programmer spoke."

- The entire town was filled with a soft hum, which intensified as we reached each building and faded slightly whenever we were between structures. "Sonic barriers," Ned told me. "A home defense system, basically. It's usually keyed to the owner's biometrics, and anyone else can walk up to the door without trouble but try approaching the building anywhere else and Zap! It hits you with enough hypersonics to stun a mastodon."

- In addition to the saloon, whorehouse, sawbones, sheriff's office, general store, hotel, stables, and bank, there were places that really did belong in a sci-fi film: "biometric adjustor," "galactic broadcast station," "shuttle teleport pad," and something called a "universal waste extraction unit." Though after a minute I realized that last one was just a public toilet. It was the crescent moon carved into the wood-plank door that clued me in.

We ignored the other places and headed straight to the general store. It had a bell on the door and everything, and a big fluffy cat that rubbed up against us as we entered. Okay, the cat had purple and green polka-dots and six legs, and said, "Hey, welcome, strangers! If you need anything, give a holler!" but it was close enough.

I gawked, of course. I couldn't help it. This place was too cool! I would have loved to set foot in a real Old West general store, complete with the glass jars of candy and the bolts of gingham and the six-shooters in the glass case up front. I also would have loved to visit a high-tech outer space equivalent, with gleaming metal counters and spacesuits and laser pistols next to jet packs and forcefield belts.

This place? It was the best of both worlds.

Looks-wise, it was the Old West general store, down to the dust in the corners and the big barrels of corn meal and flour and salt. And it did have some of the stuff I would've expected in a place like that. But most of the wares I could see were more appropriate to a space station than an Earth frontier town, and most of the weapons in that glass case up front did not look like they'd been made by Smith & Wesson.

It was amazing. I easily could've spent an entire day in there, just wandering around looking at everything.

Too bad we didn't really have time for that.

"We require new attire," Mary informed the salesman behind the counter. He had deep purple scales all over his body, bat-like ears, slit blue eyes, and a third arm sprouting out of his chest, but otherwise looked pretty normal. "For each of us. Something suitable for travel."

"No problem," he answered, hopping off the stool and coming around the counter, which is when I realized he had a tail as well. He flipped open a catalog that'd been sitting in front of him. "Travel, you say? Perhaps a karzonite coverall? Useful, durable, fits in anywhere, comes in a variety of colors, patterns, and textures."

"That will be fine," Mary agreed. She examined the catalog pages. "The Cobalt Stardust for me, I think." Then she ushered the rest of us over. "Select the style of clothing you prefer," she instructed. "And if you require undergarments, request those now as well." I definitely did—no commando for me, thanks very much! Tall apparently felt the same way, which amused Ned and Gwarmesh and Tansy to no end, but I noticed Mary surreptitiously requesting some lingerie for herself. She caught me noticing and winked, which I'm surprised didn't make my feathers turn bright red. When we'd all made our selections, the clerk returned to his original post and pulled a small lever. There was a loud clank and a soft hiss and part of the wall slid back so a silvery oblong like a futuristic shower could emerge. It had a panel on the side and he reached over to type in a few quick commands before motioning for Mary to step inside. She did and the thing slid shut once she was in. We could make out her profile, which meant we saw her shuck her prison clothes and drop them at her feet—I wish I had a camera built into my head so I could've recorded that forever. Next the chamber filled with smoke or steam or something, and we heard what sounded like clicking and ticking sounds for a few seconds. Then the pod opened and Mary stepped back out.

Wow.

She was wearing a one-piece jumpsuit, exactly the kind you see in sci-fi movies. It clung to her beautifully, close enough that you could see all her curves but loose enough that there'd still be all the fun of discovery if you ever got it off her. It was a silvery blue in color, and of some kind of shimmery fabric, which went really well with her black hair and bright blue eyes. There were pockets along the waist and over the thighs, and a few more just above the ankles and up on the shoulders, and it had a flared collar that dipped just far enough in front to give me heart palpitations. It went all the way to her wrists and completely covered her feet, too—add gloves and a helmet and she'd be sealed in. She looked amazing.

Ned went next, and it was like night and day. He'd been wearing overalls and a T-shirt and a Mets baseball cap when we'd first met, of course, so I shouldn't be too surprised that he came out wearing denim overalls, a flannel work shirt, and some kind of ribbed long-sleeve T-shirt underneath that. Oh, and steel-tipped work boots. And he'd opted for a new baseball cap—it didn't say Mets but the logo on the front could easily have been for some baseball team I'd never seen before, like a minor league one. Or one of those foreign expansion teams that seem to pop up in places you'd think had never even heard of baseball, like Tanzania. Or Boise.

Tansy hopped up next, and emerged in a cute little iridescent green jumpsuit that looked far too much like dragonfly wings for me to appreciate it properly. Tall stepped out in a U.S. Air Force flightsuit, complete with rank markings on the shoulders and at the lapel, and work boots under that. Guess we know where the Suits found him! Unless this was just him fulfilling a boyhood fantasy he'd gotten from watching *Top Gun* too many times. Gwarmesh wound up with a heavy wool kilt crossing his chest and then wrapping around his waist, in a swirling green and red pattern that made me nauseous if I stared at it too long. Apparently that was as much coverage as he wanted, but then he did have fur everywhere already.

And me?

Hell, I decided to have some fun.

"You've gotta be kidding me," Tall gasped when I exited the pod. "You requested THAT?!?"

"Sure, why not," I replied. "What, it looks bad on me?" I strutted a bit across the floor.

"I think it's very striking," Tansy assured me, the little flirt.

"Classically stylish," Ned agreed.

"Hunh," Gwarmesh grunted.

The person I most wanted to impress hadn't commented yet. "So?" I asked her. "What do you think?"

Mary continued to study me for a second. Then she smiled. "Very handsome," was her decided opinion, which made me strut even more. And this was definitely an outfit made for strutting.

Hey, the clerk had shown us coveralls. Which equaled jumpsuits. And he did say it came in a variety of colors, patterns, and textures.

They weren't quite rhinestones—something called "optical refraction arrays." But they were close enough. And the wide lapels and flared pant legs were spot-on.

I'd even selected enormous gold-framed sunglasses. All I needed now was a black pompadour and a microphone.

Hail to the King, baby.

Oh, yeah.

We picked out some other things, too, of course. We still had our dried food squares from prison, so we were good on food for a while, and I had the pharmeon loop, plus we had a few odds and ends—they'd confiscated most of our stuff when we'd entered prison but had left us with any small items they didn't consider too valuable or too dangerous. All of Ned's devices had been removed, of course, so he selected a basic tool kit and a few little gizmos. Tall wanted a pistol, and opted for a sonic variety that could stun, kill, or obliterate depending upon the setting. He wanted to replace most of his Boy Scout kit but it was too expensive, especially the finger puppets. Mary picked up a universal communicator, presumably so she could get back in touch with the Grays. I went for a packet of licorice, a yo-yo, and some Silly Putty. Tansy got some make-up. And all of us got canteens equipped with a "proximity filter" that apparently let them absorb and filter water from any nearby source, including us—the clerk and Ned both assured me it was such a miniscule amount I'd never even notice, and that most of it would come from moisture in the air anyway.

Then we walked up to the front counter to pay. The coverall salesman followed us over, and slipped behind it—I guess a place like this didn't require that many workers. The cat was nowhere to be seen, but then he'd have a hard time handling the old-style till, anyway. The clerk hopped up on a stool there, folded all three arms together—I wasn't sure how he'd get them untangled again—and nodded.

And that's when we started to run into problems.

"Galactic credit number—" Mary started, but the clerk cut her off before the first number was more than a "wah" sound. His tail uncoiled from behind him and rose to tap a sign posted to the wall, one I hadn't noticed before. Which is amazing, really, because in great big black letters it read:

CASH ONLY!

We all stared at it for a second. "Really?" I asked. "No credit?" I'd been itching to try out one of those new credit cards I'd gotten—fortunately I'd selected easy-to-remember numbers for several of them, like the batting averages of some of my favorite all-time players. But now that plan was scotched. And Mary didn't look any happier.

The clerk didn't even bother to answer. He just tapped the sign again. Below "Cash Only!" were three other words I'd somehow missed the first and second time around:

ABSOLUTELY NO CREDIT!

"Uh . . ." I glanced at the others, who shrugged or shook their heads or both. We'd just broken out of prison! What were we supposed to do, knock over a convenience store on the way here? I wondered if they had a stagecoach we could hold up.

"What about trade?" Ned asked the clerk, who nodded and tapped the sign. Below "Absolutely no credit!" it said:

BARTER CHEERFULLY ACCEPTED

I was sure it hadn't said that a second ago.

"Okay," Ned said amiably, turning back to the rest of us. "Empty your pockets! Just the stuff we didn't get here, of course."

Unfortunately that didn't amount to much.

I had the pharmeon loop, of course. I was loath to surrender it, but I pulled it off my waist and handed it to the clerk, who studied it closely. I'm surprised he didn't bite it.

"Pharmeons, huh?" he said after a minute. He squinted at me. "That'll do for you and the lady," was his final proclamation, with a nod toward Mary.

"Done!" I agreed, and stepped back away from the counter. I figured I'd done my part, and the smile Mary gave me was well worth it.

Ned offered up two of his little explosive staple-remover gadgets, the last two of the batch he'd made to break us out of prison. He also laid his old Mets baseball cap down on the counter, with clear regret. "It's authentic," he assured the clerk. "Real Earth ketchup and relish stains and everything." I didn't need to ask how those had gotten up there—I'd seen him eat.

The clerk studied the gadgets before nodding. "Those'll do for yours," he agreed. He scooped up the baseball cap and set it on his own scaly head. "Next!"

Tall had lost most of his Eagle Scout kit, of course, but the prison wardens had left a few things on him, and he piled those up on the counter: permanent marker, chewing gum, tube of skin lotion, travel toothbrush, and his handkerchief. The clerk glared at the assortment, and at Tall, before finally nodding. Four down, two to go.

Tansy didn't look too worried. "I can just summon up the cash," she assured me softly. Then she winked, crossed her arms, and did that little twitch-thing again.

But nothing happened.

She twitched harder—I thought she was about to have a fit—but still nothing. Which is when the clerk grinned at her and tapped the wall again. Now the sign was completely different. It read:

NO REALITY-ALTERATION ON PREMISES!

"Hey, that's not fair!" Tansy protested, and I wanted to agree with her out of solidarity but really I could see the clerk's point. If people could just go around altering reality everywhere, why would they ever pay for anything?

"Fine!" she huffed after a second, and pulled her stack of food squares from her pocket—we'd all transferred them over from our old clothes already. "And the old clothes must be worth something in trade," she pointed out. "Especially those slippers."

The clerk growled something under his breath, and looked about to argue. Then his nose twitched. He bent over the counter and sniffed one of the squares. "Lasagna?" he whispered.

"With garlic bread," I told him.

"Hm." One of his arms—the middle one—came up to scratch his jaw as he considered the prospect, but by the way he was eyeing that square I could tell he was hooked. "Oh, okay," he agreed after a minute. "But only because you're so cute." I'm assuming he meant that last part toward Tansy, though hey, in my new outfit I did look pretty killer.

That just left Gwarmesh.

Who was anything but cute.

Except maybe to a vacuum cleaner.

He stomped up to the counter, and the clerk eyed him warily. Gwarmesh smiled in return, and then started to cough. Well, it was more like he was getting ready to throw up, actually. I'd heard that sound before—I had a cat once. Still might, for all I know—I hadn't cleaned the guest room in a while. But I knew enough to look away as Gwarmesh coughed more, hacked more, and finally opened his mouth to spit something out on the counter. Something roughly spherical and made of matted fur.

Yuck.

"Yuck," the clerk agreed out loud. "And what's that supposed to be?"

"Gene-replicating bio-form," Gwarmesh grunted in reply. "Full sonic mimic, unlimited mobility, extended lifespan." I was impressed—put that way, it sounded a whole lot better than "it's a furball version of a pod person."

But the clerk shook his head. "Sorry, no organic life-forms accepted." He tapped the sign behind him, which now read:

NO ORGANIC LIFE-FORMS ACCEPTED

"Hey, cut that out!" I pushed my way forward and studied the sign. Then a light dawned and I reached across the counter to tap it. Instantly the last restriction vanished. Now it said:

ALL KILTS FREE TODAY!

"Perfect!" I grinned at the clerk. "Then we're all set!"

"Not so fast," he snarled. His tail whipped against the sign, and the words changed again, this time to:

SIGNAGE OFF-LIMITS TO CUSTOMERS!

"Oh, you wanna play, do you?" I pushed up my sleeves and

deliberately laid a finger on the sign, changing it to:

THE CUSTOMER IS ALWAYS RIGHT!

MANAGEMENT RESERVES THE RIGHT TO REFUSE SERVICE, he replied.

MANAGEMENT SUCKS ROCKS, I answered.

OH YEAH? YOUR MOTHER! he shot back.

AT LEAST I HAD A MOTHER, I retorted.

RRAARRRGGGHHHHHH!!!!!!

"What the hell kinda reply is that?" I asked him. But he shook his head—actually he was shaking all over—and pointed up. To where a long, curving talon had actually pierced the sign completely. A talon connected to a finger as thick as my arm, which was part of a hand as big as my head, which led to an arm the size of my torso, which led straight back to—

—Gwarmesh. Who was growling out loud now. At both of us.

"New strategy," I whispered quickly to the clerk. "Let the wookie win."

I don't know if he got the reference but he sure understood the point, and he nodded quickly. "Kilts on sale today," he squeaked in our general direction. "Free in exchange for one good sign-piercing." His eyes strayed to the sign and the talon shoved through it—I had a feeling those things were supposed to be impenetrable. "All set!"

Gwarmesh retracted his talon and pulled back his hand, but he was still growling. He shoved me aside—I collided with Mary, Ned, and a barrel of saltwater taffy, and all of us went down together—and snatched the clerk up from his stool. And started to shake him. All sorts of objects, clothing, and coinage began to rain down.

"Hey, it's enough, big guy," I managed to gasp as I righted myself and helped Mary up. Ned was busy assisting the barrel, mainly by shoving taffy into his pockets. "He said we're good! Let's just go!"

Gwarmesh kept shaking. It was like a cat with a toy. I hoped the clerk didn't have the space-equivalent of catnip inside him, or the big furball might never let him go. At least not intact.

"He's right," Tall urged, stepping up and bravely putting himself between Gwarmesh and the clerk. "We should just leave. We don't want any trouble."

That did get a reaction, at least. Gwarmesh laughed. "Trouble?" he growled. "Trouble? I'll show you trouble!" He hurled the clerk against the wall—which dented—knocked Tall out of his way with a single sweep of one long arm, and then smashed both fists down on the counter. It cracked. He smashed again, and it collapsed completely, glass and metal and wood flying everywhere. But Gwarmesh wasn't done. He turned around, those little black eyes glaring from under his heavy brow, his fangs exposed as he snarled in our general direction, and then he spotted the clothing pod. Three quick steps and he was beside it, bashing away at it with his fists. The second blow made the surface spiderweb with cracks. On the third we heard a loud crash, and the entire front shattered. He just stepped into it and started bashing on the back of it, and the wall it was connected to.

"We need to stop him!" I shouted. But Tall of all people got in my way and shook his head.

"Nothing we can do," he pointed out. "And we need to get out of here. The mission comes first."

"He's right," Ned assured me. "We have to save the universe, remember? If Gwarmesh's little tirade draws the authorities, we could wind up right back in prison. And then the invaders win. Let's go while we still can!"

I glanced at Mary, who nodded even though she clearly wasn't happy about it. "We must put the mission first," she admitted. Then she turned and led the way toward the door. I followed her out of habit. The sounds of devastation trailed us outside.

"Where now?" I asked, trying to ignore the crashes behind us.

"We are within a few light-years of the matrix," Mary reminded me. "All we require is short-range transportation to finish our journey." We all eyed the two vehicles/creatures tied to the hitching posts. Neither of them was big enough to take all five of us, but if we grabbed the mechanical kangaroo and the space-bike we could probably manage. Ned pulled out one of his new tools, walked up to the space-bike, and fiddled with something, then went over and did the same to the kangaroo. "All set," he told us after a second. "Let's go."

He hopped onto the kangaroo—which I mentally dubbed a "space-hopper" because that's how I roll—taking a place at the front of the saddle-structure. I made a beeline for the cycle, dragging Mary along with me—we reached it before Tall could, and I slid into the driver's spot, pulling Mary up behind me. That left a grumbling Tall and an amused Tansy to join Ned on the space-hopper.

"Can you operate this vehicle?" Mary asked over my shoulder.

"Oh, sure," I assured her. I wasn't even lying—except for the bell-wheels it really was configured an awful lot like a standard Harley, and I'd driven a few of those back in my misspent youth. One of them even with the owner's consent. I clicked the thing on and revved the engine. "Better hang on," I warned her. She wrapped her arms around my waist, snuggled up against me, and laid her cheek against my shoulder in reply. I was in heaven.

Ned, meanwhile, had raised the space-hopper to an upright position and then dropped it into a crouch, ready to jump. "Follow me!" he shouted, and I nodded. Then he tugged on some levers and his interstellar zoo-creature hopped away down the road and toward the spacelanes. I gunned the space-bike and took off after him, and we blew out of Proximi Garn.

I wondered how far it was to Graceland. Thank you very much.

Chapter Twenty-two
Playing the Name Game

Twenty minutes later, I pulled up alongside Ned's mechanical marsupial.

"How big was that store?" I shouted.

"What?" It's not easy carrying on a conversation when one of you's on a low-slung spacebike and the other's on a bouncing cybernetic beastie.

"The store!" I hollered again. "How big was it?"

"You saw it!" he finally replied.

"That was all of it?"

"Yes! Why?"

I jerked my head back, almost taking out Mary's eye. "He's still going!"

"What?"

"He's still going!" This was making me nuts. I hit the brakes, though I know better than to just slam then on, even on a hovering space-bike. I've been down that road before, thanks very much. One good thing the Grays did for me when they gave me this head—they took away all my old scars at the same time, including the road rash on my legs from pulling stupid bike stunts in the past. Not the way I'd recommend getting reconstructive surgery, but hey, I'll take it.

Ned's kangaroo got another hop in before he realized what'd happened. Then he must have hit some controls because the thing executed a perfect bootlegger's turn on its tail and bounced back to us before setting into a waiting crouch.

"What's going on?" he asked me in at a more conversational volume as he clambered down. Tall followed. Tansy just floated down, the little show-off.

"Gwarmesh," I explained, reluctantly climbing off the bike—reluctant because it meant detaching Mary from me. She'd seemed perfectly happy to snuggle into my shoulder this whole time, and I was more than content to let her. This felt important, though. "He's still destroying things."

The others all cocked their heads to listen. Weird that the one with no external ears had noticed it first. Must be because I don't have to deal with the wind as much. But after a second they all nodded. You could still clearly hear the sounds of things breaking, even from this far away.

"That store wasn't that big," I pointed out. "Which means he's moved on to the rest of Proximi Garn."

"Wow." Tansy shook her head. "He must have been really pissed."

"'Really pissed' doesn't begin to cover it," I told her. "I've seen plenty of guys really pissed—I take the subway to work. This is a rampage, pure and simple, like you see in the old monster movies. He's pulling a Godzilla, a King Kong, a Mothra." I scratched my bill. "And we need to stop him."

"We don't have time," Tall argued. "We've got to save the

universe. We can worry about stopping him then, if he's still at it."

Mary nodded. "The mission is our first priority," she agreed, but slowly. "But something here does not feel right." She shook her head. "This rage and destruction do seem abnormal."

I glanced at Ned. "Look, you were his cellmate. How much do you know about this guy?"

"About what you know," Ned replied. "He didn't exactly open up and tell me his life story. He's from 059-cubed—"

Mary interrupted him, which wasn't like her. "Where?"

"O59-cubed."

She was already frowning. "I have never heard of such a place."

"Me neither," Ned admitted, pushing his cap back to scratch his head, "but I just figured it was one of those little tiny places, like my own homeworld."

But Mary was shaking her head. "No. When the Grays modified me, they downloaded the entire galactic map into my cerebrum. I know every planet in the universe. Yet I have never heard of this O59-cubed."

"So maybe he was lying," I suggested. "Maybe he was embarrassed about his real homeworld, like guys from Long Island claiming they're New Yorkers when they travel. Or people from the U.S. saying they're Canadians with really weird accents."

"Maybe," Tall agreed, "but most people only hide something when they feel guilty." I could see he had his lawman cap on again. I guess he'd punched up a new one of those along with the flightsuit. "What else do we know about him?"

"Not much." Ned thought about it. "From O59-cubed, in prison for 'mayhem,' member of the 'Feharb'lanek'—"

"WHAT?!?" Tansy's shout almost bowled the rest of us over. I hadn't even known she could get that loud. Or that pale.

"What's wrong?" I asked her when I'd picked myself back up off the floor. "You've heard of them?"

"Them?" She was literally shaking. "There's no them! It's not a race, it's a thing! The Feh Har Bel Lanic."

"Oh. Oh no." Now Ned was doing the ghost impersonation. "I didn't—"

Mary hadn't said a thing, but she'd turned white as well. And I'll be damned if her eyes weren't tearing up.

Tall and I looked at each other. "Okay, for the stupid humans in the crowd," I griped, "would someone please explain what that means? We already knew he was a Feharb'lanek, so why is it suddenly such a big deal?"

Mary recovered enough to answer first. "Not a Feharb'lanek," she corrected softly. "Feh Har Bel Lanic." She pronounced each word slowly so I could hear the difference.

"Okay, so we mangled the name a bit. What's the big deal? Is the ACLU about to come after us for being un-PC?"

"Feh Har Bel Lanic is not a race," Mary explained. "It is a— thing. An entity. The name means, literally, 'that which scourges existence away.' It is in the ancient tongue of the Hem'tar Noth, a race that once ruled the universe. Until they created or found or unleashed the Feh Har Bel Lanic—no one is certain which." She actually gulped a little. "Because it destroyed them so utterly only mentions of them among other races remain."

I shook my head, trying to process all this. "So you're saying Gwarmesh—the big furball with the snaggletooth grin, the one who's been palling around with us for the past year—is actually some kind of ancient galactic scourge? That destroys whole civilizations?" Mary, Ned, and Tansy all nodded. "And we let him loose?" More nods. "Oy vey. What was he doing in prison in the first place?"

"Nobody knows how the Feh Har Bel Lanic thinks," Ned told me. "Or even if it does—until now I don't know anyone who's even claimed to see it and survive, much less talk to it and share meals with it. There are whole planetary schools devoted to the question of whether it's even a real object or just some kind of metaphor for sudden spontaneous collapse of a star-spanning civilization." He saw my look and shrugged. "Some schools will do anything to specialize."

"Oh, my!" Mary suddenly exclaimed. I swear, she curses like a character from a Pollyanna movie. "Gwarmesh!"

"Yeah, that's who we're talking about," I agreed, but she shushed me with a wave of her hand. Damn, that woman has way too much power over me. It'd be scary if I didn't like it so much.

"No, the place," she explained. "The Gewar Mesh. It is a loose amalgamation of city-states spread across the Horseshoe Nebula. An old and highly respected civilization, though one that like many had a warlike history before setting weaponry aside in favor of the arts."

"Big fighter-types that got all sappy and became hippy

painters instead," Ned translated for me. I nodded my thanks.

Mary had her new communicator out and was tapping it frantically. "They do not respond!" she cried.

"Who?"

"The Gewar Mesh! There is no answer!"

"What, from the entire civilization? Did they take a universal lunch hour?" Then I realized what she was saying. "You mean—"

She nodded. "I am afraid so."

"He killed an entire civilization?"

"Again," Tall pointed out.

"Again?"

"Apparently so." She sighed and returned the communicator to her pocket. "We thought he was telling us his name, but he was merely boasting about his most recent act of destruction."

"Which still doesn't explain why he was in prison," I said. "Though maybe he has to recharge between slaughters, or rest between meals, or whatever." I glanced back the way we'd come. "But now we've let him loose on Proximi Garn, and who knows where else. We've got to stop him."

This time Mary nodded. "You are correct. If allowed to continue unchecked, the Feh Har Bel Lanic could easily lay waste to the entire Galactic Core, killing every being within it. His is the more immediate threat."

"Right." I turned and hopped back on my bike. "Let's go."

"Let's go?" Tall was shaking his head. "And how exactly do you expect to stop him, talk him to death?"

"Do you think that'd work?"

"NO!" I could tell he wanted to hit me, then. I've seen that expression way too many times before. Mainly on ex-girlfriends. And bosses. And grocery store clerks. And those people who call asking for donations—you can hear it in their voices. But anyway.

"Okay, bright guy, what's your idea, then?"

That had him stumped. Which, honestly, wasn't the response I'd been hoping for. Because, for all his many, many, MANY faults, Tall was a federal agent. He'd been trained for this stuff. Well, maybe not for the "you've let an ancient galactic scourge loose on an unsuspecting town, and you have nothing to stop him but a handful of recently escaped convicts, a cool space-bike, and a mechanical kangeroo" scenario exactly, but close enough. And if he couldn't figure something out, I had no idea who could.

"I have an idea," Tansy announced. Which just goes to show, you never can tell.

"Great!" I turned to her. "Let's hear it!"

So she told us.

"That's the stupidest thing I've ever heard!" Tall announced immediately.

Which pretty much decided me. "I like it!" I told her. "Let's give it a whirl!"

Tall glared at me. "You're just saying that to piss me off!"

"Got a better idea, big guy?" I shot back.

"No," he had to admit. "But that doesn't make hers any less stupid!"

"Well, it's the best plan we've got so far, and we're running out of time."

"He's right," Ned agreed. "Once the Feh Har Bel Lanic finishes tearing Proximi Garn apart, he'll seek out another target. Which means we'll have to hunt him down. We need to deal with him now, while we still know where he is."

I'd already straddled my bike again, and Mary had hopped on behind me. I was starting to love this bike. "Ready?" I asked her.

"Ready," she answered, wrapping her arms around me and pressing her head into my shoulder. Yep, really loving this bike.

"Then let's go stop a scourge!" I hit the gas, or whatever this thing has in its place, and we roared off down the road, racing right back to the town we'd just left behind. Ned and his spring-footed galactic automaton were right behind us.

I had no idea what we were going to do once we got there. Because, honestly? Tansy's plan sucked. But it really was the only one we had. And we could always improvise. Hell, thinking ahead hadn't exactly worked out too well for me so far in life. Might as well try thinking on the fly instead. It couldn't really be any worse.

Could it?

Chapter Twenty-three
Thinking Like a Fly

"Well." I braked to a stop, fishtailing a little, and stared. "Well." I couldn't think of much else to say.

There'd been a town here less than two hours ago. Not a big town, at least not by Earth standards—I still found it weird that it'd been considered a "major population center" in galactic terms—but a town nonetheless.

Now?

Not so much.

Oh, there were still a few walls here and there, or at least a few supports and the odd corner. You could just about make out where the road had been if you squinted.

And had x-ray vision. To peer through all the wreckage.

Because there were building pieces everywhere. I'd seen videos of tornadoes—even went tornado-chasing once back in college, though fortunately we'd gotten drunk and lost and then more drunk and more lost and the closest we'd wound up getting to a tornado was sitting at some ancient drive-in movie theater in the middle of Iowa watching *Twister* and laughing our butts off. I knew what a tornado could do. This? This looked like Proximi Garn had been hit by a tornado, but one that'd been working out beforehand and had come in with a plan, a map, and some laser-guided missiles. A hardcore military ops tornado. With teeth.

"Right," Tall shouted as Ned's hopper came to a stop beside us. "Still think this's a good idea?"

No, I admitted to myself. But I wasn't going to give him that satisfaction. "Still don't have an alternative?" I shouted back. The glare was all the reply I needed. "Then yes, we go ahead with Tansy's plan. Come on." I put the bike in Standby mode and climbed off—I didn't want to risk it getting damaged as well. Mary was right behind me, and Ned and Tall and Tansy joined us. We all stared at what was left of the town together.

"We'd better hurry," I pointed out. "I can't imagine there's much left here for him to tear apart."

We picked our way through the debris, trying carefully not to look at anything that might be organic. I had no idea how many people Proximi Garn had had, but I didn't see anyone running away or cowering in a corner so it was a good bet the current population count was hovering around zero. And I desperately shoved away the mental reminder that this was all our fault. I'd deal with that later. If we survived.

The good news, such as it was, was that I could hear tearing sounds up ahead. So Gwarmesh—I still thought of him that way, partially because we'd called him that for almost a year but mainly because it was easier to remember and quicker to say than the Feh Har Bel Lanic, which sounded way too close to "herbal tonic" for my tastes—was still here.

Great.

"Hey, Gwarmesh!" I called out when I'd gotten about halfway down the main street. "You here, big guy? I'm pretty sure you've made your point by now."

No reply, but I wasn't really expecting any. I kept going, though. And finally reached the last building in Proximi Garn, both geographically and by virtue of being the last structure still standing. Though not for long, if the figure in front of it had anything to say on the subject.

"Gwarmesh? Hey, buddy!"

He turned and looked at me then, and I'd have backed up if it wouldn't have meant falling on my butt. First off, he was even bigger now than he'd been before—probably close to ten feet high, and at least eight wide. His fur had changed, too. It was lit now, like he was glowing from within and each hair was a fiber-optic cable. His eyes were alight too, though they looked more like the pictures I'd seen of hot lava, red and white and yellow swirled together in a super-hot liquid. And his fangs? I'd thought his teeth were messed up before! Now they shot out at all angles, a good foot or more, like he'd taken a bunch of boar tusks and just shoved them in there any which way.

He still had that cute little pink nose, though.

"I think it's enough, don't you?" I suggested quietly. I didn't really expect him to stop—scourge of the galaxy and all that—but figured it was worth a try.

He threw a roof at me.

A roof! Okay, I'm exaggerating—it wasn't a whole roof. But only because it fell apart a bit when he plucked it off the building and hurled it toward me. As it was, a section a good ten feet square still zoomed toward me like a makeshift Frisbee. Where's a golden retriever the size of Lake Michigan when you need one? Instead I threw myself down and it passed over my head—judging from the crash a minute later it went at least another hundred feet before it dipped enough to collide with the ground or the building fragments jutting up here and there.

Okay, back to Plan B. Or Plan A, really—talking had been Plan B. Though it wasn't really much of a plan, so perhaps it was more like Odd Notion B. Though then wouldn't it be Odd Notion A, since that was different from a plan and so Plan A didn't figure into the numbering scheme?

Whatever.

"Go get 'im, Tansy!" I shouted as I picked myself back up. She shot past me, wings a-blur, and hurled herself at the giant berserk furball.

Yep, that was Plan A. Sending a tiny winged faerie against King Kong from Outer Space.

But give us some credit. She didn't tackle him with her hands.

Instead I saw her nose twitch, and the air shimmer, and a gleaming metal band as thick as my waist appeared and wrapped itself around Gwarmesh, pinning his arms to his side. "Yes!" I shouted. Ned and Tall cheered as well. Even Mary let out a little celebratory yip as Tansy smiled and blushed and took a little mid-air bow.

Only Gwarmesh didn't seem pleased. Can't imagine why.

He growled at all of us, and most of all at Tansy. You could see he was trying to burst free but he didn't have the leverage.

His fists were pounding against his sides, though. And—I blinked. Then I looked again.

"Uh, guys?" I asked. "Is it me, or are his sides . . . rippling?"

We all stared. "Oh, fark!" Ned muttered. "He's using kinetic waves!"

"Kinetic what?"

"Waves. He's building and storing kinetic energy to make himself bigger and stronger." Ned had the same look I'd seen whenever the IT guys tried to debug my computer at work after I'd been downloading porn—half fascinated and half horrified. "That must be how he's done so much damage," he whispered. "He's a kinetic waveform! Anything that hits him only makes him stronger, and he amplifies the impact and spits it back out a hundredfold! If an armada tried shooting him, he'd have enough force to wipe out a star system!"

"So what you're saying is"—as we watched Gwarmesh grew several inches taller and wider, and the band around him strained, stretched, and finally snapped—"we're screwed."

Ned looked at me. "Pretty much, yeah."

"Right." Gwarmesh was free again, and we clearly had his full attention as he snarled, bellowed something loud and angry and harsh, and began lumbering toward us. "New plan— everybody run!"

You know those old Scooby Doo cartoons? How in every single one of them, there's a point where the monster o' the week is chasing Scooby and Shaggy and they're going "Yoinks!" and running like idiots, pausing frequently to dress up in silly costumes in order to confuse the bloodthirsty beastie that's always right behind them?

This was a lot like that.

Only without the costumes. None of us were that stupid.

And for a big guy made of fiberoptic fur, that Gwarmesh moves pretty fast!

"We're not gonna be able to outrun him!" Ned shouted as we all bolted down the road. "We need a better plan!"

"I'm open to suggestions!" I hollered back.

"We've got to find some way to stop him from hitting anything, or anything hitting him!" Tall yelled. "Otherwise he'll just keep getting bigger and stronger!"

"Great, let's wrap him in Saran wrap and be done with it, then!" I snapped. And then stopped short. "Yes!" I shouted. "I'm brilliant!"

"You're about to be flattened!" Tall retorted, grabbing my arm and hauling me out of the way just before what looked like a size 45 quintuple-D foot landed right where my head had been. "Keep moving!"

"Thanks!" I pulled my arm free but followed his suggestion. "But I have a plan! We need to lead him back over to the general store!" I glanced ahead of us. "Or what's left of it!"

"Then what?" Mary asked, pulling alongside me. I couldn't help noticing how gracefully she ran, even with a crazed scourge-thing behind us and a wrecked town all around us.

"Tansy!" I shouted.

"Here!" And she was, too, hovering on my other side.

"Can your reality-warping merge things together?"

"Sure, that's easy—though if they have nervous systems

it can get pretty ugly." She made a face. "Don't ask. I did have the coolest pet in second grade, though. For about thirty seconds."

"I don't want to know. I need you to book it on over to the general store," I instructed, "and find that barrel of taffy we knocked over on the way out. Then merge all of it into one big taffy-pull. Got it?"

"Got it!" She flew past us, zipping through the wreckage easily.

"We're going to offer him taffy if he leaves us alone?" Ned asked, puffing as he tried to keep up with the rest of us. He has short legs.

"Not exactly." I told them my plan, and Tall scowled and shook his head.

"That's even more ridiculous than Tansy's harebrained stunt!" he complained.

"Still waiting for a better one from you, G-Man," I pointed out. Which shut him up again.

"I think it might actually work," Ned offered between gasps. "Worth a shot, anyway."

"I agree," Mary chimed in. "I will search for the other component." I hadn't realized she'd been holding back to pace us until she sped up and left us in her dust. Which of course meant I got to watch her from behind as she ran, so I was hardly complaining. Still, it'd be nice if I was better than her at something!

Besides bobbing for apples, that is.

"He'll never fall for this," Tall groused. "He's too smart!"

"Then we need a way to trick him into it," I replied. "Too bad we don't have anybody good at sneaking stuff and planning and tactics, hm?"

For once he actually took the hint—and grinned at me. "I'm on it," he promised, which may have been one of the least antagonistic things Tall's ever said to me.

"What about me?" Ned asked.

"I need you to soup them up," I reminded him. "None of the rest of us would have any clue how to do that. And I'm sure this plan'd work against a drunken frat guy—hell, we did something similar once, with Saran wrap and oatmeal—and maybe even against a small gorilla. But against that?" I gestured back behind us, where the growls and snarls and breaking sounds were. Neither of us dared to look. "You'll have to figure out a way to super-charge them."

Ned nodded, that working-on-something look already in his eyes. "I think I can . . ." he trailed off, which was just as well since I suspected he'd been about to explain his idea to me and then my brain might have shut down from sheer futility. If Ned couldn't figure it out I don't know who could.

So now everybody had a job to do.

Including me.

I was the bait.

Which I suppose is what I get for having such brightly colored plumage.

"That's right, big ugly! Just keep right on my tail!" I shouted over my shoulder. Then, "Hey! Not literally! I don't even have a tail!" as he swiped at me and narrowly missed carving open my backside. I'm pretty sure I heard a few sequins die horrible, messy deaths. I was zigging and zagging for all I was worth, waiting for one of the others to give me the signal—not that I knew what the signal was, mind you—and trying to keep Gwarmesh from getting his massive paws on me.

I figured I could last maybe another thirty seconds. If I got lucky.

Just then I saw Tall gesturing from off to the side. Finally! "Head for the doorway there!" he shouted. I looked, and sure enough, there was a doorway.

No door.

No wall, either.

Just a doorway, standing there all by itself trying to look innocent. If it could've I bet the damned thing would've whistled nonchalantly.

I gave it everything I had, and practically flew across the rubble. "What's with the doorway?" I hollered as I ran. "Are we planning to mime locking the door on him?" I wondered if that would work—certainly those boxes could keep a mime trapped for hours, so why not an actual nonexistent door with a decent imaginary deadbolt?

Tall just shook his head. I think he was getting used to me. "Just run through it!"

So I did. I barreled along, over bits of wall and floor and ceiling and who knew what else, and leaped through the open doorway, with Gwarmesh hot on my heels. Literally—apparently being a galactic scourge and using kinetic waveforms meant you produced a whole lot of heat. I was pretty sure I'd have blisters on my rump next time I checked.

I passed through the doorway without a problem. Gwarmesh? Not so much. He was at least two feet too wide for the portal, and a good foot or two too tall, as well. Which only slowed him down a little bit.

Now here's a thing. You're standing in a field of nothing but rubble, nothing taller than a few inches in any direction. Except for this doorway, right in front of you. You're chasing a guy and he runs through the doorway, but you won't fit. So do you go around it? Or do you try to push and shove and squeeze through it anyway?

I'm not saying I wouldn't have done the exact same thing, you understand. I'm just trying to figure out why.

So there's Gwarmesh, groping for me with one clawed hand while the other tries to bend the doorframe so he can fit his bulk through it.

Which is when I finally realized something:

The doorframe? It was a bright, shocking pink. Not a color you see in nature much, except on flamingos. No, this was a shade you generally only got on Barbie accessories, little girls' lip gloss—

—and saltwater taffy. The strawberry kind.

"Now!" Tall shouted. Gwarmesh had managed to beat the doorframe into something more curved than squared, and had his head and half his body through it. Which is when Ned nodded, pointed one of his gizmos at it, and pushed a button.

The entire doorframe collapsed around Gwarmesh. And over

him. He growled and snarled and began thrashing about, but it clung to every inch of him, and his struggles only made it stick more tightly.

That was taffy for you. Tastes good, sure, but try getting it off your face or clothes or, God forbid, out of your hair.

That stuff is murder.

"Got him!" Ned whooped.

"Nice!" I agreed. "Mary! Where's the second half?"

"Right here," she announced from a few feet past the taffy-coated scourge. She was hurrying toward him, Tansy fluttering alongside her, and each of them held one end of a large cylinder of something frilly and pink.

"Great!" I ran forward to help them. "Drop it down—yeah, just like that! Here we go!" Between the three of us, with Tansy and Mary holding the roll steady and me tugging the fabric and sweeping it around, in about two minutes we had Gwarmesh the Taffy Monster completely swaddled.

In taffeta.

Tall studied the results. "You really think that's gonna hold him?" he asked.

"Absolutely," I told him. "I've seen taffeta in action before—back when I was a kid there were always a few girls who wore dresses made out of this stuff and turned up their noses at the rest of us. But they played just as hard and just as rough as anyone." I shook my head, remembering Mary Sue and Betsy Anne. "By the end of the day, our jeans would be torn, our T-shirts and sweatshirts shredded—but those taffeta dresses? Not a mark on 'em." I glanced at the writhing mass beside us.

"If it can survive two grade-school girls and a blacktop, it can handle the Scourge of the Galaxy."

"It certainly can now," Ned agreed. "I've reinforced its atomic structure—it's stronger than bifold aluminum glass. He can stretch it a bit here and there but it'll never break, and the taffy's absorbing all his kinetic energy so he can't build up a charge." He nodded. "Nice one, DuckBob."

"Aw, thanks." I shrugged. "Good to know my crazy frat days come in handy for something." I glanced around. "So, what do we do now?"

"We continue on to the matrix," Mary answered. "I have notified the galactic authorities, and they will take the Feh Har Bel Lanic into custody. With the restraints we have placed upon him, he will no longer pose a danger to anyone." She favored me with one of those killer smiles of hers. "The universe is once again in your debt, DuckBob. But now we must make sure it survives long enough to acknowledge that debt, by realigning the matrix and preventing the invasion."

"Oh, right. That." I brushed myself off, trying to look casual. "Well, I guess we've already saved the universe today. What's once more among friends?" I stepped up to her and extended my arm in my very best Clark Gable fashion. "Shall we return to our cycle, my dear?"

She giggled—actually giggled like a coed—and took my arm. "Absolutely." It's a good thing these jumpsuits were sturdy, because I'm pretty sure my knees would have gone all wobbly otherwise.

We led the way back to our vehicles and took off as quickly

as we could. No sense waiting around for the authorities, who'd only try to ask us a bunch of questions we didn't really want to answer right now.

Besides, watching that taffy and taffeta was making me nauseous. Or hungry. I can't always tell the difference.

Chapter Twenty-four
Sorry, this one's taken

It only took us another hour to reach the matrix.

Well, sort of.

"The matrix is housed in the structure just up ahead," Mary explained from up against my shoulder. "We should stop and assess the situation before approaching it."

"Assess the situation? Why?" I asked her. "We ride up in a blaze of glory, I realign the thing, the reality-fence pops back into place, the invaders get the heave-ho, and we strut out like the triumphant heroes we are." I thought about it. "Maybe the blaze of glory comes after? I guess in the movies they usually ride up in a hail of bullets, don't they? Yikes."

"Precisely," she agreed. "We do not know what will be necessary to reach the matrix, and if we simply continue on at full speed we will have no opportunity to stop and plan."

I wanted to point out that planning wasn't exactly my strong suit, and that charging in blindly had been working pretty well so far, but then I thought about the particulars: a race's history rewritten, a train crashed, a color lost, a car stolen, a shrimp killed, a prison sentence escaped, a town demolished, a scourge set loose—yeah, okay, maybe I didn't have the best track record so far. I tapped the brakes and pulled over to the side of the road, right beside what looked for all the world like one of those cheesy haircut franchises you always see in the mall. Then I made the mistake of looking in through the plate-glass windows. There were . . . people in there, all right, and they were sitting in what looked a lot like barber's chairs, with other people behind and around them, but they were . . . eating? Their own hair? I turned away quickly. Yuck. I was suddenly really happy I had feathers now instead—they just fell out and got replaced, so no barber shops. Ever.

Ned brought his mecharoo space-hopper to a screeching, tail-wagging halt right beside us. "We need to check things out before we charge in," I called up to him, and he looked at me funny. Tall nodded from behind him, though.

"Good idea." Then he frowned. "Real good idea." The frown morphed into a grin. "It was Mary's, wasn't it?"

"Oh, shut up." His grin actually got a little wider. "You're the sneaky spy-guy—get your butt down here and scout or something."

"Aye aye, sir!" he snapped off a salute and hopped down, striding past me to the corner of the shop. Then he peered around it—and whistled.

"What? What's up? What'd you see?" I crept up behind him, which was pretty silly considering I was: a) a man with the head of a duck, b) dressed like Elvis, c) riding an interstellar Harley, and d) trying to sneak past a shop with a plate-glass window. But at least it made me feel like I was being stealthy.

"Take a look." Tall pulled back so I could maneuver past

him. "At least we found our missing . . . car."

I snuck a glance. There, up ahead, was a huge . . . building? It was tall and had curving walls made from some glittering grayish-pink stone or maybe dull metal, and there were big arches carved into the sides and a few more in front, some up high like skylights and some down below like doggy doors. It had what looked like small towers running in a row down the middle, too, and those were even more glittery than the rest, except for these other shapes like narrow balconies on either side. There was something about the shape of it all that struck me funny, and not in a "oh ho, look at that space-matrix building, ain't it a hoot!" sort of way.

And then there was what looked like a miniature alien bridge sticking out of it.

"Huh." I twisted to look at Ned, who was behind me. "Guess that bridge-cluster-thingy would have gotten us here after all."

Ned peeked around me. "I knew I programmed the coordinates right!" he whispered. "If I'd only remembered to up the inertial compensators—"

"Yeah yeah, water under the bridge—almost literally." I looked at the weird building again. Whoever'd put that thing together could have used a subscription to *This Old House*. Or just a set of Lincoln Logs to practice with first. "So that's it? That's where the matrix is?"

"It is," Mary confirmed. "We must enter the structure and convey you to the matrix itself, so that you can realign it. Then the threat will finally be over." She didn't sound completely happy about that, but maybe that was just wishful thinking on my part. After all, once the matrix was fixed up again my part'd be done. They'd ship me back to Earth, back to my dead-end mind-numbing job, and all I'd have to show for it would be a cool Elvis outfit and a few galactic credit cards. Big whoop. I probably couldn't even tell anybody, at least not without everyone assuming I'd finally lost it—I still had trouble convincing people I had a duck's head, and that was when they were staring straight at me. Telling them all the weirdness I'd been through in the past year, all the places I'd been and the people I'd seen? Forget about it. Probably the closest I could manage would be muttering drunkenly about it in bars late at night, or using it as yet another way to heckle telephone psychics. Maybe Tall and I would get together every few months to sit back and reminisce like old war vets: "Yep, remember that time we were on the garbage truck and mistook that one owner for his trash? Or the little cartoon-bunny whose bridge we stole? Heh!" I probably couldn't even sell the rights to late-night cable, and that was saying something.

The job had to get done, though. I'd worry about the aftermath, well, after.

"Okay, what are we waiting for?" I flipped up my lapels and straightened my shades. "Let's go." I started to step around the corner, and Tall's heavy hand landed on my shoulder, yanking me back.

"Wait!" he hissed. "It's bound to be a trap!"

I stared at him. "What're you talking about? We finally made it! The thingy is right over there, in that big ugly pink building! We just have to walk over there, let ourselves in, find the matrix, realign it, and we're done! Easy as pie."

"Exactly." Tall let me go but shifted so he was blocking my path. "And the enemy must know that." He looked at Mary. "They know about the matrix, right?"

"Almost certainly," she admitted.

"And they know where it's located?"

A frown crossed those pretty features. "I see no reason to believe otherwise—it is not a well-known object, yet its existence and location are hardly secret. Any who wished to locate it would be able to do so with only minimal effort."

"And they must know that if we realign it they'll be blocked again."

Again Mary nodded. "If they know of the matrix's existence and function, they would certainly know of the dangers involved for them."

Tall squared his jaw—I'd never actually seen anyone do that before, but he really did. I half-expected his eyes to glint coldly any second. "Which means the invaders know we've got to get here, and they know where 'here' is. They've had plenty of time to get here before us, so they've seized the building and barricaded it against us." He shrugged. "It's what I'd do."

"Yeah, but you're an FBI guy," I argued—I knew he wasn't exactly FBI but I loved watching his left eye twitch whenever I said it. I made a mental note to refer to him as CIA next time instead, to see if I could get the right one going, too. "You're supposed to be all paranoid and conspiracy-oriented and such. You probably worry every time you order delivery that somebody's intercepted it and spiked your food with acid and truth serum and rare Australian dingo-venom." The look of utter horror on his face told me he'd never be able to order delivery again, which I simply considered a bonus. "Who's to say these guys think that way? They may not even know the matrix exists!"

"They're invading our universe from a parallel reality!" Tall all but shouted in my face. "They're a military force intent upon conquest! Of course they know it's here, and of course they've taken it hostage! They'd have to be morons to do anything else, and despite whatever you may think they are not an army of you!"

"They could be," I countered. "We have no idea who or what they are, really. Do we?" That last part was directed at Mary, who shook her head.

"The Grays were unable to observe the invaders," she said. "Every attempt was discovered and ended in the agent's termination. All we do know is that they are from a divergent plane of reality, and have broken through the natural barriers that form this universe. They intend to alter our quantum frequencies to match those of their native plane, thus merging the two realities into one and rewriting our natural laws with their own. Once that occurs they will be able to dominate the universe and impose whatever changes and rule they require."

"So they could be anybody," I pointed out. "And they could be complete chowderheads who have no idea what they're doing or how to run a war or an invasion or whatever. They could be complete blundering idiots who just crashed through the wall by sheer accident."

"Great, they really could be an army of you," Tall muttered.

"I heard that!" I peered at the pink building again. "But the point is, we have no idea how they think or what they have planned, so for all we know they really don't know about the matrix and it really is as simple as walking across the street."

"He has a point," Ned chimed in. "No point spoiling for a fight if we don't have to fight anybody."

"All right, all right." Tall sighed. "We should assess the situation fully." He glared at me again. "But you are not going anywhere until we're sure it's safe. You're the only one who can align the matrix, and I'm not letting you get your head blown off literally within sight of our objective."

"Aw, you really do care!" I batted my eyes at him—which isn't easy without eyelashes, but it's amazing what you can do with nictitating membranes if you try hard enough and if you've spent enough time drinking heavily. "Okay, you're the war chief—how do we suss this thing out?"

"We need to send someone to test their defenses," Tall answered, glancing around at the rest of us. "Someone we can afford to lose if it all goes south in a hurry." I could see the calculations in his head as his eyes moved over each of our companions in turn. No way he was sending Mary in there— she was our connection to the Grays, the only one who really knew much about the invasion, and she was smoking hot to boot. Ned was too damn useful as well. And Tansy's reality-warping powers had already saved our butts twice. Which left him, but I didn't think Tall was stupid enough to risk sacrificing himself on a slim chance. For certain success absolutely, but in a case like this where we didn't even know if there was a threat, let along how much of one? No, for that we needed somebody completely expendable. Preferably someone we barely even knew, much less liked . . .

Tall and I turned at the same time, and glanced behind us—through the plate-glass window.

"Perfect," I heard him whisper. And I'm pretty sure he wasn't thinking about a haircut. Or a quick snack.

Twenty minutes later, Ned returned from the Stellar SuperCuts. He had a tall skinny guy with him, and when I saw "tall" I mean over twelve feet and when I say "skinny" I mean maybe as thick around as my wrist. And I have surprisingly dainty hands and wrists. This guy had skin the color of butter and features that looked like they'd been molded in soft wax, like they were rough and crude and maybe a little runny. He also had five legs and three arms but I tried not to hold that against him. Or to think about how much I'd kill for some good calamari.

"This is Siden," Ned told us, almost clapping the guy on the back but apparently thinking better of it. "I explained how we're trying to surprise our friends over in the pink structure and he's agreed to help by walking over and checking to make sure they're back from lunch already." Siden nodded and let out a series of little whoots and whistles and clicks—I felt like I was listening to a clockwork owl convention.

"Thanks, you're a pal," I told him, and he nodded and whooted some more before striding out past us and toward the pink building. We all crowded by the corner and watched as he walked, calmly and in no hurry. And why should he be? Poor guy thought he was just helping some people play a practical joke or something. I didn't blame Ned for the lie, though— saying "hey, we think the building around the corner is heavily guarded by an invading force and we need someone expendable to check and see if we'll get killed for approaching it" probably wouldn't have gotten a lot of volunteers.

Siden was already about halfway to the matrix building, and there'd be no response at all. "See?" I whispered at Tall, who made a shushing gesture and didn't take his eyes off our tall, buttery, rubbery new pal. Siden took a long, loose step, raised several feet to take another—

—and turned to a puddle on the ground.

For a second I thought he'd just melted from the heat, or decided to pool himself for fun or to take a quick nap. But then I realized there'd been a brief, high-pitched whine, and the smell of burning rubber at the same time.

That hadn't been simple heatstroke. Siden had been murdered.

"See?" Tall hissed at me, but he didn't look all too thrilled at being proved right. "I told you they were guarding the place!"

"Yeah yeah," I grumbled back. "What'd they just hit Siden with? And can we do anything about it?"

"A strong-force excitation beam," Ned offered quietly. "That's my guess, from the smell and the sound and the . . . results." He shook his head. "Poor guy. He was only trying to help, and we got him killed!"

"He sacrificed himself to help save the universe," I replied.

"Even if he didn't know it at the time. So what's this excitation beam thing? That doesn't sound so bad—maybe he just got so excited he couldn't contain himself, like that old Pointer Sisters song."

"The strong force is one of the guiding forces that binds together all matter in this universe," Mary explained. "A strong-force excitation beam agitates the strong-force bonds within the target, causing it to lose cohesion at an atomic level."

"It turns anything it touches to a pile of goo," Ned translated for me.

"Oh. Got it. Any way we can protect ourselves from it?" But Ned shook his head.

"The beam operates on a subatomic level—I don't know anything that can block it, or even reduce the effects."

"So if we go out there we'll be turned to goo too?" I ground my bill together. "There's gotta be something we can do!"

"Like what?" Tall turned to Mary. "Any other ways into that building?"

"No," she replied. "When it was chosen as the site for the matrix, the structure was reconfigured to be defensible in case of attack. The apertures you see were all sealed, save only the single entrance, and thanks to its location and the local terrain there is no way to reach it unobserved."

"Great." We all looked at each other. "So how the hell're we gonna get inside?"

"What about your translocation whosis?" I asked Mary, remembering when we'd first met. "It's only, what, a hundred feet or so? Could you use that to get us in there?"

But she had more bad news for me. "The translocation device is not an option," she reminded me. "The quantum frequencies have already shifted too far for them to function. It is not a question of distance but of operation."

"Right. Forgot about that part." I rubbed my bill. "Okay, so we know they're watching, we know they're armed, we know they'll shoot anyone who tries to sneak in. We don't have any defenses, or even any weapons beyond that one gun of Tall's, and we're running out of time." I glanced around at the others. "Okay. That's that, then." And I turned and headed out across the street.

"DuckBob! Wait!" Mary ran after me, grabbing my arm. "What are you doing? They will kill you!"

"No they won't," I assured her. "I've got a plan. Trust me."

"Really?" Tall had caught up with us. "You've got a plan?"

"Absolutely. You guys hang back here, and I'll take care of it."

"Wait!" Mary still had hold of my arm. I didn't mind. "You are sure they will not harm you?"

"Harm me? No idea," I admitted. "But they won't kill me."

She stared at me for a second, then leaned in and kissed me on the side of my face, right where my bill starts. Let me tell you, you wanna talk about erogenous zones? Whoo!

"Be careful," she whispered. Then she released her grip and stepped back.

"I hope you know what you're doing," Tall warned. But he held out his hand, too. "Good luck." I shook it, and he didn't even try to crush my fingers. Much. I really was growing on him.

"Here," Ned said, holding up what looked like a fridge magnet—an H—and pressing it against the underside of my bill. "This'll let you stay in communication with us. Good luck."

"Thanks." I stretched my neck a little, but I couldn't actually feel his gizmo at all. Maybe just a mild itch. Tansy gave me a quick kiss on the bill as well—earning her a momentary glare from Mary, I noticed—and then they all drew back around the corner to safety.

I was on my own.

"Right, here I come," I muttered as I started walking again. "Get ready, because DuckBob Spinowitz is on his way!"

I waited until I was maybe a third of the way across—I could clearly see the puddle that'd been Siden, a few yards ahead of me—before slowing to a stop.

"Hello in there!" I shouted at the pink building. "Can you guys hear me?"

There was no answer, but I did hear Ned whisper, "what's he doing?" through the thing on my bill. Weird, too—it vibrated through my bill and into my head, which made it sound like I was listening to him underwater. In falsetto.

"I know you're in there!" I tried again. "My name's DuckBob! I've been sent here to stop you!" I started walking again.

"I know you could excite my strong forces or something like that," I added, "but I don't think you want to do that. Because I know some things you don't, things you'll need to know if you're gonna take over this universe properly. You can kill me but then you'll never find out what they were, and your little invasion might not even succeed. Or you can bring me in yourself, and we can talk about it."

"Not bad," Tall's voice shook through me. "Make yourself too valuable to kill—a classic hostage negotiation tactic."

"That's me—a classic," I muttered, and brightened a little when I heard Ned laugh in reply. His gadget worked! I could still talk to them! I didn't feel alone any more.

And I'd taken several more steps. All without being reduced to goo.

"I'm unarmed," I shouted next. "No weapons! I just want to talk, maybe do a little horse-trading, see if we can work things out quietly. What do you say?"

Nobody answered, but I was even with the Puddle O' Siden now, and then past it, and I was still safely unexcited. It was working!

I kept talking, telling the unseen invaders that I could help them, that I had info they needed, that I just wanted to talk, that we could work things out—that one led into me breaking into the old Beatles song "Try to See It My Way," which got snorts from Ned and Tall and quiet laughter from Mary and Tansy but carried me to within a short sprint of the pink building. And its one big, heavy metal door.

"Okay, I'm glad you've decided to be reasonable about all this," I announced as I took the last few steps. "I'm sure we can come to some kind of arrangement that works for everybody— maybe you can have the universe on alternate weekends and for holidays, but we'll split the summers and you'll have to kick in a bit for expenses. I—" I reached for the door—and it flew open in front of me. Nice.

Then a whole bunch of hands shot out from the dark past the door and latched onto me, hauling me through into the blackness.

Not so nice.

Chapter Twenty-five
What was that cereal's number again?

"DuckBob, are you there? Can you hear me?"

"Ugh."

That wasn't exactly coherent, so I tried again.

"Uh-huh."

Much better.

"Are you okay?" It was Ned, but not exactly—he sounded like he'd been gargling. Or was gargling. Or was being gargled.

He also sounded a bit like a twelve-year-old boy.

And my bill ached every time he spoke.

Oh, right.

"Yeah, I think so," I managed finally. I sat up—which was when I realized I'd been laying down—and then had to rest my head in my hands so it didn't snap off my neck and roll away like one of those horribly garish bowling balls you see at the local bowling alley gathering dusts on the racks because only crazed old ladies and former postal workers ever dare to use them.

Ouch.

"What happened?" pre-teen underwater Ned demanded. "We saw you step inside and then you stopped talking."

"We knew that had to mean things were seriously wrong,"

a more gravelly-voiced teen commented. Tall. Not surprisingly, he didn't sound like he'd ever really been young—he'd probably handed out speeding tickets in preschool to any kid who dared to do hopscotch at more than the officially regulated crawl.

"I'm fine—I think," I croaked. Which is weird, since ducks don't normally croak—that's a frog thing. But then you don't see many ducks dressed like Elvis and sitting in a pink stadium either, so I guess it's a moot point. "How long was I out?"

"A few minutes."

I shook my head and immediately wished I hadn't. At least it was still safely in my hands, though they weren't all that steady themselves. "You didn't hear me for a few minutes and figured something had to be wrong? I don't talk that much!" I could practically hear the looks on the other end of Ned's little transmitter thingy. "Oh, fine."

"Are you inside?" Mary cut in after a second. I noticed she didn't argue the whole "can't shut up thing" either, but then again if I'd been thinking clearly I couldn't have made much of a case against it my own self.

"I am."

"That is excellent! Your plan worked!"

It did? I peeked out through my fingers. There was a sparkly pink floor below me. A quick upward glance revealed equally glittery pink walls and a likewise sparkly pink ceiling. Huh. I hoped I was actually sitting up, and not hanging from the ceiling or perched on the wall. That could be embarrassing, especially if somebody mistook me for a hat rack or a ceiling fan. "Yeah, I guess it did at that," I agreed. "Cool."

"Nice work." I could hear how Tall had to force those words out past his teeth. "So now you're inside. What's the next step?"

"Next step?"

"Yes," he insisted. "You said you had a plan. Remember?"

"I remember! And it worked! I'm inside. And still alive." Which I was pretty happy about.

"Yes. Yes you are. But what's the rest of it?"

"The rest of what?"

"The rest of the plan!"

I tried to lift my head but my neck muscles were claiming they deserved an immediate holiday, they had months of vacation time saved up, and they were taking all of it right now, whether I signed off on the junket or not. "You have the rest of the plan?" I asked from where I was. "That's great—what is it?"

Now Tall sounded like he wanted to strangle me. In other words, the same as always. "No, your plan, you idiot!"

"My plan? What about it? It worked!"

"Yes, but—"

Ned cut him off. "That was the whole plan, wasn't it?" he asked. "To get inside intact?"

"Yep."

He sighed, or maybe I swallowed. The reverb on this thing made it hard to tell.

"So you have no idea what to do next?"

"Nope."

"Right." I could hear angry whispers, probably Tall. "Hang in there. We'll figure something out."

"Hanging in." I wanted to sign off but wasn't sure how. Did

this thing have an off switch? Did it deafen them every time I gulped? What would it sound like if I ate something? It'd probably be horrible, one of those things that either scarred them for life or became an award-winning documentary on one of the major cable networks. Maybe both.

They'd all stopped talking, and my head was starting to recover from the vibrations of having more than one person speaking through it at once, so I tried straightening up again. My neck muscles were still protesting and threatening to go on strike but they reluctantly cooperated, and I was able to look around a little bit.

Pink. All pink. Different shades and textures, most of it muted and shading toward the rosy hue, but pink nonetheless. All of it shiny and glossy, too, like I was sitting in the world's largest rose quartz crystal. It was even cool to the touch. Otherwise it was all on the minimalist side, no furniture just depressions and bulges you could use for chair or shelves or ironing boards. This place was a lot less like a building and a lot more like an above-ground cave system, I decided. Or an ancient Jell-O mold that'd been poked too many times with a fork.

Then something moved.

It was off to my far left, or maybe behind me—I hadn't wanted to push my neck muscles too far by asking them to turn that extensively so I'd only managed to see in front and a little to the side so far. But there was a different flicker at the edge of my peripheral vision—which is pretty wide, given that my eyes are on either side of my head—and it seemed to be vaguely person-shaped. That and all the feathers on the back of my neck suddenly stood up.

I wasn't alone.

"Hello?" I called out.

Nothing.

"Hey, anybody here?" Still no reply.

"I found this thousand-dollar bill laying on the ground just outside—is it yours?" That one always worked.

There was a rustling behind me, or at least I thought so. It was like when you heard the wind in the leaves but weren't completely sure you were hearing that or the sound of a crazed killer sneaking up the stairs, butcher knife in hand, ready to dismember you and festoon the walls with your bloody entrails.

I watched a lot of cheesy horror movies when I was younger.

Listen, there is nothing wrong with a grown man sleeping with a nightlight. Nothing!

I tried to listen harder—which is a silly phrase, really, because how do you listen harder? Do you screw up your ears or something?—and the rustling slowly resolved itself into words.

"Identify yourself."

"DuckBob Spinowitz," I answered. "Nice to meet you. If I did, in fact, meet you. Wanna show yourself? Shake hands? Get a beer?"

"Why are you here?" the rustling asked. It was still hovering just past the edge of my vision. I guess that meant no beer.

"I wanted to talk to you guys. You know, about the whole invasion thing." I didn't see much point in lying. For all I knew they could read my mind. Though why they'd need to ask my name then I had no idea. Unless they were testing me to see if I answered them honestly, and reading my mind to make sure.

Sneaky little buggers.

"Who sent you?"

"Oh, you know, the Grays. They sent me. Well, sort of sent me—I mean, they told me about what was going on and asked me to come. So did Agent Smith, though. So maybe he sent me. He's more the ordering type, when you get down to it. The Grays didn't actually demand I come, though they did say it was all up to me."

"Why did they send you?"

I scratched at my bill. "I need to realign the matrix, I think. Something like that. Have you seen it around here anywhere?" I turned my head slowly, so as not to spook anyone, and scanned the rest of the room. More smooth shiny sparkly pink. Had I fallen into the universe's largest bottle of nail polish? I hoped they tipped well, because whoever had the job of buffing all of this, they definitely deserved it!

"How will you realign it?" the rustling demanded.

"I have no idea," I admitted. "I'm kinda hoping there's a big button marked 'Realign' and I can just push it, though I suppose if that were the case anybody could have done it. Maybe there's a key code? Though they didn't give me a code. Ooh, or a musical code, like I have to whistle the theme to *Knot's Landing* to activate it—I can do that one, you know. You'd be surprised how well you can whistle through these little blowhole thingies on my bill. Listen!" I started whistling the *Knot's Landing* theme, but stopped when something zapped me in the head. It felt like static electricity, like when you give someone a goodnight peck on the cheek and get a static shock for your trouble, stinging my bill and my cheek and making my eye twitch. Yowtch.

"Where are you from?" was the rustling's next question. If a rustling noise could sound impatient, it did.

"Earth. New York City. Manhattan. Well, I mean I live in Brooklyn, because who can afford to live in Manhattan, right? But I'm in Fort Greene, it's nice, and the commute isn't too bad, so—" I shut up when it zapped me again. A shrink once told me I tended to babble when I was nervous. He also said I was one of the most nervous people he'd ever met. Of course, I was also one of the only people he'd ever met, at least professionally—he was a pet psychologist. They sent me to him because the regular shrinks couldn't look at me without frothing at the mouth and ranting about actualized metaphors and extreme self-delusion made contagious and other big phrases that sounded impressive and apparently justified their charging thousands of dollars an hour just to gawk at me. I figured if anything I should be the one charging—wasn't that how it worked in the circus? That's what the recruiters kept saying, anyway.

"What galactic coordinates?" the rustling demanded.

"For where? Earth? I have no idea." I tried to remember what Ned and Mary had said when we first met. "It's something like forty million light-years from here, I think, though that was just a guesstimate rather than an exact figure. Does that help any?"

"In what direction?"

"Hm? Oh." I thought about that for a second. "That way, I think." I gestured. "Assuming the front door is that way—is it?

Because we came from that direction."

Have you ever heard a rustling noise sigh in disgust? It's amazing, actually—the pitch or timbre or whatever completely changes, and the rustling actually slows, becomes more drawn out, kind of like an old movie ghost moan. I totally want that for my next ringtone.

"Did you come here alone?" it asked after a minute of moaning.

"What, inside? Yeah, didn't you see me walking across the street hollering at you?" Maybe it was blind. Maybe the rustling was like radar, where the sounds bounced back to it and told it where everything was. If that was the case, I was golden—I figured I could swish my pant cuffs back and forth and make it think the room'd turned into a maze somehow, or that it was stuck in the middle of a giant well, and make a run for it while it was still groping around looking for the door.

"You are in communication with others," it insisted, and I cursed under my breath. I'd always heard stories that people who lost one sense got stronger in the others to compensate. Obviously the rustling was blind but had excellent hearing. Though how it could hear anything over its own rustling was beyond me. Maybe it had special rustle-canceling earplugs, so it could filter out its own sounds. I'd kill for some of those, both one that silenced the rustling and ones that meant I didn't hear myself talking. Come to think of it, if I ever found earplugs that cancelled out the sound of my voice I could make a killing. I knew at least a hundred people who'd buy 'em, right off the bat.

I come from a large family.

The rustling was still talking, which just shows that I don't actually need noise-canceling earplugs. I'm capable of tuning out conversations all by myself. "Who are these others?" it was demanding.

"Hm? Oh, right, my friends, the ones who came with me." I ticked them off on my fingers. "There's Mary, Ned, Tall, and Tansy. Want to meet them?"

"Where are they from? Who do they work for? What are their capabilities?" Those all came in a rush of rustling, like someone had found a box of tissue paper and tossed a kitten inside to rampage around.

"Um, where are they from? I don't know, Tall's from the East Coast somewhere, I'd guess not New York because his accent's all wrong but not Midwest or West Coast either, so maybe something like North Carolina? He's not a southerner, I don't think, but he might've worked to lose his old accent as part of the job. Mary's from—I have no idea. Isn't that sad? All this time together and I really don't know anything about her. I'll have to do something about that, maybe over a nice quiet dinner in one of those little hole-in-the-wall Italian places with the good food and the dim lighting and the soft music. Ned's from Betelgeuse, or someplace nearby. No idea about Tansy—I think she may've said once but I honestly don't remember, which I feel bad about. I should make more of an effort to remember people's details, shouldn't I? Try to connect better, build a stronger bond—that's what the HR people at work keep saying. At least I think they do." I stopped talking when it zapped me again. My head was getting sore.

"What forces have been arrayed against us?" it wanted to know next. Guess it had given up asking about the others.

"Arrayed against you?" I laughed, though I knew it might get me zapped again. "Who even talks like that? Have you been watching old fantasy movies, the ones with the dragons on strings and the magic that looks a lot like silly string and smoke bombs? Because you really need to try some of the newer flicks, the action's a lot better and the green-screen stuff is actually really cool now, this one I saw the other week had—" *Zap.*

"What forces are arrayed against us?" it repeated. The rustling was louder, which I'm guessing means it was annoyed. I do seem to have that effect on people.

"How the hell should I know?" I snapped back. "What am I, the latest issue of *Newsweek*? 'Check page twelve for a full breakdown of the forces arrayed against the psychotic rustling sound from Dimension X'? Give me a break! And don't you dare zap me again! Show some manners—were you raised in a barn? A big, rustling, other-dimensional barn?"

I jumped to my feet while I was telling it off, and whirled around to face it—

—only to find myself staring at nothing.

No, not quite nothing. There was a shimmery patch in the air. Like the heatwave right behind a jet engine. I could see the room through it, but it was hazy. Something was definitely there.

Something about half my size and floating about three feet off the ground.

"Look," I started, but didn't get any farther than that because suddenly a siren went off somewhere nearby. At least it sounded like a siren—for all I knew it was one of these guys singing, or cursing because he's stubbed his other-dimensional toe.

"An intruder!" the patch rustled, so I guess I was right about it being an alarm. "It has breached the perimeter!" Which would have filled me with more enthusiasm if I had any idea where the perimeter was or what it took to breach it. If it meant someone or something had gotten inside the building, great. If, on the other hand, "breaching the perimeter" meant "someone has walked within a dozen light-years of this place," I was going to hold off on the celebrating. Though if that was the case they'd probably have that siren going off a lot more often.

"It is one of your allies," the patch informed me. It sounded way too pleased with itself. "We will question it instead. It will be more forthcoming with its answers."

"You think so? I've been pretty forthcoming," I shot back. "Is it my fault you don't like my answers? I've never tested well—give me a script and I can do better. Or let me do interpretive dance instead—I've been told my *Swan Lake* is really amazing."

It didn't answer. It was still there, or at least the air was still shimmering slightly, but that could've meant it had left the window open or the monitor on while it went off for a quick drink or a pee break or a nosh. I paced around the room, since it didn't tell me to stop, and looked for a way out, but when I tried to step into a closet-sized alcove off to one side something threw me back across the room and the same happened when I tried the one visible door. Looked like I was trapped in here, waiting on His Highness the Rustling Shadowy Thing. Great.

Since there wasn't much else I could do, I got a drink from

this one little indentation that had water trickling into it from above, then started rummaging through the little nooks and crannies that lined one wall like the cubbyholes we'd had in kindergarten. I got the feeling I was being held in the equivalent of a locker room, and these were the regular workers' lockers. Several of them had these stretchy silvery fabric thingies that I took to be work shirts and one had a great gleaming candy-apple red spiked hardhat, which I would've borrowed if it had even remotely fit on my head—that's a real problem for me these days. There were these big huge mechanical boots in a few, and what looked like a pair of worn old red velvet ballet slippers in one—I didn't ask. But the third nook from the end was the real jackpot. It held one of those bits of fabric, a wide flat rectangle of smoky glass or plastic that I thought was probably like wraparound sunglasses, a shapeless brown pouch that might have been a hat or a bag or the start of a hand puppet—and a lunchbox, the big old metal kind you used to see in commercials being toted around by construction workers. Except that this one had a grainy white and gray and black finish with veins running through it, and it was hard and cold to the touch. Marble. The darned thing had been carved out of real marble. Was there some kind of rule here that everything had to be made out of ridiculously expensive materials? I half expected to find a toilet and discover it'd been carved out of solid diamond. Well, whatever—right now I was less interested in the box's manufacture than in its contents. I grabbed it and sat back down on the bench before fumbling along its side and finally finding a narrow little depression just wide enough to slip one finger in.

I shoved a digit in there, and was rewarded with a faint hum, a popping sound that messed with my ears—and the top half of the box folding down along the sides until they'd disappeared within the rest, leaving me holding an open marble box filled to the brim. Yes! Food!

At least I *think* it was food. It certainly looked like some kind of round fruit-thing, though it had bumpy gray skin and a bright red interior. Plus there were two shiny paper-wrapped triangles I took to be sandwiches, a foil pouch of flat purple flower-shaped things I thought might be chips, and a long silvery cylinder filled with a clear liquid that smelled like bubblegum soda and left weird afterimages as I drank it from the spout that had appeared at one end when I squeezed.

I really *hope* it was food. This was the Galactic Core, after all—it's possible the round thing was an alien seedpod, the triangles data wafers, the purple flowers the compressed biological data of a dozen ecosystems, and the liquid a fuel for a faster-than-light hyperdrive.

It tasted good, though. A little too minty on the drink, and a bit squishy and salty on the fruit, and the sandwiches had this strange habit of rolling up into a ball every time I raised them to my bill, but otherwise nice. And I was too hungry to be picky.

I'd finished all but a few of the chips, some of the drink, and half of one sandwich when the door flew open and a shape landed on the ground at my feet. A tall, athletic figure wearing an Air Force jumpsuit.

Tall.

"Uh," he groaned as I squatted down beside him.

"Are you okay?"

He groaned again, and cursed a little after that. Which felt really weird because he obviously had one of Ned's little gizmos too, and so I was hearing it both through my ears and through my bill.

"What're you doing here?" I asked him.

"Rescuing you," he admitted after a second. I helped him sit up.

"Oh." We looked at each other. I wanted to say, "guess that didn't go so well, huh?" but figured he didn't need to hear that right now. Instead I said the only thing I could think of that might cheer him up even a little bit:

"Want half a sandwich and some chips?"

Chapter Twenty-six
Take two, but where will you put them?

"So walk me through this," I said a little while later. Tall had eaten the rest of the food—I know he probably had a granola bar or something on him but of course he'd want to save that for emergencies—and we were both sitting on a long straight bump that rose from the floor like a bench, legs stretched out in front of us, heads and backs against the wall. "I walk in here and get myself caught, and you tell me I'm an idiot. Then you walk in here and get caught. So how does that make you less of an idiot than I am? You'd actually be the bigger idiot, because you've already seen it doesn't work but you try it anyway!"

Tall glared at me. Sort of. He actually had his eyes closed, and didn't even turn his head. But he glared all the same. I could feel it—it was like a full-body glare.

"I," he informed me with one of those condescending tones you usually get from credit card customer service reps when they call to demand why you haven't made a payment in months and you ask them if they've never been in a tough spot and they get all superior on you and say no, of course not and then you ask them why, if they're so awesome, they're stuck working for a credit card company, "have combat training. Do

YOU have combat training?"

"Well . . . no." I didn't think District LaserTag Champion when I was fourteen would really count.

"I have extensive experience in tactics for a variety of situations, including search and rescue. Do YOU have that?"

"No."

"I have training in infiltrating and taking out hostile encampments. Do YOU have that training?"

"I have the head of a duck," I shot back. "Do YOU have the head of a duck?"

That shut him up. Actually, I've found that shuts almost everyone up. Particularly useful if you're in a packed movie theater and you get some of those idiots in front of you, the ones who think the theater is actually their living room and they can carry on a conversation with their buddies right in the middle of the pivotal scene. I recommend everyone get their head modified into a giant duck head just for the satisfaction of completely shutting those people down, leaving them staring and drooling for hours after the movie's ended.

That, plus then I'd have someone to talk to.

And we could all take up synchronized swimming together. Move over, Rockettes! The Duckettes are coming atcha!

"Okay, so we're both stuck here." I glanced around the room again, hoping that maybe a door would have appeared while we were bickering, "Swell. What about the others?" Ned and Mary had been strangely quiet.

"No response, and no sound," Tall confirmed, tapping his earpiece. "My guess is the invaders figured out that we were talking and blocked the transmissions."

"Damn." I scratched at my bill. "Guess we're on our own."

"Best to think that way," Tall agreed. "Don't rely on anyone who could screw you over later, whether deliberately or by accident. We need to do this ourselves."

"Okay, I have a strange idea. What if—" I didn't manage to finish my thought—not just my words, I tend to just say whatever I feel or see or hear, like I don't have filter in there, no buffer to let the thoughts stew a bit and mature or wither and die before they get spit out. But this thought faded into the air as the door creaked open, and something slid through. Something tall and broad and squared. And no, it wasn't the NFL's Mensa representative. It was some kind of machine, with straps and wires and hoses sticking out every which way and knob and dials and switches all up and down one side.

At least it wasn't glittery and pink.

"We have you and your friend both now," the rustling sound had returned, and I didn't much care for the way it sounded, all slick and oily and nasty. "Now you will tell us everything you know or he will face the consequences."

The room honestly seemed to blur all around me, like I'd suddenly taken fifteen Jell-O shots intravenously and then gone on a merry-go-round at the state fair. I couldn't find the skateboard or the feather duster this time, though. Don't ask. Whatever caused it, I felt lightheaded and blinked a few times to clear everything out—

—and somehow I was alone on the bench.

"Tall?"

A string of profanity drew my attention back to the machine, now standing in the middle of the room.

Tall was strapped to it.

And not just jury-rigged, either. Those manacles looked heavy-duty, and they were bolted securely into the machine's frame. I know how to check that sort of thing. I'd had a girlfriend once who was really into bondage. And blacksmithing.

"What the hell?!?" Tall was fuming. I circled the machine, looking for some way to shut it down, but didn't see anything with big red letters on it saying "Push me!" or "Pull me!" or "Hazardous Waste—Do Not Eat!"

"Tell us: what forces are arrayed against us?" The rustling demanded.

"Oh, come on!" I replied. "Didn't we go through this already? I have no idea!"

Zap!

"Aaaahhhhhh!" That last contribution came from Tall as blue lightning forked across him and through him. I had a feeling from his response that being attached to that machine made the zaps considerably more powerful. And more dangerous.

"I don't know!" I shouted. "I swear it! Just leave him alone! Leave me alone! Leave all of us alone—pretend we're Australia and we're playing Risk!" That never works for an entire game, of course, but I hoped the metaphor still held.

"We shall allow you time to reflect," the shimmering announced after a minute. "To decide for yourself what path you must take. But do not reflect for long." Then it faded away. We were alone again. Being monitored, possibly, but I was sure somehow that our nasty little shadows had left the building.

'Quick, let's get you out of this thing," I told Tall. I stepped around to the front and studied all the dials and knobs and switches. Still no big red letters. Darn.

"Do you know what you're doing?" Tall asked me in a whisper. He was still shaking from that zap. Wow.

"Sure," I assured him. "I just need to flip this switch—"

"Aaahhhh!"

"Okay, maybe not that one. How about this switch instead?"

"Aaahhhhh!"

"No? Darn. Okay, how about this one?"

"Don't touch that!"

"Touch what?" My finger was already on the button.

"That! That!"

"This? You want me to touch this?" I know, I'm a terrible person. Besides, I figured one of them had to work.

"No! Not—aaahhhhh!"

"Oh. Sorry." Apparently not that one.

"Stop doing that!"

"Doing what?"

"Touching that!"

"Touching this?" I selected another likely looking button.

"Aaahhhhh!"

"Oops." Maybe one of the levers instead?

"Enough!" I couldn't see Tall, since he was on the far side of the machine, but I could guess his expression.

"I said I was sorry."

"Can we just get on with this?"

"With what? Did you want me to—?"

"No! DON'T TOUCH ANYTHING!!!"

"Well, that's going to make this more difficult, don't you think?" Honestly, I'm not sure why he was quite so upset. What's a little electrocution among friends? And I really was trying to help. Is it my fault I can't resist fiddling with things? That's why all my old co-workers had learned long ago never to leave their clock radios or MP3 players sitting out where I could reach them.

Or their pets.

We stood in silence like that for a few seconds. Which was about as much of it as I could stand. "Now what?" I said finally.

"Just—just be patient, okay? Don't do anything stupid."

"Oh. Sure. Right. No problem. I'll just—hey, what's this?" I hadn't noticed that button before. I was sure it was the right one!

"Aaahhhhh!"

I straightened up quickly. "Sorry!"

"Just leave it alone!"

"Okay, okay. I was just trying to help. Sheesh." I stepped around to the side, resisting the urge to flip one more switch or push one more button. Tall glared at me as soon as I came within his field of vision. "What?"

"You're a menace, you know that?" he gasped.

"Hey, I'm not the one who put you in those shackles," I pointed out. "Or brought that machine in in the first place!"

"No, but you are the one who kept zapping me with it!"

"I was trying to get you loose!"

"Yeah? Great job!"

"Fine, next time you try to rescue me I'll be sure to leave you alone!"

"Good!"

"Great!"

"Excellent!"

"Superb!"

"Fantastic! O!"

Tall stopped just as he was getting ready to shout a reply. "O?"

"Fantastico." I shrugged. "I like it better that way."

"Fantastico isn't a word."

"Is too."

"Is not."

"Too."

"Not."

"Tootootootoo!"

"Notnotnotnotnot!"

"Too to the infinity!"

"Not the infinity plus one!"

"Too to the infinity plus infinity! Hah! So there!" That stopped him. And Mrs. Scandariotto had said I'd never master math!

I was trying to think of something else we could argue about when the air near the machine started shimmering again. "Uh oh, they're back," I whispered to Tall, who nodded and put on his best stoic expression. Which is what he usually had on when he wasn't dealing with me.

"Have you reconsidered your refusal to reveal your knowledge?" the shimmering patch of air rustled. "Will you spare your companion further pain by relinquishing your information?"

"I already told you, I don't know anything," I said yet again. "You can torture him all you want"—that earned me a furious glare from Tall—"but it won't change anything. I can't tell you what I don't know."

"They would not have sent you so ill-prepared," the rustling countered, and I felt but couldn't see someone or someones stepping up beside me and taking hold of my arms. If I squinted I could make out hazy outlines, but nothing more.

"Oh, you should have seen me when I first hit the road," I told them. "You think I'm unprepared now? Ha!"

"Listen," Tall called out, "I can tell you a lot more than he can! Release me and I'll tell you whatever you want to know."

"You only wish to evade your confinement," the rustling accused.

"No, I'll talk!" Tall insisted. "I really will!" He managed a small smile, though it faltered quickly—that might have just been from lack of practice, though. "If I'm lying, just do that weird flickering thing again and put me back in these cuffs. What've you got to lose?"

The shimmer faded for a minute, and I could almost hear several voices speaking all at once. It was like I knew they were there but couldn't quite hear them clearly.

"Very well," the rustling stated just I was getting ready to sing to break the near-silence. "We will release your shackles and you will answer our questions fully and truthfully. Fail to do so and we will attach you to the machine once more and torture the information from you."

"You got it," Tall assured them. "No funny business, no evasions. Done."

There was that flickering again—it was like I passed out for half-a-second, between blinks, or like somebody rewrote the world while I wasn't looking—and Tall was standing next to me. Then he was on the ground.

"What is this?" the rustling demanded. "Return to an upright position and answer our questions!"

"Give me a break," Tall gasped, rolling over onto his back and folding his arms over his chest. "I've just been tortured for twenty minutes!" The look he gave me showed he hadn't forgotten that at least half of that time had come from me. "I need a few seconds to catch my breath, otherwise I won't be able to tell you anything!"

Silence. Then, "very well. You may recover first. But do not try our patience." This guy or guys or patch of crinkly paper or whatever really did talk funny.

Tall lay there, eyes closed, his breathing slowing little by little until it was steady again. Hell, for a second I actually thought he'd gone to sleep. But then he opened his eyes and nodded.

"Okay." He levered himself to his feet, though I noticed him wincing a little as he did, and straightened up. "I'm ready."

Then he winked at me.

Uh-oh.

A wink like that was never a good sign. Okay, almost never. A wink like that from a hot chick in a seedy bar was a completely different matter, though sadly I tended to get them far more often from plain chicks in the avian sanctuary at the zoo—and not all from the human variety of "chick," either. But from a guy, and especially in a hostage situation? Never a good thing.

Sure enough, Tall opened his mouth as if he was about to spill his guts—and bolted for the door.

Oh crap.

"Escape attempt!" the rustling roared, the sound of it cutting into my head. "Stop the prisoner from escaping!"

I felt the shapes next to me release my arms. They were going after Tall! And while he wasn't my favorite person in the universe by any stretch, he wasn't really all that bad a guy and he had come in here to rescue me. I couldn't let them grab him. So I turned, squinted at the hazy outlines, and kicked the nearest one.

Hard.

"Aaahh!" It went down in a heap, which is when I realized it hadn't been touching the ground in the first place. These things could fly! I didn't have time to think about that, though. The other one was still moving, and it was like trying to track a fly—if it got too far from me I'd never be able to spot it again. So I threw myself after it, arms outstretched, bill open. My arms got nothing but air, but I felt something against my bill. Contact!

So I bit him.

Hey, let me tell you, you don't want to get stuck in a duck's bill. We've got some serious torque going on there. I had to learn real quick, after this first happened, not to try impressing people by opening bottles with my bill. Because broken glass? Not a turn-on. At least not for anybody I'd want to impress.

Cracking nuts is always an icebreaker, though. So, for that matter, is breaking ice. Especially those swan ice-sculptures—somewhere there's a picture of me doing that at an avant garde gallery opening, with the caption "Duck vs. swan as life imitates art." I sent that one to my mom.

This time I wasn't going for tearing anything open—yuck!—but I did clamp down, and I heard a squeal of pain. Then I hit the ground, and something smaller than me hit the ground right by my head with a muffled thud. Gotcha!

I spit out what I'm pretty sure was a leg, leaped to my feet, and kicked down hard. Another squeal as my boot connected, and then I saw a hazy outline collapse on the floor. Two down!

Tall had made it to the door and gotten it open, but now it looked like he was doing one of those "punching-himself" mime fights. By squinting until I could barely see through the slits I could just make out the outlines all around him. They were practically swarming the big guy.

"Hang on!" I shouted. "I'm coming!" And can you believe it? I actually ran forward to help him. Wild what enforced captivity and taunting can do to a person. I'm never gonna make faces at the bears and gorillas ever again.

The orangutan, though, I can't pass up. Besides, he makes faces right back at me.

Tall was lashing out around him for all he was worth, and I heard several meaty thunks as his fists and elbows and knees and head connected. He couldn't really see what he was fighting, though, and they were all over him, so it wasn't going well. I waded in, squinting and grabbing and kicking and sometimes biting, and between us we managed to clear a space around us, at least for a minute.

"Okay," I said, wiping my bill on my arm. "We've made it to the door. Now what?"

"Hold them as long as we can," Tall replied. "Can you actually see them?"

"Not really, no, but when I squint I can make out outlines."

He squinted. "Hey, yeah! That helps!"

"So your plan is to hold them off as long as we can? What kind of a plan is that? Eventually they'll just take us down, chain us back up, and torture both of us."

Tall grinned. "No they won't," he assured me.

Then they were on us again, so I didn't have a chance to ask him why not.

We fought them back a second time, and they paused to regroup.

"Is there more to this plan you're not telling me?" I demanded as soon as we were clear.

"Of course."

"What? Well, tell me what it is!"

Tall laughed. "Why would I want to do that?"

"Damn it, Tall, how can I help if you don't tell me what's going on?"

"Just keep fighting," he countered, and kicked out at an outline that had crept back within range. It went flying, and the others surged past it as it fell.

It seemed like there were more of them this time around,

and I had several hanging on each arm, one wrapped around my neck, and a few trying to scale my back and head. Tall wasn't faring any better. How many rustling patches did it take to invade the galaxy, anyway?

"Whatever else you've got planned," I managed to gasp, "I suggest you do it now!"

"Good idea," someone agreed.

But it wasn't Tall.

"Ned!" I half-shouted, half-croaked as he burst in through the door. Mary and Tansy were right behind him. Ned had what looked like a tricked-out firehose in both hands, and he twisted it on, flame-colored water spraying from it. Or maybe flames spraying from it like water. I'm not sure. Whatever that stuff was, the intruders recoiled from it, hissing and screaming like it burned them, but when droplets touched me they just felt a little tingly.

"Charged relativistic particles," Ned shouted over the noise. "Burns like hell when in contact with anything from a different reality, but completely harmless to us!"

"Awesome!" I could move again, and so could Tall, so we quickly stepped over beside the others to give Ned an unobstructed shot. Mary wrapped her arms around my neck and kissed me soundly on the cheek as soon as I was within reach.

"I was so worried!" she told me breathily, which almost made me forget all about this whole life-or-death battle thing.

"Yeah? Thanks! I'm okay, though." I glanced past her at Tall. "So this was the plan all along?"

He nodded. "I was the distraction, made them focus on me so the others could slip in undetected. Ned needed time to get that hose thingy built."

"Nice." I slipped my arm around Mary's waist. She didn't object.

The last of the outlines stopped moving, and Ned shut off the hose. "Need to conserve the supply," he explained, gesturing to a tank on his back. "Wasn't easy filtering the particles into a usable form and applying the charge." He grinned. "Looks like it did the trick, though." Then he held out his hand. "Glad to see you're okay."

I shook it happily. "Thanks to you guys I am." Tansy was the only one who hadn't welcomed me back yet. "What's up, Tansy?" I asked her. "Aren't you happy to see me?"

"Sure," she answered, smiling. "Of course I am!" She fluttered over and gave me a quick peck on the cheek, which made Mary snuggle up against me more possessively. Damn, life was suddenly good! "I just—" she gestured down at the barely-seen figures on the floor. "What are we gonna do with them now?"

"Get rid of 'em," Tall growled in reply. "Maybe keep one or two for study. Destroy the rest."

Tansy sighed. "I was afraid you'd say that." She wrinkled her nose like something smelled bad—and suddenly Ned's firehose and tank were in her hands. Another twitch and they'd crumpled into a ball. "Sorry, guys," she said, and she actually did sound sorry, "but I can't let you do that."

"What?" Tall demanded. "Why the hell not?"

But I got it. All the little things I'd been noticing finally came together. Small, winged, reality-warping—"you're one of them, aren't you?" I asked her. "You're one of the invaders."

The others stared at me, then at her. Tansy glanced down. Finally she spoke. "Half," she admitted softly. "On my mom's side."

"That's why we can see you normally, and hear you without that weird rustling."

She nodded.

"But your reality-warping stuff, that comes from them."

Another nod.

"And now, what? You're siding with them? They're trying to take over the universe, Tansy! They're gonna destroy everything!"

"No!" she shouted, finally meeting my eyes. "They're not like that! It's not about destruction! It's just about expansion— and change! They need our reality! Theirs is old and tired and can't support them anymore!"

"So, what, they get to come in here and take ours instead?"

"They're not taking anything!" she argued. "They're just changing it, so they can live here too! We'll all still be here! YOU'll all still be here!"

"Tansy," Mary said quietly, gently, "they have misled you. Their goal is conquest. And they consider us, all life here, to be the enemy. They seek to exterminate us, and to alter this reality until it is utterly inimical to all life but their own." She held out a hand to Tansy, but the little flutterbug backed away.

"No!" she insisted. "That's not true! You just don't understand!

You can't understand! But I can! I'm one of them!" She looked around, and managed a weak smile. "And now we have you surrounded."

Damn. I had a feeling this time there wouldn't be any sandwiches.

Chapter Twenty-seven
And the color of the day is—

"**Okay, I'm** fresh out of ideas," Ned admitted. "Somebody else's turn."

He was still taking the loss of his charged-particle spray pretty hard. The intruders had all recovered—most of them, anyway, since I think I may have stepped on one by accident while they were herding us over toward the bench—and had been intent upon swarming us when Tansy talked them into backing off. She convinced them to just keep us hostage instead, at least for now—I think she was hoping to show us both that she was still our friend and that her family weren't actually as awful as we'd heard. I understood that desire—I'd once gone out bowling with some friends, back in high school, only to have some of my cousins show up at the same bowling alley, and I'd been torn in exactly the same way. Turns out that stopping your second cousin from lighting her bowling ball on fire and hurling it into the concessions stand instead of down the lane toward the pins? A real good way to show just how crazy she really is, and convince your friends that you're only half a step away from that yourself. Yeah, that was a lonely year. My cousin, though, she got asked out a lot after that. Lots of sudden fires that year, too.

Anyway, I felt bad for Tansy, but I couldn't completely forgive her. We were her friends. Hell, we'd broken out of prison together! According to every cheesy movie I'd ever seen, that was supposed to forge an unbreakable bond between us! When I pointed that out she just shrugged and looked miserable.

"I'm sorry," she told me. "I really am. But they're my family! What am I supposed to do? Just sit back and let you destroy them?"

"No, you do what everyone does with family," I told her. "You disown them and then you call the cops on them. What?" That last was to Tall, who was staring at me again, but he only shook his head.

"Let us go, please, Tansy," Mary pleaded. "We need to stop them! If they bring through enough of their kind they will complete the convergence and transform our reality into their own, destroying every living thing native to our own plane of existence!"

"That's not true!" Tansy snapped. "They don't want to hurt anyone! They told me so!"

"They sure have a funny way of showing it," Tall commented, rubbing the many bruises he'd gotten during the fight.

"You didn't exactly give them a choice," she pointed out sharply. "What were they supposed to do, let you attack them and not defend themselves?"

"Would have been nice," I muttered. I had more than a few bruises of my own.

"It'll be okay," Tansy assured me. "You'll see! You all will!"

I was too tired and too depressed to argue.

"What do they look like, anyway?" I asked her after a minute. "Your relatives, I mean. You can see them, right? And not just as hazy outlines?"

"Of course I can," she answered with a laugh. "I can see them just fine! You could too if they wanted. They can look like anything. Actually, they can be anything! My reality-bending? Nothing compared to theirs."

"Anything? Really?" There was something kicking around in the back of my head. I wasn't sure what it was yet, but I figured if it rattled around long enough it might roll into view. "There must be something they can't do."

"Nothing!"

I glanced around at the hazy shapes filling the rest of the room and clearly listening closely to the conversation. "Is that true?" I asked them all. "You can do anything?"

"Yes," came the rustling reply, only now it echoed several times as more than one of them answered me together.

"You can turn into anything?"

"Yes."

Hm. "What about an elephant? Can you make yourself into an elephant?"

There was some hushed rustling, like whispering, and the hazy shapes coalesced, coming together and growing larger and clearer and darker until suddenly there was an elephant in front of me! A big, dark gray elephant, with baggy skin and watermelon-sized eyes and dull ivory tusks. Amazing! If we'd had a small white mouse right about then the invasion'd be over, but oddly I found it more comforting to have them all looming over us in elephant-form. At least I could see them now. I hated not being able to see something—it made it hard to be sure it was really there.

Which is when the idea finally bounced its way to the front and burst into my thoughts like a sugar-overloaded kid leaping into the neighborhood pool. Blam!

"Okay," I admitted slowly, "that's not bad. But that doesn't really prove much. Turning yourself into an elephant? That's easy!" The others were all staring at me like I was nuts. And maybe I was. We were about to find out. "Now, turning yourself into raccoons—that'd be something."

The elephant stared at me for a second, its trunk waving idly, and then it collapsed in on itself, its body crumbling to pieces which spilled out onto the floor—and shifted on their own, each one developing whiskers and fur and bushy tails and masked faces. The room was now filled with beady-eyed raccoons, each one staring at me like it was debating whether to steal me, eat me, or ignore me.

"Yeah, okay, so you can do raccoons," I announced, trying to sound like I saw a room full of large conquest-crazed vermin every day. Actually I'd been through Wall Street more than once, so I guess it wasn't a completely new thing for me. "Still, wildlife's one thing. Becoming something inanimate, like a lamppost—that takes talent."

More rustling, and then the raccoons leaped onto each other's shoulders, forming swaying, furry columns that narrowed and rose and widened at top. A second later and there was a forest of old-fashioned lampposts filling the room, each one shedding a soft light upon us and our bench.

"What exactly are you doing?" Tall whispered to me. "Trying to wear them out?"

"No," I replied out loud. "I'm just curious if they really can do anything, like Tansy had said. I mean, okay, they can do wildlife and they can do street fixtures, but those are pretty easy, right? Now if they really wanted to impress me, if they really wanted to show off—but nah. There's no way. Nobody could do that."

"Do what?" the rustling demanded.

"Nothing," I answered. "Forget about it. It's impossible. Even for you."

"Nothing is beyond our capabilities!" the lampposts replied. "We can do anything! We can become anything!" Apparently including lampposts that could talk. I mean, it's not like they had mouths any more! Because a lamppost with a mouth—that would just be wrong.

"Really? Anything? Anything at all?" I pretended to think about it. "Yeah, but even so—I doubt even YOU could become this!"

"What? Tell us!" they demanded. It was just like dealing with my kid sister. Only without the BB gun.

"Well, if you really can do anything," I said slowly, "let's see you make yourself—mauve!"

Ever see a lamppost blink in surprise?

"Mauve?" they repeated.

"Yeah, you know, the color mauve," I said. "Not a shape, or an animal, or a thing, just a color. The color mauve." For a second they didn't answer, and I shrugged. "Well, like I said, that's a pretty tough one, so I understand. But hey, the lampposts are really nice, right guys? Don't sweat it. You did a good job with all that other stuff."

"NO!!!" the lampposts roared. "We can do anything! We can become anything! Even mauve!" They all merged together, into a single large shapeless blob, and began to shift color, from gray to dusky pink to more rosy-hued, and then—

—they were gone.

Not just invisible, either. There was a faint popping sound, like when you shake the water from your ears or blow to clear the pressure from your sinuses during a plane flight. The room was suddenly empty, except for the four of us on the bench—and Tansy fluttering nervously in front of us, glancing around behind her and growing more panicked by the second.

Right up until Mary hauled off and slugged her. Tansy folded like a letter and crumpled to the ground, where Ned quickly tied her with some streamers he claimed were hardened relativistic particles and immune to her reality-warping.

Then we all just sat there for a second, staring around us.

Finally Mary turned to me. "How did you manage that?" she asked softly. "They are gone—you got rid of them. How?"

I shrugged. "It was an idea I had," I told her. "Remember that traffic court judge stole the color mauve from us?" She and Tall and Ned all nodded. "Well, I figured that meant not just that we couldn't see it anymore, but that somehow it didn't even exist for us. We no longer have the color mauve in our world. I tricked them into turning themselves into mauve, but since that color can't be around us and suddenly they were that color"—I shrugged—"they couldn't be around us. So suddenly they weren't. The universe decided it couldn't have them here anymore, not near us, and it tossed them back out."

The three of them stared at me for a second.

"That—" Mary began, then stopped. "It—" she started again.

"It doesn't make any sense," Tall finished for her. "In fact, it's flat-out ridiculous. You convinced them to turn into a color we can't see, and so they were ejected from reality? How could that possibly work?"

"How the hell should I know?" I retorted. "Do I look like some egghead quantum physicist or something? Or one of those new-age philosopher types? All I know is, we and the color mauve can't co-exist, and they're mauve so they can't be here." I scratched my bill. "I was hoping the universe would decide that, since we'd been here first and they were johnny-come-latelies, we'd get priority. Seems like it worked."

"That it did," Mary agreed slowly. "I still do not completely understand the how and why of it, but it seems you forced an existential conundrum upon our reality and it protected itself by shunting the invaders back into their own plane of existence."

"So that's it then," Tall half-asked. "We won? They've been sent packing?"

Much as I loved to watch her move, I hated it when Mary shook her head.

"DuckBob has banished them temporarily," she informed us. "But they will be able to return once they recover from their forced expulsion. And this time they will be angry and will return in force."

Wait, that whole mob of rustling patches that had swarmed us earlier, that wasn't "in force?" It had seemed pretty forceful to me!

"Okay, so how do we stop them from coming back?" I asked. Then I smacked my forehead. "The matrix!"

"Exactly." She turned that kilowatt smile of hers on me. "You have granted us a reprieve. Now you can realign the matrix, which will restore the barrier between their reality and our own. Once that is in place again the invaders will be unable to return."

"Right!" I hopped up off the bench and offered her my hand. "What're we waiting for?"

Mary accepted my hand with a smile. "This way." Ned and Tall pulled themselves to their feet and followed us as Mary led us out of that room and down a short tunnel into a big, wide-open space at the center of the building, shaped like an oval with flattened sides a huge domed roof way up above. There were several other openings at various points, none of them very regular in size or shape, and again I thought it looked more like a sparkly cave than a building. But at the moment, the architecture wasn't important.

Because there, at the center, was the quantum fluctuation matrix.

It was beautiful. Like a band of shimmering silver and gold ribbons, all woven together and circling round and round, but with computer cables and monitors and processors mixed in. There were things in there that looked for all the world like massive piston engines, seeming delicate against the open backdrop, and other shapes that resembled blown glass vials and elegant pinwheels and curving horns and sparkling fans. If someone had taken props from a Victorian murder mystery, a period martial arts film, a modern-day IT department, and a high school marching band, and woven all those pieces together into something beautiful and glorious and seamless, that would be the quantum fluctuation matrix. It was the single most amazing thing I'd ever seen.

And it wasn't working.

I could tell that right away. It was circling, but slowly, and there was a weird hitch to it, like watching a man with a limp trying to dance. The rhythm was off. And for all my other faults, I've got excellent rhythm. I have to—I spend half my life almost-falling and catching myself just in time, so I've learned how to dance around my own clumsiness.

"Wow." I whispered, unable to tear my gaze from it. "Just—wow."

"Yes," Mary breathed beside me. "It is truly spectacular." She gave me a gentle push between the shoulder blades. "Now realign it, and secure the safety of our reality once and for all."

"You got it!" I started forward, and got about three steps before I slowed to a halt again. "So, uh—how do I do that, exactly?"

I glanced behind me, and saw Mary staring at me, open-mouthed. My heart sank. This didn't look promising.

Chapter Twenty-eight
Anybody got a Phillips head?

"**Tell me** you're kidding."

She shook her head. "I truly wish I was. I thought—"

"What, that there'd be a big red REALIGN button on it? Swell!" I didn't want to admit I'd just spent the past ten minutes searching for the exact same thing. No such luck.

"The Grays indicated that you would simply be able to realign it by virtue of your modification."

"Yeah, and they're always so clear and concise about everything! These are the people who invented the crop circles, for heaven's sake! Giant signs carved into the ground, when they could've just popped down and said, 'Hi, we're aliens, can we borrow a few of you for experimentation? Oh, and some beef, please?'"

I looked to our resident techie. "Ned? A little help here?"

But he shook his head, too. It was becoming an epidemic. "Sorry, no idea. I'm just a tinkerer and a fix-it guy. The matrix is way beyond me."

"Some suggestions, at least? A place to start? Something to look for?"

He shrugged. Was that a step up from a headshake, or a step

down? "Look for anything that seems particularly off?"

"Okay, that's something, anyway." I sighed. "Spread out, everybody. Scan it for anything that looks 'particularly off.'"

Tall frowned. "I'll look," he agreed, "but I doubt it'll do much good."

"Why's that?" I demanded. "Your defeatist attitude blocking your eyes?"

For once he didn't rise to the bait. "No. But I'm not attuned to the matrix. You are. So I'm guessing I won't be able to notice the problem because I don't have an existing connection to it."

That actually made sense, unfortunately. I glanced at Mary. "Any chance we can get the Grays to kidnap Tall here and whip up a last-minute mod for him? The tail of a Pekingese or something?"

"No, I am still unable to contact them," she replied. Turned out she'd been trying since before we reached the building, actually, but hadn't mentioned it because she didn't want to upset any of us. Great.

Which reminded me of something. "They modified you, too," I told her. "So doesn't that mean you're attuned as well?"

But she shook her head again. "No, my modifications are of a different nature," she explained. "They involve cerebral upgrades only." Which answered the question about her looks, at least—all natural. Impressive. "Only bodily modifications like your own require attunement to the matrix."

I turned to Ned. "And you completed my modification, but I'm guessing you can't start one on your own, so you can't attune the rest of you." He nodded. I wasn't sure where that landed in the hierarchy of body language for a screwed-up situation, but I knew what it meant. I was on my own.

Okay, I told myself. That's okay. You can do this. You can look over this incredible piece of advanced alien machinery, suss out the problem, and fix it. You can save the universe from a horde of flying, near-invisible, reality-shifting invaders. All by yourself.

Aw, who was I kidding?

Just then a soft hand came to rest on my shoulder. "You can do this, DuckBob," Mary told me quietly. "I believe in you." And she kissed me on the cheek.

Okay, as motivators go? Encouragement and smooches from a gorgeous dame? Pretty high on my list.

"And you'd better hurry up," Ned added, fortunately without the touching or kissing. "Because I'm guessing we only have a few minutes before the invaders start popping back in again."

Threat of imminent doom? Also high on my list. Though I prefer the kissing.

"Right." I rubbed my hands together and studied the matrix again. "Okay, big boy, Doctor DuckBob is here. Tell me where it hurts." I was half-expecting and more than half-hoping it to answer. Hey, you never know! But not a peep. So much for the easy way out.

I began walking a circuit around the matrix again, moving a little more slowly than it was rotating so I could study each section for a bit before it undulated past me. It was hypnotic, and I had to force myself to focus. Where was the problem?

"It'd help if I knew what it looked like when it was working properly," I called out to the others, who were leaning against one of the walls, where rows of ridges sat one behind and above each other, almost like stadium risers. If only they'd come with one of those guys who walked around selling hot dogs and beer! "Anybody got a snapshot?"

"Sorry," Ned replied. "I've never been here before."

"Nor have I," Mary agreed.

"I've never been anywhere," Tall added. "Well, not past Lunar orbit, anyway."

I spared him a quick glance and he shrugged. Then I went back to looking at the matrix.

There was definitely a problem here somewhere. I could feel it. Hell, I could see it, in that weird hitching half-step it was doing. I just had to figure out exactly where the problem started. And then how to fix it. Great.

Piston-engine thingies—check. Fans—check. Horns— check. I studied each component in turn. Monitors—down, but that's probably a symptom of the problem rather than the cause. I could try randomly pushing buttons and tapping gauges but I remembered what'd happened to Tall the last time I did that and shuddered. No way I wanted to start accidentally zapping the entire universe!

Besides, I had a feeling buttons weren't the problem. They wouldn't cause this hiccupping movement. There was something else going on here.

"Um, DuckBob?" Ned hollered. I was on the far side of the matrix, sidestepping a small mountain of cigarette ash—some people are so inconsiderate!—so he had to yell for me to hear him.

"Yeah? What?"

"You might want to hurry!"

"I'm looking as fast as I can!"

"I know, but you really might want to hurry." I was rounding the far curve again, and froze as Ned and the others came into view. They were all on their feet now, and Tall was—

Well, Tall was pummeling the air.

Or something fluttering in the air. Something we couldn't see.

Oh, hell.

"They're starting to come through again!" Tall shouted, stamping on something else I couldn't see. "Hurry up and do whatever it is you've gotta do!"

"I agree!" Mary added, smashing a surprisingly effective-looking right hook into something unseen near her left side. "They are clearly agitated and in full aggressive mode!"

Pissed off and on the warpath. Gotcha.

I forced myself to turn back to the matrix instead of running to their aid. They could handle themselves. And they needed to keep the intruders at bay. I had to figure this thing out while I still had the chance, before the invaders broke past them and swarmed me as well. Because once that happened it'd all be over.

I focused on the matrix again. Where was the problem? Where? My eyes glided over it, past the ribboning cords and cables and streamers, along the curls and sweeps and bows, over the gap between—

Wait.

Gap?

Why was there a clothing store in the middle of the matrix?

I sprinted a few paces to catch up to that spot again. Yes! There was a gap in the matrix! It was between one of the fans and two of the streamers, and at first I'd just thought it was part of the design but it was the only space I'd seen between the components anywhere around. This had to be the problem!

Now I just had to figure out how to fix it.

I reached out and grabbed one of the streamers in one hand and the fan in the other. Yowtch! It was like trying to hold a live wire. Two of them. My whole body tingled, and my hands felt numb. And the matrix's rotation slowed. Damn, had I just drained the power somehow? Tripped a breaker circuit or something? But no, it was still moving, just not as fast. And the rhythm—was it my imagination, or had it gotten a little bit smoother?

"What'd you do?" Tall shouted. I could tell from the way he was gasping that he was talking in between beating on things.

"I found the problem!" I yelled back. "I'm just not sure how to fix it!"

"Well, figure it out!" he replied. "And fast!"

Okay, I had the two separated pieces in my hands. The jolt had faded, though I could still feel that tingling sensation. So I tried to pull my hands together.

No go.

I tried again, putting all my strength into it.

Still nothing. I'd never been able to win the kewpie doll at those "Test Your Strength" things at the circus, actually. And that was before the modifications—now I had trouble swinging anything overhead. Not enough leeway.

Okay, I couldn't just pull them back together. So what could I do instead?

"DuckBob!" Mary called. "Please!"

Damn, my lady friend was in distress! Yeah, I was calling her "my" lady friend in my head—let's hope the Grays hadn't made her telepathic, too! But I had to do something! And fast!

There had to be a way to bridge the gap here!

Maybe if I took a closer look . . .

I stepped in a little close, and craned my neck to peer into the space between the two pieces. Maybe there was some way to extend one or both of them . . .

. . . which is, of course, when I tripped.

"NO!!!" I heard Mary scream. Then I didn't hear much of anything except—

ZZZZZZAAAAAPPPPPPP!!!!!

Ow.

Owowowowowow.

And, also?

Ow!

Because, of course, when I tripped, I stuck my entire head into the gap. Yep. Me. Whole head. In gap.

Great.

There was a loud whine, and a thunk, and then a single melodic note—I know because all of it was echoing through my head and my entire body.

And then the matrix stopped moving.

"He killed it!" I heard Tall shout, though it sounded like he was far away. Y'know, because I had streamers shoved into one ear and a fan in the other.

"DuckBob! Speak to me!" Mary sobbed. Aw!

"Hey, wait a second . . ." Ned said. Thanks, Ned.

But he was right.

Because shoving my head into the matrix?

Maybe the dumbest thing I've ever done in my entire life.

Or possibly the smartest.

You've heard a computer start up, right? That little chime it makes, one if it's a Mac and one if it's a PC? Okay, imagine if that chime is an entire symphony instead.

Now imagine the computer is the size of a small building.

And that your head is stuck inside it.

I've never felt that musical in my life.

And then—

Lights!

Colors!

More music! But not as loud this time, thank God! And quickly settling down into something like background noise, even. But prettier.

"I think—" Ned offered slowly. "I think he did it."

"He did?" Ah, thanks, Tall. Always my biggest fan. Still, I was right there with him. I did? Did what? I didn't mean to! I'll put it back, honest! It was only for a second! It was a mistake! An accident! You can't even prove I was there!

Oh, wait . . .

Thinking with music vibrating through your body? Not as easy as you might think.

At least there weren't any lyrics.

"Did it work?" I asked. I may have been a little loud. I was shouting to be heard over the music, but judging by the way the others stared at me I'm probably the only one who can hear it.

I remember, when I was a kid, wondering if I could cut out the middleman—in this case my crappy headphones—and just plug myself directly into my stereo system. Didn't work so well then. Apparently I just needed a big enough opening.

Or to have my head rebuilt by aliens. Whichever.

"It's not moving!" I pointed out, then lowered my voice when I saw they were still flinching. "It's not moving. Is that good or bad?"

"Everything's lit up," Ned answered. "All the monitors are online again, every piece is glowing evenly—I really think you did it."

"And no more invaders," Tall added, mopping his brow and then wiping his hands on his legs. "It looks like they've stopped." He gave me a grudging nod. "I think Ned's right. I think you fixed the matrix."

"You did it!" Mary was, not surprisingly, the most enthusiastic. "You realigned the quantum fluctuation matrix!"

"Apparently you were the missing piece," Ned mused. "The invaders must have somehow torn a hole in the thing and set it wobbling, and your modified brain chemistry allowed you to function as a bridge. Once you inserted yourself—bold move, by the way!—and completed the loop the matrix shut itself down and rebooted, which reset its frequencies and resealed the barrier between the dimensions. Nice work!"

"Thanks." I was starting to feel pretty good about myself. I'd stopped the alien invasion! I'd saved the universe! Me! DuckBob Spinowitz! That called for some celebrating. "Hey, Mary, how about a hug for the conquering hero?" I asked. I'd have fluttered my eyelashes at her if I had any.

She laughed. "Happily!" she said, and started toward me—

—but Ned pulled her back.

"Sorry, it might not be safe," he pointed out. "DuckBob's been attuned to the matrix and can handle the energies coursing through it, but I'm not sure the rest of us would survive the contact."

"Oh. Right." I twisted my head slightly to glance around. "Okay, so how do I get out of this thing, then? Guys? Guys?" There wasn't any answer, and when I turned back to them I saw they all looked pretty sad, even Tall.

My heart sank.

"Oh, come on!"

"I'm sorry," Ned told me. "We'll have to run some tests, check some readings, but right now you're part of the matrix. Removing you would leave a gap again."

"Yeah, but they're gone, aren't they? And the wall's back up?"

"For now," he agreed. "But who knows what'd happen if the matrix was thrown off again? It might shut itself down until it could be repaired properly. Or it might just wobble like it did before, leaving enough of a gap for the invaders to find their way through a second time."

"And this time they'd hit us fast and hard," Tall added. "I would if I were them."

"So you're saying I'm stuck here? With my head in this thing? Forever?"

Ned looked away. "I don't know. Hopefully not. But I can't promise anything."

I looked at Mary. She had tears in her eyes. "I will confer with the Grays," she assured me. "There must be something we can do."

"I hope so. I don't want to be a permanent piece of the hard drive!"

She nodded and tried to smile. "We will do all we can. But no matter what happens, DuckBob, you have saved the universe. We are all in your debt."

Yeah. Great. In my debt. If that was anything like any other kind of debt, it would mean years of letters back and forth, lots of "it's in the mail" and "my dog ate it" excuses, a bunch of trumped-up late fees and other silly charges, and not a whole lot of result in the end.

I'd prefer the cash.

Hell, right now I'd settle for a tuning knob. Surely this thing, which was the focus of the universe and maintained the quantum frequencies and all that, could get some classic rock?

Or at least talk radio?

Epilogue
Stuck in a soap bubble

Okay, so things aren't quite as dire as I made out.

Yes, I am stuck in the matrix.

Sort of.

Ned did some checking, and confirmed that yes, the matrix does need a living component. Turns out, that pile of ash I saw before? Yeah, not from a sequoia-sized cigarette. We're not sure if the previous matrix operator got shot and killed, maybe by an intruder-sympathizer like Tansy, or just overloaded and went up in smoke. Regardless, that's all that's left of him.

Some retirement plan, huh?

Still haven't found out why the Grays didn't just tell me up-front that I needed to interface with the matrix directly. Would've saved us a lot of time and trouble, not to mention a few pants-wetting moments.

Maybe they figured I wouldn't do it if I knew I was being asked to play the high-tech equivalent of Atlas.

They might have been right, too.

At least, back then.

I think I've grown up some, though. Or maybe just learned to contain my more childish impulses from time to time. In public.

Which may be the same thing, anyway.

Thing is, they offered me a choice. The Grays. After the matrix was running again, so was their translocation doohickey, so they popped right up for a quick inspection tour. And congratulated me on "accomplishing my goal, albeit in a roundabout and much delayed fashion." So yay me, passing marks, something I never got in college!

Then they told me that I'd displayed "a surprising degree of intelligence, coupled with impressively creative strategic problem-solving." Which I took to mean I wasn't as dumb as I looked, and that I sometimes had these crazy ideas that actually worked. Mostly.

Anyway, they told me I'd "performed admirably," and "justified their practice of bodily modification," and that if I wished to I could go home now.

And go back to being normal.

I don't just mean my definition of normal, which includes prank calls to nature shows. I mean NORMAL normal. No duck head, no feathers, no webbed feet. REAL normal.

No-more-DuckBob normal.

I thought about it. I did. But honestly? What did I have going for me back there? A dead-end job, some loser almost-friends, a squalid apartment, an endless succession of boozy nights and possibly loose women? Okay, the last part didn't sound so bad—or wouldn't. Until I'd seen that there was more out there.

Until I saw I could be more.

So I said no, I'd stay this way, thanks. And stay here. Why

not? I'm actually *needed* here. That's pretty much the first time that's ever happened.

They gave Mary a choice, too. Told her she'd "performed exceptional service"—I try not to think about that one too much—and that if she wished it, they could undo her modifications and return her to her old life. She didn't even need two seconds to turn that down flat. Seems that, before they got to her, and despite those twin degrees (I know, right?), her last job? Hooters. Because every time she did get an interview for a real academic job, the fuddy-duddy old-guy professors wouldn't take her seriously. At one school they even tried stuffing dollars down her shirt!

Nice to know I'm not the only one around here who's banned for life from certain college campuses. Hell, all *I* was doing was cadging free food. They're *allowed* to feed the ducks!

Anyway, she said no, too. Which means she's still their intermediary to the human race, and sort of an advance scout and problem-solver on other jaunts.

She's away about half the time, but she tries to come back some nights, and weekends.

Guess who else stuck around? Tall! Yeah, he says it's just to keep me from screwing up again, but I know that's not it. Well, not entirely. I mean, you can't go through as many weird and dangerous things together as we did and not bond a little, right? Deep down, I think he really likes me.

He's still a MiB, of course. But his bosses agreed that they should have a liaison to the Grays, and an eye on the matrix, and it made sense to assign Tall since he'd already, y'know, been here. So now he drops by maybe once a week to check in, see how things are going, and all that.

Mostly that means he shows up with a six-pack of Omegan fire-beer ("You'll burn up from the inside out!") and watches Madrigoran spikeball with me. That's like hockey only the players are all a cross between a bull and a really big guy and a tank, and the ball has spikes and can move on its own and occasionally explodes, and the sticks are more like the Grim Reaper's scythe crossed with a lightsaber and a cattleprod. Fun to watch but they go through players pretty fast—each team's bench is something like a hundred deep. Anyway, we have fun, even if half the time we're rooting for opposite teams ("Let's go, ChaosFiends!").

The good news is, Ned—who asked to be assigned as the matrix's new resident techie, so he pops in on a regular basis as well—managed to rig up a helmet for me, and spliced its cord into the juncture. At least I can walk around a bit. The cable for it is thin and looks like it's only about twenty feet but it stretches to twenty times that length, so I can literally reach anywhere in the main matrix space and some of the adjoining rooms besides.

Including the bathroom they set up for me. Ain't that a relief!

He's looking into a wireless setup, which would give me the run of the entire skull.

Because that's what it turns out this place really is.

A skull.

The crystallized head of some ancient and impossibly huge beastie. Those towers along the top? Spines. The balconies off to the sides? Horns. The openings here and there? Eyes, nose, mouth, ears, a few others I don't recognize.

I'm living inside the biggest head in all creation.

I feel like I should have a shirt that says, "Hey, I'm your subconscious" and should go around whispering naughty thoughts and snide comments.

Yeah, all right, I do that part anyway.

Regardless, it's not like I can find new digs. I'm skullbound for the foreseeable future.

Still, it ain't so bad. I've got a nice little bedroom set up in a nook right off this main area, and a mammoth projection TV at the far back end. I get cable from over five hundred different worlds and civilizations. Over thirteen million channels. And guess what?

There's still nothing on besides reality TV, soaps, and cooking shows.

I am getting to be a fair hand at making a Janalusian trill-flip omelet, though. The trick is not to blink. Or stop whistling.

So this is now my new job. Guardian of the Matrix. It's a lot like my old job, in that I don't really have to do anything except show up. I surf the Internet a lot—you don't even wanna know what some of those porn sites are like, though the spam emails are pretty damn amusing, especially the ones that start "Dear Mrs. Matrix!"—and watch TV when I can stand it. Ned managed to connect Earth's networks up here as well, so I can watch movies on InstantView, and catch up on American TV shows on the network sites.

I've also got a blog. It's on my website. DuckBob.com.

Yes, I get bored a lot.

Oh, here's one really good thing, though. That truck stop diner, Red's?

Turns out they deliver.

Yep.

Some other good news—turns out I may not be all that special after all.

More to the point, Ned's figured out that, while my modified noggin was needed to jumpstart the matrix, now that it's running smooth again any old brainbox will do. At least for short periods. So he, Tall, and Mary take turns spelling me at least once a day so I can get out of my skull—like that?—to wander over to the shopping center and generally just get away from all that pink. I can't stay away too long, but I can get a few hours out, which is enough time for Mary and I to go out for dinner or catch a flick or go particle-sledding or something.

Yeah, Mary and me.

No, I'm not going into details.

Yes, she really is all-natural.

That's all I'm sayin'.

Most of the time, of course, I'm here on my own. But that's okay. Like I said, I've got the run of the main room and a few of the nearby alcoves. I've set up a pool table in one, and a dartboard. I've got a Jacuzzi in that locker room place we were held in first. There's a wet bar in a nook off to one side.

In case you're wondering, I got my mail forwarded. That took a little doing, but Tall smoothed things over for me. Arranged it all with my old job, too. And told my mom I'd been tapped on a matter of national security, so I couldn't come visit but I could call and email.

But yes, I got my mail.

Including all those credit cards.

I've got about twelve different game systems, though some of them I can't play too well because I don't have the right number of limbs. Or sensory organs. I've got a gazillion different games. I've got books, and movies, and the Internet. I've got an entire stadium-sized space to run around in.

Of course, sometimes I still feel the need to cut loose a little bit. Go off on my own, even if it's just for a smoke break. No, I didn't ever smoke before—always thought it was an ugly habit. But then I discovered these jewel-light sticks from Bennoit 6. They're amazing! Make you feel like your entire body is made of clouds and vapor and fine, faintly lilac-scented mist! Good stuff. Mary doesn't approve, says she doesn't know how it'll react to my modified body chemistry, and she's gotten Ned and Tall to side with her, so I can't smoke them anywhere around any of them, or even in the skull.

So I sneak out from time to time.

Turns out, you can take a metal guitar string and run it between the leads in the helmet. Works like a charm. Strictly short-term, of course, but there haven't been any problems so far.

At least I don't think so. I haven't seen any more invaders, anyway.

But the other day?

I thought I saw a shape moving toward the door, just out of the corner of my eye.

It was mauve, though, so I can't be sure.

Oh well. I'm sure it was nothing.

Gotta go. One of my shows is on. It's a triple-daytime talk show from Deceter Epsilon. The host drills each visitor on their problems—literally. The show's slogan is "sometimes you've got to dig past the surface to find the root of the problem."

It can get a bit messy, but at least it's all in good fun.

I think.

About the Author

Aaron Rosenberg has not been altered by aliens, as far as he's aware. He is, however, very silly, and he and DuckBob share similar taste in shirts. When Aaron isn't busy taste-testing fried chicken and barbeque or watching movies or sleeping, he's writing. So far he's written roleplaying games (including the award-winning *Gamemastering Secrets*, plus work for *Warhammer, Dungeons & Dragons, Deadlands, Vampire: The Masquerade*, and many others), children's books (among them the middle-grade series Pete and Penny's Pizza Puzzles, and books for *iCarly, Ben10, Chaotic*, and *Transformers Animated*), educational books (including books about cryptology, the Bermuda Triangle, and various biographies), and of course novels (like his two WarCraft novels, his Warhammer trilogy the Daemon Gates, the Stargate: Atlantis novel *Hunt & Run*, and the Eureka novels *Substitution Method* and *Road Less Traveled*). He is also the author of the Dread Remora space-opera series and one of the creators of the O.C.L.T. paranormal thriller series. If he did meet Grays, he'd probably ask them to increase his typing speed. Aaron lives in New York City with his family, and makes sure to always have a MetroCard and a finger puppet handy. You can read more about his life and his books at gryphonrose.com or follow him on Twitter @gryphonrose.

Want more DuckBob?
No problem!
Check out the first chapter of
DuckBob's next exciting adventure:

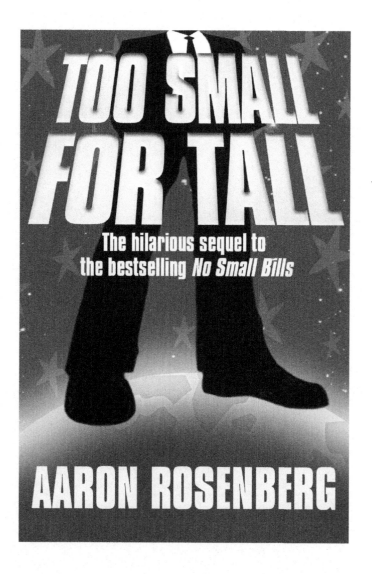

TOO SMALL FOR TALL

The hilarious sequel to
the bestselling *No Small Bills*

AARON ROSENBERG

Chapter One
If I wanted one of those, I'd order it

Tall is trying to kill me.

No, he really is.

Oh, sure, he calls it something else:

"Exercise."

Yeah, right.

I call it "Tall shouting and screaming at me like my step-dad used to, and making me run around and do jumping jacks and a lot of other hideous and evil things designed to kill me by making my heart burst out of my chest and dance the watusi around the room."

When I tell him that, he just laughs at me.

And then yells at me to get off my fat butt and do some pushups.

Have you ever tried to do pushups when your bill sticks out past your elbow? It ain't fun. I can manage the full extension part, but dropping back down I get stuck halfway. And trying to lever yourself up when your arms are already partially extended? Not fun.

Once he realized the pushups weren't going to work, Tall switched to sit-ups.

Uh huh.

Most people, they've got maybe half their weight above
the waistline. Me? Two-thirds. And half of that is my head.
Hey, duckbills aren't light! So here I am, lying on my back on
the floor, Tall standing over me yelling, and he wants me to
lift around a hundred and sixty pounds using just my stomach
muscles? Even if they got out and pushed that's not going to
happen!

"Don't you want to get in shape?" he demands. "Don't
you want to look good and feel good?" That expression that
flits across his granite features is supposed to be sly, I think,
but when you've got the same face as Mt. Rushmore (he's got
Lincoln's jaw and brow but Washington's nose) it's tough to
manage the subtle stuff. "Don't you want to look good for
Mary?"

Okay, that's low. "Mary likes me just fine the way I am," I
reply from the floor. Y'know, it's surprisingly comfortable down
here. I guess that's because instead of carpet it's actually like
grass or little fuzzy caterpillars or something, so laying on it
you feel like you're getting a massage from a thousand fingers
all at once. Small, soft, squishy fingers.

Right, getting up now. Ick.

"Look, I'm trying to help you," he says, and the funny thing
is, I know he means it. We didn't start out as friends—hell,
I'm pretty sure Tall started out thinking of me as something
between a juvenile delinquent, a lab rat, and a loaded gun—but
during our trip across the galaxy, well, we kinda bonded.

What can I say? I'm a people person.

"I'm just not built like you," I tell him, limping over to the couch and plopping down on it. "You're, like, modeled after a Greek god or something. I take after Mr. Potato Head. Or Donald Duck." All of which is more or less true. Tall's a MiB, a Man in Black, and I guess they've got even tougher entry requirements than the FBI or any of those agencies people actually know about, both mentally and physically. You've gotta be in good shape to chase after little green men, or something. But I met a few other MiBs and Tall could probably take 'em all on in arm-wrestling, using only his pinkie, and still win. While distracted. And feverish. He's not only tall, he's got the broad shoulders, the thick upper arms, but then the narrow waist and the long legs—he's like an Olympic athlete, if they had an event for skulking and brooding and shooting things.

Me? Even without the whole duck-head thing going on, I was never like that. I'm a decent height, but I was always a little on the doughy side. Having all this happen to me hasn't really changed that any. If anything, I'm more sedentary now—I figure I lied, cheated, snuck, stole, conned, fought, and fled my way across the galaxy, battled a race of invaders from another dimension, restored the Matrix, and saved our entire reality. That's gotta be enough exercise for anyone. I deserve to take it easy after all that.

Still, I can see this is killing him. "I appreciate your concern," I promise him, and I really do. It's nice to know he cares, if in a gruff and borderline homicidal fashion. "But don't worry about it. I'm comfortable with who I am and how I look." I am, too. That's why I didn't have the Grays change me back after the whole invasion thing, despite their offer. Who wants to go back to being just another pudgy guy with a weak chin and pug nose and watery blue eyes and a receding hairline? I'm resplendent in my feathers, my coloration is striking—once literally, when I found out that the people from Rasmussen Nine-Five-One actually experience physical pain from bright colors, and accidentally knocked out an amiable pair of floating noodles who'd come to see if I wanted a magazine subscription—and I've never met anyone else who looks even remotely like me, at least away from a duck pond. I'll take that over "pudgy and boring" any day.

Besides which, Mary does like my looks. And my feathers. Hey, once you've slept on down, you never go back!

And then there's the job. As the Matrix's Guardian and "sentient operator"—read here, "living component"—my staying plugged into it via the Mad Scientist wired headband Ned whipped up keeps it running, which in turn keeps the universe balanced and safely sealed from outside intrusion. But I couldn't do that if I got changed back to the old me—it's the fact that the Grays had altered me that made me suitable to be the human plug-in in the first place. Give that up and I've got to go back to Earth and find another boring, normal job, probably another cubicle somewhere. I think that'd kill me.

"Yeah, yeah." Tall drops onto the couch beside me. "Fine, we'll call it quits for today, but this isn't over. In the meantime, when you run out of breath climbing the stairs, or drop a jar of pickles because they're too heavy for you to manage, don't come crying to me." He gives me one last chance. "Come on, just a little more today. Three months and you'll have a six-pack and killer guns, I guarantee it."

"Dude, if I want a six-pack I'll just order one, and I hate guns. Besides, who would see it under all these feathers? But thanks."

"What about swimming?" he suggests. "You're good at swimming, right?"

"Yeah." And it's true. Hell, with these webbed feet and the feathers, I could probably outrace Michael Phelps—hell, I could probably get to the end, double back, stop to do a quick water ballet routine, and still beat him. Though that might come across as gloating, I'm not sure. There's just one problem. "You see a pool around here anywhere?"

"Oh. Right." He actually looks abashed, which is pretty funny on him—it's like a dragon after a major browbeating. But the thing is, he's knows I'm right. Being Guardian of the Matrix is a cool gig, and looks great on a resume, but it's very much on-location—as in, I'm actually wired into the damn thing at all times. And even with the tether our tech-buddy Ned rigged up, I still can't leave the Matrix building. Which is odd and sparkly and pink—and doesn't have a pool.

"Don't worry about it." I scoop up the remote. "Now, you wanna watch the game, or what?"

"Who's playing again?" He eyes the remote warily—after that one time, he tends to steer clear of the tech around here. Hey, I warned him to stroke it before trying to push any of its buttons. It's sensitive. And it gives off one hell of a shock.

"The Yarmoths versus the Ma-bin-yo."

"Right. And what're those, exactly?" It does get hard to keep track sometimes.

"The Yarmoth are those little guys that look like they're made of marshmallows and toothpicks but can melt anything with a touch," I remind him. "The Ma-bin-yo are the ones that look like emo Goths drawn by a six-year-old with sticky fingers, purple crayons, and a lot of glitter."

Tall shakes his head. "I don't know how you can keep all those straight." He glares at me for a second. "Especially when you can't remember which temperature to use for laundry."

What? You've never gotten confused and washed reds—and maybe a few whites—on hot before? So his shirt shrank a little. And turned sort of a tie-dyed pink. It was a whole new look for him. That was the last time Tall brought his laundry over—now he does it at home or something, though I suspect he has his mom do it for him. If he has a mom. It's possible he was born from a granite quarry, a chisel, and an overly ambitious sculptor.

"Different kinds of knowledge," is all I tell him. "I've got a vast capacity for useless trivia." Which is true. It's why I'm so good at Trivial Pursuit. That and whenever I'm not sure about an answer I go with either "Whistler's mother," "the Himalayas," "butterflies," or "The War of 1812." You'd be surprised how far you can get with just those four.

We turn on the game and settle in to watch for a bit. There're over a thousand different televised sports in the galaxy, it turns out, and I can get all of them here. One of the advantages of being "the guardian of the Matrix"—I'm at the very Core of the galaxy, smack dab in the middle of everything, so I've got phenomenal reception. There's always a game on somewhere.

And, oddly enough, most of them look an awful lot like football. Oh, the uniforms change, and the fields, and the balls, and the use of additional weaponry, but underneath, they all boil down to the same thing—Team A is trying to get past Team B to score points, and then Team B tries the same thing with Team A. As long as you don't try to remember all the smaller rules and especially all the penalties, you're fine.

But Tall's not really into it today. Usually he gets psyched— he picks a team, more or less at random, and roots for them, and he gets pretty vocal about it, cursing out the other team and threatening their lives and waving his pistol about and the whole bit. Kinda reminds me of the sports bar I went to back in college, only without the cigarette smoke. Today, though, he's just staring at the screen, and even when a dozen of the Yarmoths surround this one poor Ma-bin-yo and swarm all over him, melting holes through his torso until he looks like he's made of Silly String, Tall doesn't react.

"You okay there, amigo?" I ask gently—gently because he is armed, and I've seen him punch reflexively. That poor old lady just picked the wrong time to ask directions, is all.

He sighs, and starts to nod, then turns it into a shrug, which then becomes a shake of the head. Yeah, he's off his game. Either that or he's developed palsy overnight. "I don't know," he admits. "It's just—work's been getting me down lately."

"Work?" I click off the game—this is way more interesting. Tall's usually real close-mouthed about his job, which I get—without being all spooky and secretive the MiBs are just undertakers with sunglasses and guns. Which could be cool, actually, but not the same thing. So if he wants to tell me something about being a MiB, I'm all ear canals. "Do tell," I urge. "Lay your troubles at my feet, my friend, and I'll happily squash them flat." I wave one pontoon-sized webbed foot at him. "Free of charge."

He sighs, and for a second I think damn, he's gonna clam up again like always. But then he starts talking. And once he starts, it's like he's never going to stop.

48291203R00199

Made in the USA
Middletown, DE
14 June 2019